# THE 38 IMPOSSIBLE LOVES OF NAOKO NISHIZAWA

MONNA MCDIARMID

HOUSE OF WINTERPORT PRESS

*For Douglas Reid McDiarmid who was as kind and funny a father as any I could have written.*

# CONTENTS

# CHAPTER 1
# IN WHICH SKYE LEAVES PARIS

've tried to hold everything in place, exactly the way it was. For months I've tried to stop the clock from sliding forward, to pull the kite of time backwards by its tail, but it turns out that time is not particularly interested in the wishes of sixteen-year-olds. The truth is that my old life is already unravelling as I hurtle towards the inevitable.

Dusk falls as the airport-bound, black SUV makes its way slowly through the Paris neighbourhood where I've lived for the last four years. I can't process that this is the last time I'll see the small bakery where they make the perfect croissants, the fresh produce stall where it took Yoko two full years to jackhammer her way into the heart of the owner, and the flower shop where Giselle sets a bouquet aside each Thursday, knowing that Yoko will pop in before closing.

Back in April, the school counsellor met with all the kids who were leaving at the end of the year. She urged us to build a metaphorical raft to help navigate the move and said we should celebrate the time we'd had in Paris and prepare to grieve what would be lost. Uh, no thank you. While this was probably excellent advice for those other kids, I'd already locked in a foolproof plan based on the complete denial of the move to

Japan, in favour of the fantasy that these days with my friends would stretch on forever. I managed to skillfully overlook all evidence, including the fact that my parents were actively packing up the house, and that my father had already spent a few weeks in Tokyo transitioning to his new job and looking for a home and school. It was like I was watching a film about some other girl who was leaving. Of course, I didn't do any of the goodbye stuff the counsellor recommended. I didn't have one last meal at my favourite restaurants or sit in my favourite parks, and I absolutely should have known better because this is our second international move. Four years ago, we left Ottawa, Canada, where I'm from, to move to Paris. That was rough. Maybe the only thing worse than moving to a new country when you're sixteen is completely changing your life when you're twelve.

During those four years in Paris, I met Claire, became Queen of the Knock-Knock Joke, finished middle school, became a pro at taking the Paris metro despite some serious navigational challenges, started babysitting, ate what my dad calls an unholy amount of cheese, learned six different ways to tie a silk scarf, became fluent in French, started and then quit playing three different musical instruments (piano, violin, and flute), dragged my parents and friends to every romantic comedy released over the last two years, went to therapy, started a journal, and started writing stories. There have been some hard times, too, but I don't really want to think about those. It doesn't help. In science class, we learned that the cells in the body replace themselves every seven years or so, which means that I'm at least fifty-seven per cent a new person since we moved to Paris.

Sometimes I wonder what kind of person I'll become in Tokyo, but the truth is that I am very tired of growing and learning new things. Maybe I could just stay the same for a while.

We pass the Seine on whose banks I've read two million books, more or less, where I've sat, hundreds of times, talking with my friends (which my dad calls gossiping. Rude!) and where, one very hot afternoon last August, I jumped into the river to cool off. This is super illegal and probably a huge health risk, and my parents will be furious if they ever find out. We pass the bridge where Claire made me laugh so hard the water I was drinking actually came out my nose, which is way more painful than you'd think! This is the moment that I realize I'm doing exactly what the counsellor recommended but cramming the whole experience into this one drive. Dad, who is sitting in front with the driver, keeps turning around to ask if we remember this day or that thing, and Yoko does the work of responding for both of us while I stare out the window. He seems sad to leave and, at the same time, eager to get to Japan to start his new job. He's a weirdly happy and resilient guy. I look over at Yoko and she's laughing at his story, and I wonder how she feels about returning to Japan after not having lived there for twenty years. I want to ask her, but maybe not right now.

I wonder what Claire is doing tonight. The last time I saw her, she hugged me and whispered, "There isn't a single time-line in which we aren't friends, Skye." I really want to believe that, but things have been awkward between us for the past few weeks. As always, it's my fault. When Yoko wanted to invite Claire to dinner last night, I didn't know what to say. I just couldn't face her. Yoko made me a grilled cheese sandwich, which is one of her love languages.

My dad has asked the driver to take the scenic route, so we continue along the Seine where the grand buildings are lit up like an outdoor wedding at night, and those miles of lights are reflected in the river, and I think that while Paris is always pretty, the evening is when she shines. The French are deeply committed to beauty, and I wonder if the Japanese are similarly obsessed. It's not that Canadians don't care about beauty, it's just that we have more plaid and polar fleece in our version. This makes me think about my passport, and I open my backpack and pull out the bag containing my stuff for the airplane: passport, novel, journal, pen, headphones, sleep mask, lip balm, and a warm wrap just in case the plane is cold. Yup. It's all here and, as I look up, I see Yoko smiling at me. This is all her doing, this award-winning level of preparedness.

We pass Shakespeare and Company on the right and Notre Dame on the left and I think about all the quiet hours I've spent in these two churches, one grand and airy, the other small, crammed with bookshelves and cosy reading nooks. For me, this is the most sacred block of the city. I don't even realize I'm crying until Yoko places her hand over mine and tells me for the millionth time that I'm going to be okay.

# CHAPTER 2
# IN WHICH AKARI MEETS THE NEW GIRL WITH THE RED HAIR

The first day of school is always about managing expectations. At least that's the case for me. After two months of sleeping in, doing absolutely no homework, and meeting up with our friends in Tokyo parks while cicadas screech the soundtrack to our summer, we arrive with new haircuts and a belief that anything could happen. New year, new me. On my way into the building, I see a student who grew six inches over the summer, and I know someone else who fell in love, and they feel suddenly wise but, in reality, not that much has changed. We continue to do exactly what we did last year and, for most of us, exactly what we'll do next year. In recognition of this fact, I try to keep my expectations in check. The first day of school means same situation, new grade.

I am doing what I always do which is to say that I'm sitting with my back against my locker and my legs straight out against the cool floor, with my sketchbook on my lap, working on a new comic strip I started during the summer. I read a lot of manga but most of it isn't exactly "smart girl" friendly, so I've been working on some ideas for girl superheroes. This one is my favourite. It's about this girl named Chiyo who can fly and is strong enough to stop trains. Her superpower is to stop people, mostly young people, from dying by suicide. I know that's a little dark. A few times every semester, I am late for school because someone has ended their life by throwing themselves in front of a train, and while we sit in the train waiting, I wonder what happened in the life of that person, and if it could have been different for them.

I draw Chiyo with red hair. I'm not sure why, exactly, although I've always been fascinated by red hair. It is possibly the least Japanese thing in existence but since that is how she showed up in my mind, that's how I draw her. I colour in her hair with a red charcoal pencil, then smudge it with my index figure so it looks fuller and wilder, like your hair would look if you were in the middle of swooping in to stop a high-speed train with your bare hands.

The hall is becoming crowded now and people are bumping into my legs, so I know it's time to get up. I sit cross legged while I pack up my pencils and sketchbook. I push myself up to stand against the bright purple locker, and that's when I see her.

"Chiyo?" I think I must be losing my mind. Walking down the centre of the hallway is a round, pink-cheeked girl with long, curly, red hair. A constellation of light brown freckles travels from one cheek to the other via the bridge of her small nose.

"That girl has the reddest hair I've ever seen," Kimi says.

"You wouldn't think that's a colour that occurs in nature. You've got to love an international school," Reika says.

My two best friends have just arrived from shooting hoops in the gym.

"You see her too?" I ask.

"Of course. She's standing right there," Kimi points at the red-headed girl who has stopped to read something on her phone. "You okay, Akari?" Kimi is both small and mighty. In volleyball, she can spike and block like someone a foot taller, partly because she believes she can and partly because she practices relentlessly. My favourite thing about Kimi is that she always tries to see the other person's perspective. She also makes the most amazing chocolate chip cookies and brings them to school to share. Not just for special occasions but just because. Kimi's kids, if she decides to have them, will be very lucky small humans to have such a kind mom.

"How could we miss her?" says Reika, our resident queen of snark, who is tall and willowy, like bamboo. She's not just the tallest girl in our grade anymore, but taller than most of the seniors, and some of the teachers. Her long hair is always pulled back in a ponytail. She plays on the volleyball team with Kimi and is a talented player, but her true passion is her cello, which she carries on her back like a twin. She is also the scariest girl I know by a factor of ten. When we first met, I was afraid to even talk to Reika, and if it hadn't been for Kimi, I don't believe we would have become friends. My theory is that Reika must be descended from a long line of warriors. Being friends with her means that nobody bothers Kimi and me even though we aren't even remotely close to being cool.

"Chicas, let's not be late for homeroom on our first day of junior year," says Kimi, herding the three of us down the hall and into our homeroom. We choose seats in the centre of the classroom, a compromise between the front seat I would have chosen and the back row that Reika naturally migrates towards. I hang my backpack on the back of my chair, turn off my phone, and drop it inside my bag. It's a school rule, but I am with the only two people who ever call me aside from my mother.

As the bell rings, the girl with the red hair enters our classroom and stands just inside the door. She looks startled and unsure. Suzuki-Sensei says, "Students, please take your seats. I hope you've all had a good summer." She addresses us in

English, like all our teachers do, except in Japanese class. "We have a new student with us this year ..." She scans the room, and her eyes finally rest on the new girl near the door.

"Skye?" she asks. The girl smiles broadly. It's not the cautious smile of a student on her first day at a new school, but a smile that says she's all in. "Students, this is Skye and she's from Canada, but her family has most recently lived ... my apologies, where are you moving from, Skye?"

"Paris." The new girl looks the teacher squarely in the eye. I glance over at Reika, who is rolling her eyes.

"Paris. Yes. Students, thank you in advance for making Skye feel welcome." The teacher points to an empty seat at the back of the room.

Skye smiles and waves at us. This girl is nothing if not consistent. Hers is not the sedate wave of a senior member of the royal family but more like that of a little kid riding a carousel for the first time, waving crazily at her parents every time they come back into sight. For a moment, I feel as though I'm seven again and not a junior in high school. I want to laugh out loud but resist the impulse. The other students smile or bow their heads slightly in gestures that look like the welcome Suzuki-Sensei requested, but the truth is that the other students and, by the look on Reika's face, even my friends, are already judging her based on the few things we know, or think we know, about her: a round body, a friendly nature and the fact that she moved here from Paris. From the satisfied look on her face, Suzuki-Sensei seems proud of her introduction, and I wonder how teachers can be so utterly clueless about how high school actually works.

But whatever the others are thinking about her, I'm curious about this new girl with the uncanny resemblance to Chiyo. Skye seems kind. And that hair. It's transcendent, like she's growing a head full of roses.

The cafeteria is already filling up as Reika, Kimi, and I arrive. Many of the foreign students are lined up at the counter to buy their lunch while most of the Japanese students go directly to a table with our packed lunches. There are three long sections of tables and benches that run between the kitchen and the stage where the seniors eat, and since we are juniors now, we move to a table just below the stage. I am unaware of how old this tradition is, who started it, and all the other details that some people seem to care so much about. Last year, the ninth graders staged a coup and took over the stage for a week. I was secretly very impressed with their attempt. In the end, they relinquished the stage because the seniors were a little scary, with their feelings of entitlement to those particular tables and seats. I couldn't care less where we eat lunch.

My mother has wrapped my bento box in a furoshiki, which I unwrap, lift the lid off and place it upside down on the handkerchief. Reika and Kimi do the same. Our friend Fiona used to say that our lunch table looked like an elegant Japanese picnic. Pork cutlet and rice are my favourites, and mom has made it specially for the first day of school. Things are complicated with her sometimes, but I cannot help but smile, thinking of her making this for me. I was not aware of feeling hungry, but as I look down at my lunch, I realise I am ravenous, and I pick up a piece of cutlet with my chopsticks. Kimi points at the cloth my bento box was wrapped in. "Panda bears, huh? Your mom's choice?"

"Yes. She likes the cute things." Reika and Kimi nod knowingly.

I look up to see the red-headed girl enter the cafeteria. As she walks between tables, students avoid making eye contact.

Some people even turn away from her. "The way everyone is ignoring her is so mean," I say.

Reika seems to read my mind. "No, Akari. Don't. We don't have the time to train another new girl. Plus, there's no way she speaks Japanese." says Reika.

"I think she seems interesting," says Kimi.

"I agree, Kimi. I am going to invite her to sit with us." I raise my hand and wave Skye over to our table.

Skye runs over to us, places her tray on the table, drops her backpack on the floor, and swings her legs over the bench. Her skirt flies up in the air exposing her thighs, but she doesn't seem to notice. All three of us look away for a moment.

"Hello!" she says. She smells like chocolate chip cookies. "I'm Skye. I think we're in the same homeroom," she says.

"I am Akari," I say, switching into English. "This is Reika and Kimi." They nod at Skye but remain silent.

"You are from Canada?" I ask.

"Yeah. My dad's Canadian and my stepmother is Japanese, so I don't know exactly what that makes me."

"Hafu," says Reika.

"Hafu ... as in half?" says Skye.

"Yes. It's the word Japanese people use to describe someone who is only half Japanese," explains Kimi.

"It is not necessarily meant as a compliment." I glare at Reika, who glares right back.

"Really? Why not?" Skye asks, as she picks up her ham and cheese sandwich from the orange tray and tries to extricate it from its plastic cocoon.

"Hmmm. This is a bit difficult," I say. Kimi nods. Skye looks up and meets my gaze as I struggle to explain. She sets her sandwich down on the tray and then begins to nod.

"Oh, right." Skye says. "Well, I'm not sure I qualify as hafu anyway since my biological mom was Canadian. And then there's this hair. It makes it pretty hard to blend." Skye reaches into her backpack, pulls out a set of glossy black chopsticks, and deftly employs them to tear open the plastic wrap on her sandwich. She smiles as she pulls it free. "Hey, maybe a better word for a kid who is half Japanese and half something else would be double. You know? Anyway, thanks for inviting me to sit with you." Kimi nods at Skye, while Reika crinkles up her nose like my mother does when the garbage needs to be taken out.

———

In period eight, I have English Lit. Neither Reika nor Kimi love reading in English like I do, so they take a less challenging course. English Lit is my favourite part of the day.

In middle school, I felt shy about my English. I would say as little as possible, just enough to answer questions directed at me and to avoid the dreaded report card comment, 'Does not participate sufficiently in class.' Then, in grade nine, a new teacher arrived. She was taller than most of the teachers and she wore the same thing every day. If I ever had an invisibility cloak and a non-creepy opportunity to snoop around Ms. Barrett's home, I am certain I would find, in her closet, five crisp white cotton blouses and five navy skirts, all of them lined up and waiting like soldiers ready for battle. She is a highly efficient person and, from what I can tell, not bothered by what other people think of her or her uniform. I imagine Ms. Barrett ironing her blouses on Saturday mornings with the windows wide open. She would be listening to opera. Ms. Barrett is a classical music person in a J-pop era. She's very stylish in her own way, the way she turns up the collar of her blouse, changes up her jewelry, and adds a cashmere sweater or a tweed jacket when the weather gets cooler. She has a collection of silk scarves, and she wears one every Friday. I can't discern any kind of pattern, so I'm left to conclude that she chooses them based on her mood. Her shoes range from sensible flats to patent leather red pumps to a pair of leopard print slingbacks. Those leopard slingbacks are not sensible shoes by anyone's definition.

As a teacher and a person, she is a gust of fresh air. She asks questions like, "What does the sky taste like?" and "What would strawberry jam say if it could talk?" and "What accents do polar bears speak with? Do you think they would wear berets if they could get away with it?" Back in grade nine, I made the mistake of telling my parents all about my new English teacher and her amazing questions. What was I was thinking? My dad said, "Akari, it is not clear how these questions will help you with your English." My mother said Ms. Barrett sounded creative, but her eyebrows were raised, so I knew she meant crazy. I came to the logical conclusion that Ms. Barrett's miraculous class would need to be my own little secret.

Then, in grade ten, I had another English teacher who, while fine, was no Ms. Barrett. I did well in the class, but I didn't feel my heart race as I headed to class. That brings us to just a few weeks ago, when I received an email with my schedule for grade eleven. My heart felt like it would explode as I checked the name of my English teacher, and there it was: Emily Barrett. It was a leopard print slingback kind of day.

As the bell rings for period eight, I rush to English class and choose a seat in the front row. Although I recognize that this is a tremendously geeky move, I no longer feel worried about being called upon in English. I look around at the other students in the class, mostly academic high-flyers and Model United Nations big talkers. Most of these students aren't particularly soulful about literature; they just want the most rigorous English class listed on their transcript for their university applications. Ms. Barrett begins taking attendance and, as the bell rings, Skye sails through the door.

"Sorry I'm late."

"Skye, is it?" Ms. Barrett approaches Skye and stops just a few inches away from her.

"Yes." Skye's eyes are wide with something that should be fear but looks more like curiosity.

"Scottish?"

"Canadian with Scottish ancestors. How did you know?"

"The Isle of Skye is in Scotland. Take a seat and don't be late again." Skye drops into the seat beside me and shrugs her backpack off her shoulders.

"She's cool but she hates tardiness," I whisper.

"Noted." Skye pulls her laptop out of her backpack.

"You are juniors now and, as your people say, things just got real. You will do more work in English class over the next two years than you have done in the past five combined. I say this not to scare you but because you need to understand that you will need to work faster, become more organized, and be ruthless about your priorities. Is that understood?"

Skye nods appreciatively.

"Good. Let's not waste any more time. You can play those get-to-know-you games in other teacher's classes. You know, the nice ones." A wave of laughter travels from the back of the class all the way to the front.

"Is she kidding?" asks Skye.

"She's making a joke but no, she's not kidding."

"Hardcore. I like it," says Skye.

"American scholar Joseph Campbell coined the term monomyth which is commonly referred to as the hero's journey. Campbell identified a pattern of narrative that described the adventures of the hero archetype in drama, storytelling, myth, religious ritual, and psychological development. Most of you should be familiar with this theory. Skye?"

"Oh yeah. Campbell and I go way back." I hold my breath, waiting for Ms. Barrett to react, but nothing happens.

"Excellent. All right, everyone is invited up to the white-board. Let's begin by brainstorming the various stages of the hero's journey, then we'll arrange them into the proper order. Well? What are you waiting for?"

Skye is the first person at the board. She wasn't joking when she said she'd heard of him, and she knows the stages even better than I do. I realize I should not have been surprised. There is something about her.

As we leave class and merge into the deafening end-of-day hallway traffic, I shake my head at Skye. "You are one auda-cious person, Skye MacTavish."

"If by audacious, you mean bonkers, then I hear that a lot ..." Skye pauses, raises the index finger on her right hand, and stops to take a long drink of water from the fountain. She wipes her mouth with the back of her hand. "Sorry. Which particular craziness are you referring to?"

"Nobody talks back to Ms. Barrett."

"When?" says Skye.

"When you talked about you and Joseph Campbell going way back."

"That wasn't back talk. That was just a little light-hearted banter. In fact, my performance in today's English class would have made me the most engaged student at my old school in Paris."

"But not here. Not at this school." We stop at my locker, and I turn to face her.

"I'm gathering that," Skye says.

"I know this is just the first day of school and we've just met so this is probably none of my business, but you may need to dial things back a bit here ... try to be a bit more cautious," I say.

"Cautious?" says Skye.

"Perhaps respectful would be a better word."

"Hm. Is this a Japan thing?" asks Skye.

"Yes." I laugh out loud. "I guess it is a Japan thing, but our school is relaxed by Japanese standards. In a Japanese school, I would be considered a rebel."

"A rebel, huh?" Skye's whole face lights up.

"You are laughing at me, now. I apologize for raising the issue." I turn to open my locker and Skye puts her hand on my shoulder.

"Hey! Don't be sorry. I really appreciate the warning. I know I'm like a fish out of water here. Like I'm so out of water, I might be in milk." I laugh as I pull a textbook off the top shelf.

Closing my locker door, I see Reika and Kimi approaching us. Although Kimi is almost a foot shorter than Reika, she has no trouble keeping up with Reika's longer strides. Reika marches into battle while Kimi bounces along cheerfully.

"Algebra homework on the first day back. Ouch," says Reika. The rest of us nod in solidarity at the Math teacher's bold but not entirely surprising move.

"So, are we on for Starbucks this afternoon?" asks Kimi.

"Sure," I turn to Skye. "Would you like to join us?"

"Actually, I've gotta get home and help Yoko sort out our apartment. We just got our shipment, and everything is still in boxes. It's kind of a disaster."

"I understand, Skye. Perhaps you can join us the next time," I say, ignoring Reika's glare.

"Thanks for the pro tips, Akari. I'll see you all tomorrow." Skye walks down the hallway and students stop to watch the departure of the chubby new red-headed girl with the strange name.

# CHAPTER 3
# IN WHICH SKYE GOES SHOPPING

Outside my apartment building, I pause to dig my keys out of my bag. When Dad visited Tokyo in the spring, he called us to say he'd found the perfect apartment in the neighbourhood of Roppongi. He was super excited because it was large, light-filled, and close to his work at the Embassy and to my school. Yoko was not having it. She said Roppongi was home to a lot of sketchy bars and clubs, and that it was a bad neighbourhood in which to raise a teenaged girl. When he got back, he became like a walking, talking advertisement for Roppongi, telling us about all the museums, shops, and restaurants he'd discovered, then he would turn to me and wink. My dad almost never asks for anything, so I promised Yoko that I would keep my clubbing to a minimum. Both dad and Yoko laughed out loud, and, in the end, Yoko relented, and my father rented the place he'd fallen in love with. I totally get why he loves this place. It's a super modern corner apartment with floor to ceiling windows along two of the four walls and a view that takes my breath away every single time I walk into the living room. My bedroom is pretty big, and it has its own bathroom which I'm quite certain will make everyone in our family happy. In my mind, I've begun writing a fairy tale about how the apartment is enchanted and how nothing bad ever happens to anyone who lives here, but I already know better than that.

As I let myself into the foyer, I hear the distinctive rustle of bubble wrap. I drop my backpack at the door and follow the sound until I find Yoko unwrapping dishes in the middle of the light-filled living room. The sofas and chairs are piled high with boxes, so I join Yoko, who is sitting cross-legged on the floor. I lean over and kiss her on each cheek. For a while we work in silence, unwrapping our family's dishes.

"We have a lot of dishes for three people," I say. I grab my phone out of my pocket and take a photo of the mountain of bubble wrapped dishes. I tap on Instagram, skip the filters and write, *Unpacking. Tokyo.*

"I was just thinking the same thing, Skye. But we do throw some big parties and it's good not to have to rent dishes. Okay, that's enough small talk. How was your first day of school?"

"Yeah. It was okay, actually," I say. The look in her eyes is one of unadulterated joy, like she's jumped way ahead to the happy ending of this high school story of mine. "Yoko, please don't get too excited. It was just the first day. Anything could happen," I unwrap teacups and mugs while Yoko excavates our plates from layers of plastic.

"You're absolutely right! What was I thinking … getting excited for my daughter who just started at a new school in a new country?"

"As I said, it was okay."

"What was the best part?" Yoko gets up and folds the pieces of discarded bubble wrap before placing them into a large cardboard box.

"Best part? I don't know. There was this funny thing that happened during Orientation this morning. The principal gave all the eleventh graders a big speech about FULFILLING our

POTENTIAL. It's hilarious how she talks … like in all caps. She's a real ball buster."

Yoko looks up from the box of bubble wrap. "Don't say that in front of your father, Skye. He won't like it."

"But I learned it from him," I say.

"I know. What else was good?"

"There's this girl in my homeroom. She invited me to join her and her friends for lunch. She's smart and kind of sarcastic. She doesn't seem like the other Japanese girls at school. No disrespect intended, Yoko."

"None taken." Yoko drops back onto the floor and leans back against the sectional. She closes her eyes and sighs. "Sometimes I struggle with how much to tell you about Japan."

"Why?" I ask.

"Japan is complicated, my love. It appears a certain way on the surface, but you must go very deep in order to understand the culture. I'm also aware that for you and your dad, your experience of living here will be quite different than that of Japanese people."

"I'm starting to see that already," I say.

"Ultimately, I will try to mind my own business so you can have your own experiences. Over time, you will develop your own understanding of Japan and I don't want to clutter it up with experiences from my past that have nothing to do with you." Yoko closes her eyes again and I'm not sure if she's tired or just lost in her thoughts. I wonder about these experiences from her past, but I know that when Yoko is ready to tell me, she will.

As quietly as possible, I stack my sheets of bubble wrap inside the box. When I get to the last one, Yoko is sitting up again so I pass her a sheet of bubble wrap and she begins to pop each of the small plastic-wrapped pockets of air. Each time she bursts one of the bubbles, the popping sound makes her giggle and, finally, she begins to laugh loudly and without restraint.

"Ah! Therapy," says Yoko, wiping tears from the corners of her eyes.

"Hey, thanks," I say.

"For what, exactly?"

"Not treating me like a little kid."

"You're welcome. You didn't mention the name of your new friend," says Yoko.

"Akari. Does it mean something in Japanese? Or is it just a name?" I ask.

"It means something like glimmer," says Yoko. A reminder flashes up on Yoko's phone and she picks up her phone and reads the message. "Skye, an old friend has opened a clothing boutique this afternoon and I told her I would check it out today. Would you like to come with me?"

"Sure," I say.

"Perhaps we can pick up something for you too, like some linen for the August heat." I look at Yoko, my tiny bird-like stepmother, and wonder if she's forgotten how hard it is, outside of North America, to buy clothes that actually fit me.

We take the train to the neighbourhood of Daikanyama, which is filled with interesting shops and cafes, and Yoko enters the address of the shop into her phone. It's on a little backstreet, and a small bell jingles as Yoko opens the door and we pass into the cool air of the shop. The vibe is super relaxed, the walls have been painted a soothing cream colour, and the furniture is wooden with mid-century modern lines. I feel immediately at home. Yoko waves to a woman coming out of a back room.

"Skye, this is my friend Saka. We went to university together." Saka wears a long dusty rose tunic over a pair of beige linen pants. She bows towards us. "Come here and give me some love," says Yoko, stepping forward and folding the woman into her arms. I'm not sure that Saka is accustomed to being hugged in this way, but she's not hating it. When Yoko finally lets go, Saka extends a hand to me. "It's good to meet you, Skye. Yoko has told me so much about you. Based on what Yoko said you might be looking for, I've put some things in a change room for each of you."

There are six items hanging up in my change room: two pair of linen trousers, two blouses, a skirt, and a dress. Saka has beautiful taste but, as I get closer, I notice that these clothes look small. Like way too small for me. I check the labels and they all say XL, which would be the right size at home in Canada, but these look more like a medium. I lift up my arms to slip on the first blouse but, by the time it's at my elbows, I can tell it's too small. The second shirt fits, technically, but it's so tight across the chest and upper arms that I would never be comfortable wearing it.

"How are you doing, Skye?" says Yoko.

"Oh, you know. Okay." I can feel a line of sweat forming in the centre of my back, so I carefully remove the top and hang it back up. I try on the pants but both pairs are too snug across my butt and upper thighs. My grandmother MacTavish calls this singing tight. The dress has a fitted bodice, so I already know it's too small for me. I don't even try it on.

"There's a large mirror out here if you want to see how things look," says Yoko.

"Thanks." I pull a small pink handkerchief out of my knapsack and wipe the beads of perspiration from my forehead. There's a gentle knock on the door.

"Skye, can I come in?" I open the door for Yoko. "Is everything okay, love? Saka told me she had some beautiful things in your size."

I know that if I try to talk, I'll start crying and then Yoko

20

will feel bad, and her friend will feel bad, so I just stand there in my underwear willing the tears to stay inside me.

"Would it be better if I gave you a little space?"

I nod, and Yoko backs into the hallway. "I'm so sorry, Skye, if I screwed this up." I gently close the door behind her and let the hot tears arrive. I sit on the tiny chair in the change room and practice my breathing. Deep inhale. Longer exhale.

After wiping my face with my handkerchief, I pull on the skirt which is a deep pink with large lime green polka dots. It's an A-line skirt, and with the right boots and a baggy black tee, this could work. It wouldn't be terrible. Despite the elastic, the waistband digs into my belly and the fabric is tight across my abdomen. I'd have to lose a bit of weight to wear it.

I find Yoko at the cash register and add the pink and green skirt to the three items she is purchasing. "I'm so pleased you found something," says Saka. Yoko places her hand over mine on the counter and leaves it there longer than she needs to.

# CHAPTER 4
# IN WHICH AKARI NAVIGATES FRIENDSHIP

At our regular table at Starbucks, Reika slams her mug of soy latte down on the small round table with a loud *thwak*. Kimi jumps a little and then laughs. "So, the thing you've been dying to say since lunch is ..."

"This Canadian girl ..." says Reika.

"Her name is Skye. Let's use her name," I say.

"Okay. The thing is ... um, well ... I don't know exactly what to think of Skye," says Reika, tripping over her words.

"Of course, you don't. None of us do ... because we just met her," I say.

"Akari, you don't have to be snotty about it," says Reika.

"Really? Was I being snotty?" I turn to Kimi who is, as usual, quietly observing Reika and me bump heads.

"Maybe just a little," says Kimi, frowning slightly.

Following the rules of the girl-friendship code book, I apologize to Reika, but she can probably tell that my heart isn't in it. She gives me a 'whatever' look. We've been through this so many times before.

"Reika, what is really happening here? That hafu stuff in the cafeteria today was passive aggressive at best. If I were Skye, I would have been hurt by what you said," I say.

"Akari is right, Reika. You were mean," says Kimi, nodding. She breaks her large chocolate chip scone in three and places a piece in front of each of us.

"Maybe. I think we have a good thing, the three of us. We know and trust each other, and I don't think we need a fourth friend," says Reika pushing away Kimi's scone-gift. "Plus, with her around, we'll always have to speak English even though it's way easier to speak Japanese to each other."

"I have to call your bluff, Reika," I say. "We constantly shift between Japanese and English, like most of the students at our school. Also, Skye speaks Japanese. I overheard her in the hallway. Her Japanese isn't perfect, but neither is my English."

"You're going to have to get over that old story, Akari. Your English is better than most of our teachers. Do you know that Reika and I call you The Thesaurus?" says Kimi. Reika laughs.

"You could lean into a contraction a little more often, though," says Reika.

"Hey, mean-girl," Kimi turns to look at Reika. "Does your objection to Skye have anything to do with Fiona?"

Fiona had been the fourth girl in our friend group, from kindergarten until the end of ninth grade, when her family moved back to Australia. Even though most of the foreign girls hung out together, Fiona chose us. When she moved away, we struggled to figure out how to be just three friends. Over the year since Fiona left, I have sometimes felt left out because I live in Yokohama, which is almost an hour away from our school in central Tokyo, so I spend almost two hours on the train every day. It's not so much that I mind the commute, but Reika lives in Den-en-Chofu, which is only about fifteen minutes from school on the train, and Kimi lives in a creaky one-hundred-year-old wooden house in Ebisu, close enough to walk to school. Sometimes I get this strange feeling that three is an inherently awkward number in the arena of friendships. Perhaps four just works better. But I keep this to myself.

"We all miss her sunny goodness, Reika, but she left more than a year ago. Besides, I like Skye," says Kimi.

"You do?" Reika turns in her chair to look directly into Kimi's face.

"I do," says Kimi. "She's unique, and I think she seems kind."

"That hair, though!" says Reika. Kimi punches Reika gently on her shoulder. Reika grabs her shoulder and begins to fake-cry which makes the two women at the table beside us stare. I kick Reika under the table. She drops the act and sits up in her chair. Kimi stifles a laugh.

"I think she's courageous," I say. "Like the way she walked into the cafeteria today. The way she looks people in the eye. I wish I could be more like that."

"Look! It makes me crazy that you two are so much nicer than I am," said Reika. "This isn't about Fiona. The truth is I just don't like Skye, and I don't know why or how to explain it. Like when she joined us for lunch, did you see how she swung her legs over the bench? Her skirt flew up showing her thighs, but she didn't even notice. And she's a BIG girl."

"Reika, what's her size got to do with anything?" I can feel my heart pounding in my ears.

"I just get a bad vibe from her, like maybe she doesn't know herself. I think she's trouble," says Reika.

"For what it's worth, I think we should give her a chance," says Kimi.

Reika stands and drops her empty cup on my tray. "You two can be friends with whoever you want but that doesn't mean I have to like her or hang out with her." She grabs her bag and heads for the stairs

I raise my eyebrows at Kimi. "What was that?", I say.

"I'm not sure," says Kimi.

Reika and I disagree about things all the time, but this bump, this barrier between us, feels different, like it will be harder to come back from. As much as I want to make Reika happy, I have this feeling that I'm meant to be friends with Skye. I can't get it out of my head that I drew her before I even saw her. Kimi rests her hand on my back for a moment, then we finish our coffees and eat Reika's leftover scone.

# CHAPTER 5
# IN WHICH SKYE GETS A LETTER

When we get home from shopping, Yoko remembers that a letter came for me. There's only one person I can imagine that it might be from. Who else would contact Yoko or my dad for our new address and send me a letter so soon after we'd moved into our new place?

Claire.

I find a small blue envelope on the pillow of my meticulously made bed, which definitely did not look this way when I left the apartment this morning. I really should remember to make it myself. I'm too old to have it done for me.

The air conditioning unit in my room is set to an ecologically friendly twenty-four degrees which, in my opinion, does not actually constitute air conditioning at all, so I turn it down to twenty-one degrees, change into a pair of shorts and a T-shirt, and lie on my bed. I tuck my thumb gently inside the flap of the envelope to pry it open. There's just one page and the writing is tiny and beautiful and so very familiar.

Dear Skye,

A letter. An actual letter. I know you must be shocked at its arrival. I had to go all the way to the Latin Quarter to find a package of those light blue envelopes with the navy and red airmail border. Apparently, that's not a thing anymore.

It's so weird to think of you starting school in Japan while everyone in France is still having their long August vacation. We just got back from my grandmother's house in Provence, and I think she's starting to lose her mind a little. It's like she's finally saying all these things she's been dying to say for her whole life. From the moment we arrived, she told me how many calories were in everything I ate, lectured me about portion size, and when I took a second helping, she'd say, "No one wants a fat girlfriend, Claire." Those. Exact. Words. So freaking hurtful.

I was hoping that my parents would intervene on my behalf but, as usual, nothing.

Then I heard your voice in my head and you said that setting a boundary is a way to teach others how to treat us. So, one night, as she was washing the dinner dishes and I was drying, I said, and I am totally quoting here, "Grand-mère, I know you love me and you want me to have a good life, but extreme thinness is not a requirement for finding a life partner. Please stop making comments about my body." There was a long pause followed by the sound of my grandmother sucking in air followed by the sound of her stomping out of the kitchen. The good news is that she stopped talking to me about food after that. Actually, she stopped talking to me about everything. This visit with my grandparents helped me understand a bit more about why my mother is so angry all the time but she's an adult now so I don't think it's fair to use her own crappy childhood as an excuse for being a terrible mother.

Anyway, I felt proud for standing up for myself. Thanks for being the voice in my head telling me that I deserved better.

What's it like there? Have you made friends? Even as I write that question, I feel so conflicted. Of course, I hope you are starting to make good friends at your new school. You deserve kind people in your life. There is also a (small-ish) part of me that hopes things don't work out in Tokyo so that your family decides to return to Paris. Listen, I know that's awful and selfish and highly unlikely but having you as my best friend for the past four years made life bearable. I'm not sure how my life works without you. My apologies. I'm feeling sorry for myself which is not fair to you.

I know our last few weeks were awkward. I wish there was some way I could make that better.

I've sent you a polaroid of the Eiffel Tower. We took my cousins on a tour of the Seine and one of them had this old polaroid camera. I think it turned out pretty well. Seeing the Eiffel from the river made me feel melancholy and I knew you would understand.

I'm loving your Instagrams. They make me feel like I'm there with you. That and listening to Nina Simone.

Sending you lots of love.

Claire

I read the letter a second time, then fold it up, slide it back inside the delicate airmail envelope, and stash it in the drawer of my bedside table. I pick up my laptop and open my email.

Dear Claire,

I just got home from my first day of school to find your letter, a real letter that crossed half the world to get here. It's so great to hear from you.

Your grandmother doesn't mean to be wicked, does she? I mean, probably not, right? Like she's just a person from her generation. Still, I'm really sorry she was cruel and that your mom didn't have your back. Again. You deserve SO MUCH BETTER and I'm so proud of you for speaking up. I'm sorry it's so hard. Just hang on, Claire. In two years, you'll go to university, and you'll get to live by your own rules. You can do this!

Yoko said it would be hot when we arrived but 'hot' doesn't even begin to cover it. It's like August in Paris times one million. The backs of my knees start to sweat just standing waiting for the train. You know how directionally challenged I am, so I've gotten lost a bunch of times, but people here are really nice and helpful although they do seem surprised when I start speaking Japanese. I'm not going to lie ... I enjoy that part! Mostly we've just been unpacking and getting settled. Our apartment is cool and I think you'd love the view.

Tokyo is so many things. It's loud but it's quiet and crowded while also being empty. Every time I come out of the metro, the city is different. Like really different but the architecture all feels kind of the same, so I don't know how that differentness works. I miss the oldness of Paris, but I know Tokyo is old too, even older maybe, but all that history is buried underneath shiny new apartment buildings and posh shops and neon signs. But then you'll pass by some small side street and catch a glimpse of a wall of cigarette packages behind glass and there's a window and, behind the window of the shop, there's an old man selling cigarettes and you know he's been there forever. This happened to me just the other day and the old dude behind the window smiled at me, just a little, and I was certain he invented the universe. I don't think I could find that street again if you offered me a million euros, but I felt really peaceful in his presence. That's weird right?

It's too soon to know about friends. I can say the kids weren't terrible so that's something. I like most of my teachers.

Thank you for wanting good things for me. You know that's what I want for you too, right?

If I could live my last few weeks in Paris over again, I would not have told you how I felt about you. My confession wasn't strictly necessary because I knew you didn't feel the same way. Still, I thought maybe you should know, like maybe you would want to know. It probably wasn't my finest thirty minutes. Maybe I could just call you and we could talk about it. You know, if you want to. Or not.

Whenever you see a peony or a firefly, that's me sending you love.

Yours,

Skye

I only have to type the first three letters of Claire's name before my email recognizes who I'm writing to and auto-fills her address. My heart beats loud and fast as I move the cursor towards the blue send button. I take my fingers off the keypad. It's too much. I can't. I hit the X at the top of the message and the email slips, like a ghost, into my drafts.

———

In the morning, I wake before my parents and make a cafe latte with my dad's very expensive, excessively shiny, red espresso machine. As hard as I try, I can't manage to create the shape of a heart with my milk. The baristas in Paris made it look so easy.

The living room is starting to resemble a room where people might actually live. Yoko and I finished unpacking the kitchen and decorative stuff after dinner last night, and Dad unpacked and shelved our enormous library. The built-in bookcases run from the floor all the way to the ceiling and, for the first time in four years, we have room for more books than we own. Although the big sectional is now back in the seating business, I prefer to sit cross-legged on the soft Moroccan rug in front of the living room window, where the window ledge offers a perfect place to set my mug. Although the sun rises early in Tokyo, most of the city has not yet started its day.

Sometimes I forget that I now live in the most populated city on earth but then I stumble upon some random factoid like metro Tokyo alone has almost as many people as all of Canada, and my mind explodes. Not far from our apartment, millions of people travel through Shibuya Station every day. The odd thing is that the city just works. There are rules that govern everything. Before our first trip on the Metro, Yoko gave Dad and me a little pep talk outside the station. "If you're standing on the escalator, always move to the left so that people who are running for their train can move more quickly on the right. It's essential that you two get this right." Dad laughed but Yoko shot him a look that made him stop laughing. I noticed that almost everyone inside the station seemed absolutely certain where they were going and those who weren't stepped out of the flow of traffic to look at their phone.

This city reminds me of a scene from an animated film I loved as a kid. These insects are standing in the middle of the road and one of them wonders if their society isn't a little too perfect while all these cars travel around them. They are completely unaware of the danger they're in because everyone else is working so hard to protect them. That's how I feel after a few weeks of living here; it's the most perfectly functioning place on Earth. There are a lot of rules to protect me, and I don't even know what they are yet.

I miss the extravagant beauty of Paris, the cafe-au-lait-ness of it, but I find Tokyo lovely in its own way. It took months to adjust to living in Paris and I try to remember that it's okay if Tokyo takes time as well.

I grab my phone and take a photo of the still-pink skyline. I Instagram it with the caption, *Wish you were here*, and tag Claire. Then I go into edit mode and delete the caption and the tag. Leaving Claire is the jagged edge of this move.

My dad appears at the entrance to the living room wearing plaid pyjama bottoms and a T-shirt. His feet are bare, and his short red hair sticks out in every direction.

"Good morning, daughter." He ruffles my hair on his way to the sofa. He stretches out as though there isn't a place in the world where he's uncomfortable. "Good first day, kiddo?"

"Yup."

"Starting at a new school can be challenging, right?"

"Yup." I suspect we're both thinking about my exceedingly rough landing at my school in Paris.

"You would tell me if things were bad, right?" he says.

"I would try, Dad."

"Alright, Daughter. That's all a father can ask." He sits up, leans forward, and kisses my forehead, which still feels lovely.

"Hey, Dad. Knock knock."

He sits up, rubs his hands together and leans towards me. "Who's there?" he says, as he has a million times before.

"Hike," I say.

"Hike who?"

"I didn't know you liked Japanese poetry." He roars with laughter at my Japan-specific joke and, when he finishes wiping the tears from his eyes, he grabs a pillow and throws it at me.

"Well done, my girl. Very well done," he says as gets up. He crosses the room to the kitchen where I can hear the whir of the espresso machine as he hums this old song he loves. *Ahead by a Century*.

# CHAPTER 6

# IN WHICH AKARI INTRODUCES A FOURTH

I wake up before the alarm but keep my eyes closed for a few minutes. It's only the second day of school and Reika is already angry with me. What is she angry about? I don't remember right away. There it is. Skye, the new girl. I feel the same lump in my throat I felt in Starbucks yesterday afternoon, and the anxious feeling keeps growing, so I get up and get dressed in my school uniform. I tuck my white cotton blouse inside the plaid skirt. Kimi and Reika wear their skirts short, but I couldn't be bothered to shorten mine, so it ends just above my knees. I pull on my navy socks and check myself in the mirror. There I am. Short black hair. Round face. Medium height. Average in absolutely every way.

My backpack is already packed with my books, computer, and sketchbook, so I grab it and descend the stairs quietly so that I don't wake my dad if he had a late night at work. I can smell the fish grilling before I turn into the kitchen. Mom always makes a full traditional breakfast of rice, miso soup, natto, grilled fish, pickled vegetables, and salad. I've never been a big fan of natto, which is fermented soybeans, and that makes me feel like a traitor to my people, but what can I do? The heart wants what it wants, and since I started high school, I prefer to eat toast or a bowl of cereal. Unfortunately, this has made breakfast a bit of a battlefield.

I say good morning to my mother as I enter the kitchen and she nods in my direction. "Breakfast?" She's wearing the bright pink Minnie Mouse apron that her sister brought back from Disneyland in California last year. She's a serious person with a weakness for cute things. If this preference is genetic, it skipped a generation with me.

"Thanks, Mom. I'm just going to have a bowl of cereal." A dark shadow crosses her face, but she says nothing. I pour myself a bowl of granola and then take a moment to put the box of cereal and milk away before sitting down at the table. We're a clean-as-you-go kind of household. We are also a clean-as-you-go kind of nation. "Itadakimasu," I say, giving thanks for my meal. My mother nods and fills my yellow mug with coffee.

"Coffee is terrible for you. I shouldn't be making it for you."

"I know. Thank you, mom." She shrugs but I know there's a smile buried deep inside that gesture.

"How are Reika and Kimi and their families?"

"Reika and Kimi are fine. They didn't mention their parents." These words are still hanging in the air when I realize I have said the wrong thing. I should have just said they were all fine. My mother frowns and I quickly add, "I am sure everyone is fine, Mom. If not, Reika and Kimi would have said something." My mother nods. What I don't say is, *Teenagers don't really talk about our parents unless we are complaining about them.* For just a moment, I feel a tiny bit superior for keeping that to myself.

I'm just finishing my cereal when we hear my father's slippered feet on the stairs. He appears, already dressed in his work suit, and takes his seat at the table. On the table my mother lays several small plates containing the various parts of their breakfast. Unlike me, my father is a huge fan of natto and fish in the morning, and he's also a person of few words so after his "Itadakimasu" the kitchen is quiet except for the sounds of my father eating and my mother washing up the dishes.

"Dad, you're going to work early this morning," I say.

"Big meeting," he says. I nod. "How was the first day?

"Fine, thank you."

"Your mother and I are hoping for a very successful year," he says. Mom drops her towel on the counter and quickly turns to face me. Her eyes narrow. I swallow the *Me too!* that was on my lips and say instead, "I promise that I will work diligently."

———

Skye says she is free after school and the four of us head to the coffee shop. As we enter, Reika complains that she is running short on money, so Kimi buys Reika's coffee. When we get up to the third floor, we grab a table for four.

"Tell us about Paris, Skye," says Kimi leaning forward. Whatever is happening with Reika, Kimi does not seem infected by it.

"Have you visited?" Skye asks. All three of us shake our heads. "There's this quote by James Thurber: 'The whole of Paris is a vast university of Art, Literature and Music. Paris is a seminar, a post-graduate course in Everything.' The first time I read that quote, I nodded my head. Like I actually nodded my head. That's exactly how it feels. Like it's this city where you live but it's also a living museum and people come from all over the world to visit that museum."

"What was your family doing there?" asks Kimi.

"My dad worked at the Canadian Embassy, so we were there for his work. Yoko, my stepmom, is a Japanese translator so she can work from anywhere. We moved at the beginning of grade seven. It was a pretty terrible time to move," says Skye.

"Our friend Fiona moved back to Australia at the end of grade nine. She said that was bad too," I say. Kimi and Reika nod their heads in agreement.

"What do you miss about Paris?" says Kimi.

"Definitely the food, like even the most basic stuff like bread and cheese. Canadians take those two ingredients and make grilled cheese sandwiches. But in Paris, the bread is heavenly. Like God baked it or something. There are a zillion different cheeses. At first, I didn't like the strong ones, the ones that smell like feet, but eventually, I even started to like blue cheese. I miss chocolate ... oh, and macarons. At Ladurée they make these salted-caramel macarons that I'm sort of addicted to."

"We have a Ladurée Teahouse in Ginza. Let's go sometime," says Kimi. Skye extends her closed hand for a fist bump and Kimi responds immediately, stretching out her own arm and gently bumping Skye's fist. Even Reika laughs.

"Wow! You are some nerdy girls!" says Reika. Four armchairs have opened up, and Reika pops over and leaves her phone on the table while we gather up our bags.

"What's with the phone?" Skye asks.

"That's our very sophisticated table reservation system," says Reika as she wedges her cello into the space between her chair and the wall. Skye drops her bag on the floor, but I shake my head and she picks it up and places it between her back and the back of the armchair as Kimi, Reika, and I have done.

"Wow! In every other nation state on the planet, that would be an invitation for someone to steal your phone," Skye says. The three of us nod.

"Sometimes we forget how safe it is here," I say. "It can be difficult to see things clearly when you are in the middle of them."

"My Philosophy teacher would say something like, 'To

what extent is it possible to ever see something clearly,'" says Skye. Our laughter draws the attention and frowns of two older women sitting nearby.

"What else do you miss about Paris?" whispers Kimi.

"Visiting museums and galleries with my parents. Buying records at this old shop in the Marais. Crepes, I'm not going to lie. Sitting in the Tuileries, just people-watching, you know? Around four o'clock at this time of the year the sun is all golden and you think there can't possibly be a more beautiful place on earth. Hanging out with my friends." Skye looks out the window and takes a deep breath.

"Yum. It sounds perfect," says Kimi.

"Some of it was. Some of it, not so much. For example, I won't miss the smell of thousand-year-old cat urine." Reika, Kimi, and I wrinkle our noses. "Also, the metro is filled with sketchy characters and there are parts of the city where I wasn't allowed to go on my own, which made me feel like a little kid. The worst part was that sometimes, before they knew I spoke French, some people were sort of obnoxious to me."

"Yuck," says Reika. I raise an eyebrow at Reika who pretends not to notice so I clear my throat and Skye asks if I'm okay. I nod and take a sip of tea.

"They're not very interested in hiding their disdain," says Skye.

"If hiding one's disdain were an Olympic sport, the Japanese would win the gold, silver, and bronze medals. For all eternity. Eventually other countries would just stop competing against us," I say. Kimi laughs particularly loudly while an evil grin spreads across Reika's face.

"Yoko says that French and Japanese cultures have some things in common," Skye says.

"Really? Do tell," says Reika. Kimi kicks Reika's foot under the table and Reika flashes her a big smile in return.

"She says that in France and Japan, many people are obsessed with beauty in design, fashion, and architecture. They care about food, about knowing where their food came from. Both cultures value knowing what is correct, like what fork to use for dessert, and then always doing the correct thing," Skye says.

"Actually, that's true," says Reika. "I'd never thought of it that way before."

"Seriously, though, I've been talking way too much about myself. What will the three of you miss the most if you go to university outside Japan?" Skye asks.

"Ramen," we answer in unison and then laugh.

"There's this place called Ippudo. They serve ramen in these big red bowls, and you can choose what kind of noodles you want, and each bowl comes with this perfectly cooked hard-boiled egg. But not hard ... still soft and gooey. Trust us. It's that good," says Kimi.

"We'll take you," I say. "We go all the time."

"Yes, please! Have you three moved around with your parents' work?" Skye says, taking a sip of her latte, which must be cold by now.

"Nope. We've all been at this school since kindergarten," says Reika.

"You've known each other since you were five?" Skye's eyes widen.

"Yup. Pretty boring, right?" says Reika.

"Are you kidding? It sounds amazing to me."

"You got to live in Paris for four years," says Reika. "That sounds pretty great to me. I'd give anything to get out of here."

"Yeah, I know it sounds weird. I definitely feel lucky to have lived there and now here in Tokyo, but sometimes I feel like I don't belong anywhere." I try to send Skye a look that conveys kindness and reassurance, but I worry it looks more like pity.

Reika and Kimi talk about their upcoming volleyball tryouts, but Skye seems far away. After a round of byes and see you laters, Reika and Kimi drop off their cups and plates at the recycling station and disappear down the stairs.

"Hey," I say. "I noticed that you seem a little sad. Do you want to talk about it?"

"Not really ... but I wondered if you'd go shopping with me some time. I need to buy a new bag and I'm sort of what you might call directionally challenged."

———

I hardly ever come to Shibuya except on my way somewhere else. Shibuya Crossing is one of the few things that most tourists know about Tokyo. I can't really blame them though. What do I know about New York City? I doubt New Yorkers spend much time in Times Square or at the Statue of Liberty. From the second floor of Starbucks, Shibuya Crossing looks epic but when you walk through the crossing, it doesn't feel crowded at all. It just feels like crossing a street. Life is like that. What seems magical to one person is just regular life for another.

Skye and I made plans to meet outside the coffee shop, because you literally cannot miss it, and then we're going to a thrift shop which strikes me as particularly funny given that most Japanese people don't like used things. I wonder if Skye knows that. Even if she does, she probably won't care. From what I know of her thus far, Skye is her own country.

I look up to see her running towards me. She runs past me by a bit then turns right, tilts her arms like the wings of an airplane, and makes a large loop back to where I'm standing.

"Hey! Sorry I'm late. Shibuya Station is kind of a nightmare."

"Really?" I say.

"Totally lost. Had to ask a guard for directions. Okay, three guards. Those guys know everything."

"I am sorry that happened to you, but perhaps you will be comforted to know that my sense of direction is extraordinary. It is almost as if I have a chip in my brain that gives me access to Google Earth through my eyeballs," I say.

"Show off."

"I like your new hair style." Skye had pulled her massive head of hair up into a large, floppy red top knot.

"I saw a girl pull up her hair like this while waiting on the train platform last night. And I want to be super-fashionable for our shopping expedition," says Skye.

"Excellent. You can check that item off your list."

"Yup. You're lucky to have short hair," says Skye.

"It wasn't luck. It was a decision," I say.

"So, where's this place?" says Skye. She looks like she's getting ready to sit down on the ground, so I start to move.

"Pretty close. About six or seven blocks."

"Really. Since when is six or seven blocks considered close?"

"It just feels longer because it's so hot."

"No kidding," says Skye.

"My father says, 'Tokyo in August ... welcome to hell.'"

"Your dad and I are on the same heat-wavelength." She pulls a paper fan out of her backpack while laughing at her own joke.

It turns out to be ten blocks to the shop. I know this because Skye counts them out loud. When we stop to buy water at a convenience store, Skye stands directly under the air conditioner, pops up on her tiptoes and sighs loudly.

The vintage shop is on the third floor of a building with no elevator and Skye groans when she sees the flights of stairs.

"Come on, Skye. You can do this."

"No pep talk required. Sorry. Did I mention this heat makes me cranky?" says Skye.

"There was no need for you to mention it."

The store is cool, both in terms of the temperature and the vibe, and is well stocked with vintage clothes, shoes, and vinyl. There's an entire wall of hats and another wall of purses. A young saleswoman greets us as we enter.

"Wow!" Skye walks between the rows of clothes. "It's like being lost in a vintage forest. A really orderly forest." Skye takes her phone out of her back pocket.

"It's not permitted," I say.

"What?"

"You looked like you were going to take a photograph. Businesses don't allow customers to take photos of their merchandise," I say.

"Okay. Thanks." Skye pops her phone back in her pocket and begins moving hangers to get a better look at the clothes. "Hey, here's a cute top for you." The top is light pink with tiny pineapples.

"Thank you for thinking of me, Skye, but I do not really get the kawaii thing. It's cute. So what?" I say.

"Really? That's your stance? You don't like cute things. I think you just lost your citizenship," says Skye. I laugh out loud and cover my mouth with my hand.

"Possibly," I say.

"What do you like, then? Like what do you wear when you're not at school?" says Skye.

"Anything in black."

Skye holds up a sequined black flapper dress.

I screw up my face. "I amend that statement. Simple and black. Jeans and a black turtleneck, for example."

"So ... boring and bleak. Remind me, is black an absence of colour, or all colours at the same time? I can't seem to remember," says Skye.

"Black absorbs light and is an absence of colour. It is the visual impression experienced when no visible light reaches the eye," I say with a smile.

"Good to know. Hey what about this?" Skye holds up a black cashmere cardigan. "It's your style and it's a pretty good price for cashmere." Skye hands me the cardigan and I make eye contact with the saleswoman at the front desk. The woman nods her head.

"Hey! What was that?" Skye says.

"I was asking her permission to try it on."

"Cool. In Paris, I wouldn't have even picked this up off the shelf. The salesgirl would have done it for me," Skye says. I unbutton the sweater and slip it on. "It suits you. It's a bit big but in that cool 'this is my boyfriend's sweater' kind of way."

"I think so too, but I will probably not buy it. My mother would not like it. She is distinctly anti-germ and used things. I think of them as her Ebola-fears."

"No problem. Don't tell her it's vintage," says Skye

"No such luck. She would know."

"Yeah. My mom would too."

"What happened to your old purse?" I ask.

"It got all moldy in the shipment. We had to throw it out."

"Oh! That is a shame. I'm sorry."

"No big. They're just things, right?" says Skye, a little too breezily.

I survey the bags and find a brown leather one that looks a bit like a doctor's bag. The leather is quite hard, and the purse is in good shape. I lift it off its hook and pass it to Skye.

"Hey! That's cool," says Skye. She carries it up to the mirror and holds it in front of her with both hands. Then she hooks it over her right forearm and laughs. "I don't get why women do that," she says. "It looks ridiculous and must be torture for wimpy forearms." I nod. I don't even own a purse.

We look through the rest of the bags but none of them comes close to the bag Skye is holding. It is definitely her style.

"It makes me feel super grown-up, and it'll look cool with my red Converse," says Skye.

"Everything looks good with red Converse. It is a universal law," I say.

Skye, who is already on her way to the counter to pay for the bag, turns back towards me.

"Get out of my head, Miss Akari."

# CHAPTER 7

# IN WHICH SKYE GETS MORE THAN SHE BARGAINED FOR

O n the train ride home, I hold my new purse inside a brown paper bag on my lap.

"You can put that on the shelf if you want," Akari says, as she looks up at the metal rack above our heads.

"While my head knows that's true, four years of Paris metro training will not be so easily undone."

"Are you saying you never stored your bag on the shelf on a Paris train?" Akari says.

"Oh my God, no." A couple of people look up from their phones. "Stealing is an art form in Paris. You can't even leave your umbrella up there. Oh, there's another thing I won't miss about Paris. The thieves." I pull the package towards my chest. "Hmm. That's odd." I pull the purse out the bag and look inside.

"What are you looking for?" says Akari.

"I don't know exactly. I felt something hard inside," I say.

"Is there something in the side pocket?" she says.

I open the zipper in the satin lining and thrust my hand inside the pocket. "Nope, nothing."

"Skye, get up. We are at Roppongi Station." Akari is on her feet, headed for the exit.

The doors *bing*. We jump off the train and sit on the closest bench. I place the carrier bag and my backpack on the ground. Akari picks them up and puts them on the bench beside her.

"Okay, Mom," I say.

"Sorry. Habit. Is it possible to turn the lining inside out?" says Akari.

"Should be." I turn the purse upside down and the lining slides out of the leather with a thud.

"There is definitely something in there." Akari clasps the lining between her hands. "It feels like a book. Hey, there's a rip in the bottom of this pocket. Put the lining back inside the purse and let me see if I can get whatever it is out."

"If you can't get it out through that rip, I've got a Swiss Army knife with me," I say.

"Shhhh! Skye, you cannot carry a pocketknife in Japan! It is against the law. Like really, totally against the law." Akari's eyes are wide.

"Even a little Swiss Army knife? It was a gift from my dad," I say.

"Yes, even a Swiss Army knife. Promise me that you will leave it at home from now on," says Akari.

"Okay." I tuck the lining back inside the purse and hand the bag to Akari, who reaches into the side pocket and starts to wiggle the object loose.

"I have almost got it. Oh, I'm afraid I am going to tear the fabric a little," says Akari.

"Go for it. Remember, I was ready to cut it open," I say.

Akari has her right hand wrapped securely around the top of the object. She takes a deep breath and yanks it out of the pocket.

"It's a book," I say. "Open it!"

"What if the contents are private?" says Akari.

"Well, it's inside a purse I just bought, so that makes it not so private," I say. Akari hands me the black medium-sized hard-cover book. When I open it, I discover that the letters are written in kanji, so I flip it over and open it to what is still for me the back page.

"It looks like a journal. It's the same brand as the one I've been buying for the last few years," I say.

On the first page there is only one phrase, and it has been written in blue ink, in larger than average characters. The handwriting is not exactly messy, but it seems confident. Not worried about the rules. On the first page of the journal someone has written, "The 38 Impossible Loves of Naoko Nishizawa."

"Akari, I already know what you're going to say," I say.

"Do you? Can you feel it in your Scottish blood and bones?" says Akari. I laugh at the wonderful strangeness of her question.

"Yup. You'd like us to take the journal back to the store."

"Indeed. You have the perceptive qualities of a Betazoid," says Akari.

"A what?"

"Commander Deanna Troi from Star Trek: The Next Generation. She was an empath. You are going to need some serious pop culture training. How do you not know this stuff?" says Akari.

"We don't own a television," I say.

"Now that is interesting," says Akari. "A North American who doesn't watch television."

"Stereotype much? Listen, I don't need to be a Betazoid to read the disapproval forming between your eyebrows. When does the store close?" I ask.

Akari does a quick search on her phone. "Oh. The shop closed at six o'clock."

"Okay, I'll take it back in the morning," I say.

"Excellent. They open at ten o'clock."

"Slackers," I say.

"Are you certain you can find the store on your own?" says Akari.

"Piece of cake. I'll use Google Maps. If I get really lost, I'll catch a taxi."

"I really would like to go with you, but I have to spend Sunday with my family. It's a family rule," says Akari.

"Sure. I get it."

"Skye?"

"Akari?"

"Promise me that you will not read the journal, okay? It is private," she says.

"I promise." I place it inside the purse and close the clasp.

Suddenly, Akari jumps up and runs for the train to Naka-Meguro. Just before she steps onto the train, she mouths the words, "Good luck with that."

———

At nine o'clock, I text Akari and say:

SKYE

I'm a terrible person.

AKARI

Please be more specific.

I read the journal.

Yes. This was anticipated.

Just the first entry.

And?

I think you should read it.

You are not a good influence.

> Probably. But I really think you're really going to want to read this.

See you tomorrow.

––––––––

It's the end of the day and I'm melting in the afternoon heat as I wait for Akari at her locker.

"Hey!" I say.

"Cool hat," she says.

For a minute, I don't know what she's talking about but then I remember that Yoko found this straw hat I love when she was unpacking yesterday. It's got a wide brim and a thick black ribbon.

"So, about the journal," I say. "Does reading it make me a bad person?"

Akari straightens up and looks at me. "Not bad, exactly."

"Curious, right. Inquisitive?"

"Impatient. Impulsive. Lacking in discipline," says Akari.

"Okay. Guilty as charged. And, for the record, I really am sorry. I had every intention of leaving the journal closed and returning it to the store on Sunday. I tucked the journal inside my new purse, and then I placed the purse inside the carrier bag, which I stored at the very back of my closet. I secured it away. But during the night, it started to glow," I say.

Akari raises her eyebrows and her eyes twinkle. "If I understand your story correctly, the journal glowed through the purse, the carrier bag and your closet door? And you were able to see this even though you were sleeping?"

"It glowed like the green light from an alien spaceship. It woke me up and I couldn't fall back to sleep. The glowing was like a pulsating message: Read me. Read me. Read me," I say.

Akari shakes her head and laughs.

"Listen, I'll take the journal back to the shop if you really want me to, but I want to ask one favour first," I say.

"Yes? I am listening," says Akari, as she carefully slides her laptop into her backpack.

"Would you just read the first entry?" Akari pulls her violin case off the hook, closes her locker, and leans her head against the metal. She closes her eyes.

"What good would that do?" says Akari.

"Then we could start looking for clues to find her. This woman. Naoko Nishizawa." I hold out the journal, and Akari takes it from my hands.

# CHAPTER 8
# IN WHICH NAOKO NISHIZAWA WRITES ABOUT HER FIRST LOVE

My first love was also my first impossible love. I'm sure this is the case for most people.

That first love was impossible on so many levels that I find myself embarrassed now, just writing about it. We were completely unsuitable for each other. He was from a poor family, and he'd decided to change his destiny. He described the Japanese socio-economic system as a feudal one and he was about to change lanes. I had nothing to say about the feudal system, as it had worked so well for my family.

Kenji was convinced that if he worked hard enough, he would get accepted to the University of Tokyo, where so many of the Prime Ministers go to school, and he would become acquainted with these sons of important men, and they would take him with them on their journey to the top of the nation.

He sat near the front of our classrooms. While other students dozed and zoned out, Kenji recorded every word our teachers said, more like a court reporter than a high school student. Of course, I never complained because he was always happy to give me the notes. After finishing his homework every evening, he went over that day's notes, constantly revising what we had been taught. He became adept at understanding the mind of each teacher. Eventually, he was able to anticipate what questions we'd be asked on a test.

Kenji powered through high school. A coal-powered locomotive. I floated along on the breeze of his knowledge.

He had no time for fun. Aside from school, which we attended six days a week, he had only two activities: karate, at his local dojo with an 88-year-old sensei who was the person he loved most in the world, and violin, which he had played since he was four. Technically, he was very good. Everyone said so. Although I was no expert on stringed instruments and it felt terribly disloyal to see it so clearly, there was no heart in his performance. He had learned the notes, learned the correct placement of his fingers, and practiced, practiced, practiced until the piece flowed like a river. But there was no joy in it. No despair. No transformation. Just notes, perfectly executed.

He had no friends except me and I'm not even sure I was a friend. I was his girl. He had never asked me, and I had never accepted, but we had been together since we were fourteen. We had known each other since we were six.

From my description, you may picture him as a slight and serious-looking young man in glasses, but Kenji's insides didn't match his outsides. His skin was smooth and tanned even in the middle of winter. He had a heart shaped face and upper arms the size of tree trunks. He towered over the other boys, brooding and magnificent.

That was my Kenji.

I will never be able to say which part of him I loved more ... his intellect and staggering determination to change his stars, or the sheer beauty of him.

On the streets, girls in their school uniforms of navy-blue socks and blazers stared at him. Older women, in their kimono, were not immune to his charms. I never felt angry though. He was beautiful and he was mine.

Kenji's social experiment proved successful. He was admitted to Todai with a scholarship. His mother, dressed in a light pink suit, cried through the entire graduation ceremony. I was also admitted to Todai, partly because of my proximity to Kenji's brain and his encyclopedia of class notes, and partly due to my own family's connections. A member of the board of trustees of the university owed my father a favour. As I crossed the stage to accept my diploma, my father wore a smug smile that suggested that he was both impressed with his mastery of the art of persuasion, and relieved that the long and glorious line of Todai graduates from our family would not be broken on account of his only child, a frivolous daughter.

That evening, after the mandatory family celebrations, we snuck out of our respective homes and met in the park that marked the midway point between his family's apartment and my family's house. He took my hands in his and said, "I am very glad, Naoko, that we will attend university together in the fall."

It was the most romantic thing he had ever said to me. I felt as though he'd proposed marriage. Perhaps, in the serious world that Kenji inhabited, he had.

Two weeks later he was dead. Struck by a delivery truck while cycling to the store to buy his mother some rice.

# CHAPTER 9

# IN WHICH SKYE DOES WHAT SHE WANTS AND NOT WHAT SHE SHOULD

At nine o'clock I video-call Akari. Yoko says that to call any later is rude. There are so many rules to remember. The red rug from my room in Paris came back from the cleaners and when I got home from school, it was stretched out beside my bed as if it had been there the entire time. Before I call Akari, I pull some throw pillows onto the rug and make a little fort against the bed. No. More like a castle.

Akari pops up on my phone. She's at her desk. I wave at her, then she disappears for a minute, and I hear her bedroom door close. I notice there's nothing on the wall behind her, just that oatmeal-coloured wallpaper with the tiny squares that Yoko says is used in almost every home in Japan.

"Sad, right?" I say, as Akari sits in her desk chair.

"Beautiful," says Akari.

"And sad," I say.

"I am not yet certain. I am thinking." Akari closes her eyes. "I'm still taking it in."

I grab another pillow and prop myself up against the bed. After a few moments Akari opens her eyes and asks, "Do you think she is real? That she's a real person?"

"Naoko? Absolutely," I say.

"And that she is still alive?" says Akari.

"I'm certain of it. The kind of journal she used, they started making them in 1997. I looked it up. That's not so long ago."

"Skye, I feel guilty about reading the journal but also ..."

"Curious? Giddy with anticipation?" I say.

"Both of those things. Then I remember that these words are someone's most private thoughts and I feel uncomfortable that this journal is out here in the world. All her secrets, these observations about her first love, for anyone to read."

"Not anyone. Us," I say.

"I know but still, if this happened to me, I would die of shame."

"Akari, do you want me to take the journal back to the store?" I move my face closer to my phone, which makes Akari laugh.

"I did at first, but I have to admit I loved the first entry. It reads like an amazing novel I borrowed from my mother's book-shelf without her permission. There is something compelling about Naoko's voice and I want to know what happens next." Akari sighs.

"That's it, exactly. I'm already addicted to the story, and we've just begun reading it. There's this quality in her writing that says, 'I trust you, Reader.' Listen, I know she doesn't know me, and she probably never thought a Canadian kid would read her journal, but I feel like she's okay with it and that she trusts me to understand her story. Does that make sense?"

Akari smiles.

"My parents are always saying that I'm a shameless roman-tic, so the fact that there are thirty-seven more love stories is like catnip for me. I'm dying to know what makes them impossible. Are they all impossible or is there one that sticks, or maybe more than one?

"Naoko had you at konichiwa," says Akari.

"Exactly! Akari, listen, I know you are not super comfortable with my decision not to take the journal back to the store, but I want you to know that I genuinely believe that Naoko is out there somewhere, and if anyone can find her, it's us. You should know that I am both sleuthy and deeply stubborn as a person."

"As much as I believe in your sleuthiness and your stubbornness, locating her seems unlikely. Yet I find myself wanting to believe that it is possible," says Akari.

"Great! Then believe it! With your super-tingly sense of direction and my absolute inability to take no for an answer, I think we're the best people for the job," I say.

Akari chuckles and covers her mouth with her hand.

"Should we create some guidelines for reading the journal?" I say. "For example, we should only read one entry per day so we can take in the information and record clues."

"Excellent idea. Hold on a moment." Akari disappears for a moment and returns holding a notebook and pen. She begins recording our guidelines. "Okay. Two. Thou shalt not tell another living soul about Naoko Nishizawa's journal. No one. Not our friends or our parents. Capiche?"

"I'm curious. Are you going to write down the word 'capiche'?" I ask.

"No. Everything up to that point. Your turn," says Akari.

"Three. Akari and Skye will share custody of the journal, but Skye will keep it on the weekend."

"That is fair. It was inside your purse. Four. As soon as we locate Naoko Nishizawa, we return said journal to her in person. Together," says Akari

"As long as she lives in Tokyo, right? If she lives in Okinawa or California, we might have to mail it to her," I say.

"Four B. Should Naoko Nishizawa live in a location other than Tokyo, Skye and Akari will assess the viability of travel to her location. If this option is not possible, they may have to return the journal via Postal Services," says Akari.

"Wow. You should be a lawyer," I say.

"Maybe I already am one!" says Akari.

"Or maybe a junior in high school ..."

"Killer of dreams. Anything else?" says Akari.

"Not that I can think of, but we should be free to amend the list as we go," I say.

"Agreed," says Akari. "One issue remains. How will you cope with the green light on the nights that you have custody?"

"What green light?" I ask.

"Seriously?" Now Akari's face grows much larger as she leans closer to the camera in her laptop. She glares at me. "The glowing green light emitted by the journal last night. Through your closet door." Finally, I catch her meaning.

"Right!" I say. Akari laughs.

"Do you think you will be able to sleep through the night?" says Akari.

"It shouldn't be a problem now that the journal has gained our full attention," I say.

# CHAPTER 10

# IN WHICH AKARI REFUSES TO BECOME ONE OF THOSE PEOPLE

At lunch I join Reika and Kimi in the cafeteria. They are both eating salad and I have a hamburger, french fries, and a glass of green tea on my tray.

Reika raises an eyebrow and says, "Really?"

"Are you referring to my hamburger and fries?" I say. She nods in the direction of my lunch.

"Listen, I refuse to become one of those people, Reika."

"What people?" she says.

"You know what I mean. Those totally boring humans who talk incessantly about food and calories and workouts and are always comparing themselves to others."

"Oh. Those people." Reika drags out the word "those" and cackles loudly.

Kimi sighs deeply. She's spent the duration of our friendship putting band-aids on everything unpleasant and uncomfortable between us.

"What's wrong with you two?" she asks. "Akari, I think Reika just meant you normally bring your lunch from home." Reika nods. The truth of this misunderstanding takes a moment to sink in. Reika wasn't judging what I ate for lunch. I'm the one who jumped to the wrong conclusion.

"Sorry," I mumble. No one says anything and I can feel my face flushing hot.

"Where's Skye?" asks Kimi.

"She has a session for new students. Something about laptop training." I take a huge bite of my hamburger. Reika seems like she's about to say something and I say, "Please don't start complaining about Skye."

"I wasn't going to," says Reika. "Listen. About that ... I want to apologize for some of the things I said about Skye. That big girl stuff was out of line," says Reika.

"It was all out of line," I say pushing away the tray with my half-eaten hamburger.

"Akari, do you want to be right, or do you want to be a friend to Reika right now?" Kimi has lowered her tone and is leaning towards me.

"Do I need to choose?" I say huffily, and there's something about this that Reika finds hilarious. I watch the smile developing on her face like a polaroid, then she's laughing and Kimi's laughing and now I'm laughing.

"Hey, can I have your burger if you're done with it?" says Reika.

"Sure," I say. Our laughter has burned away the terrible feeling I've been carrying around in the pit of my stomach for the past few days.

"Really, though. I'm sorry I was so rude. I don't know what's going on with me," says Reika between big bites of the burger. When she finishes eating, she picks up the tray and stands. "Okay, I'm going to take this tray to the kitchen before the duty teacher has kittens." I nod my head in gratitude. This is an uncommonly thoughtful gesture for Reika.

After she leaves, I place my hand on Kimi's arm. "Thank you. I am not asking you to confirm or deny anything, but

Reika's apology had your fingerprints all over it." Kimi smiles and says nothing.

# CHAPTER 11

# IN WHICH SKYE WONDERS IF SHE IS THE LIGHT OR THE WINDOW

"Hey, Skye-girl. It's pretty dark in here." I'm napping on the sectional when Dad arrives home from work and flips on the light.

"Ouch. Dad!"

Yoko, who has been putting away dishes in the kitchen, goes to the light switch and turns off the overhead light in the living room. There's a new round knob beside the light switch and Yoko turns it ever so slightly to the right. The dining room shimmers with echoes of glass and whispers of Venice.

"Yoko, you got the chandelier wired!"

"Apparently, I am very persuasive," says Yoko.

"Did the electrician fall in love with you?" I ask.

"There were two, and I believe that one did, yes," says Yoko.

"Yoko, you are a scoundrel," says my father, kissing her on the tip of her nose.

"But a scoundrel for the good. Only for the good," says Yoko.

I pull out my phone and photograph the chandelier from below. I Instagram, *The light is beautiful here. From Venice to Paris to Tokyo.*

Dad orders pizza for dinner, and we sit at the dining room table under the dim light of this chandelier we bought in Venice three years ago. It's made of six heavy glass rectangles, each of which increase in size until the fourth piece, which is the largest in the light fixture. The fifth is smaller, and the sixth and bottom piece is the smallest. From the first moment I saw it, I thought it was bold and modern and still super romantic.

We saw the chandelier from the sidewalk outside a shop in Venice, and Yoko and I fell in love with it immediately. We entered the shop to take a closer look, and my father asked if we realized how much this glass monstrosity would cost. Yoko said yes. He asked if we were aware of the exorbitant fees the shop would charge to ship it to Paris, and Yoko said we were. He asked us if it would make us happy, and I said yes. Yoko said, "Immeasurably," then she strode to the counter and purchased the chandelier herself. I couldn't tell if Dad was proud of her or just happy that he dodged the expense.

Later that evening, Yoko came to my hotel room to say good night. My duvet cover was shiny and gold and it rustled with every movement as Yoko dropped onto the bed and tucked her feet under her knees so that she sat cross-legged facing me.

"I thought Dad was going to have kittens when you bought the chandelier with your own money."

"Yes. He was a bit surprised, wasn't he? When I was growing up, most women did not work outside the home, but when I moved to Canada, many of my colleagues at the embassy were women. Some were married, some were mothers, others were not. Working with those women helped me see things differently. I think it's important for women to make their own money."

I felt my heart leap sideways. "Is everything okay with you and dad?"

Yoko cupped my cheek with her hand. "Of course. Your

father and I are very happy together, but we are both parents to one remarkable young woman named Skye, and I want to make sure that you are always well cared for. Also, sometimes a woman wants to buy a chandelier."

"Sometimes a woman wants to buy a chandelier," I repeated, and we both laughed at the truth and sassiness of that statement.

"I am also reminded of something my grandmother told me when I was a girl. Maybe a bit younger than you are now. This was my mother's mother." I nodded. "She said sometimes we're the light, and sometimes we're the window." Yoko closed her eyes for a moment.

"I'm not sure what that means," I said.

"I didn't understand the meaning for a long time either. My understanding now is that sometimes we're meant to be the star, shining brightly for everyone else to see, and sometimes we're meant to be the window through which others can shine brightly." She kissed me on the cheek.

Dad puts another slice of pizza on my plate. "Skye, you seem very far away," he says.

"Sorry. I was just remembering the day Yoko bought the chandelier," I say. Yoko flashes me a smile and a thumbs up.

"I wondered if you'd like to invite a friend over for dinner on Friday night," says Yoko.

"Um, I'm not sure," I say. I focus on the linen napkin in my lap.

"Why's that?" Dad asks.

"I have a lot of homework." I pick up my fork and move the Greek salad around, creating a small, lopsided green mountain.

"My love, you haven't even opened a book yet," says Yoko with a chuckle.

"But I should ... or else I'll get behind," I say.

"Did you have a disagreement with Akari?" says Yoko. Her eyes are no longer twinkling.

Dad looks up. "Who is Akari, and how could Skye have possibly had a disagreement with her? We just moved here five minutes ago."

"Dad, calm down! Akari's a friend and there hasn't been a disagreement. I'm just not sure about having anyone from school over yet." I push my plate away.

"Fine. As you wish," he says. He folds his napkin and places it beside his plate.

I clear the table and stack the plates beside the sink. As I turn on the tap, Yoko calls out, "Thanks, Skye. It's your dad's turn to clean up." As I go back through the dining room, Yoko has her arms crossed and she's giving Dad a look. He knows it too.

———

In my room, I rummage through my backpack until I find my headphones. I scroll through the music on my phone until I find a jazz playlist I made last Christmas. I let myself fall backwards onto my fluffy bed as Billie Holiday sings, *I'll Be Seeing You*. When I open my eyes, Yoko is standing in the doorway. "Is this an okay time?"

I nod and pull off my headphones. Yoko sits on the edge of the bed.

"I'm sorry if you felt pressured," says Yoko.

"I didn't. Not by you anyway. Everything is fine with Akari. It's just that I ..." Yoko sits completely still while I search for the right words. "I haven't known her very long and I've already been a bit impulsive, a bit pushy. You know?"

"I do," says Yoko, attempting to smooth out my curls with the palm of her hand.

"It's possible that I've been too much already. I'm just not sure if Akari is ready for dinner here."

"Skye, you are such a lovely person. I think you underestimate your own goodness. My wish for you is that you would see yourself as your father and I do." She speaks quietly but deliberately, holding my gaze, and I know she means it.

"Thank you, Yoko."

"Your father and I just want you to know that your friends are welcome here any time."

"I know."

"In case you change your mind, I am making Julia Child's beef bourguignon for dinner on Friday night." I smile at Yoko's unflagging ability to say the right thing at the right moment.

# CHAPTER 12
# IN WHICH AKARI SLIDES INTO AN ORANGE VINYL CHAIR

"Did you know that the average person spends two weeks of their lifetime waiting for traffic lights to change from red to green?" I say. Skye looks up from her novel. The air conditioning is set on high which must be making Skye very happy, and the room is hushed with occasional bursts of laughter rising up from the far corners of the room.

"Random much?" says Skye.

"I cannot help but notice you've found the library!" I say.

"I can't help but notice you're stalking me," says Skye.

"Hmm. I have studied at this school for twelve years and you have been here for two weeks so who, exactly, is stalking whom?"

"Two and a half. I've been here for two and a half weeks," says Skye.

I slide into the orange vinyl chair beside Skye and hang my backpack on the back of my chair. Although there are loads of empty study carrels, Skye has chosen to sit at a round table for eight in the very centre of the library.

"Based on your seating choice, I would guess you are not an

introvert?" I say. Suzanne from our English class walks by, and Skye gives her a high five.

"Nope. Not even remotely. It's my superpower. Super-friendly Canadian girl. Warming even the coldest hearts for sixteen years."

"Skye, I would like to ask you about something. Obviously, please tell me if this is not okay but last week, at Starbucks ..." I lean towards Skye and lower my voice, "you said something about not feeling like you belong anywhere."

"I shouldn't have said that."

"Why not?"

"Obviously crazy. Unbelievably ungrateful."

"Fiona used to talk about the feeling of not belonging. She was born in Australia, and she really missed it when she first arrived. But then she lived here for ten years, so she said she felt more Japanese than Australian even though she's this white, blonde surfer girl. She felt different from her parents because when they talked about moving back to Australia, they always called it home. Nothing was ever going to change that for them."

"That's true about my dad. You know ... about how he feels about Canada. He spent most of his life there so it's always going to be home for him," Skye says.

I nod. "Yes. I think many students at our school feel this strange homelessness."

"So, you're saying that I'm not special after all." Skye's eyes dance.

"Yes. That is exactly what I am saying."

"You sure are mean for a Japanese kid!" says Skye.

"And you show a shocking lack of gratitude for a Canadi-an," I say, and we both laugh. I grab my bag from the back of my chair and stand up, shrugging my arms through the straps, one at a time. "Seriously though. You can talk to me if you want to, Skye. I am happy to listen." Skye's eyes fill up with tears and I have one of those terrible moments where it is unclear if I should stay or leave, so I offer her the palm of my hand and she delivers an excellent, smacking high five.

"Thanks, Akari. Um, I get the feeling that Reika doesn't like me very much. Sorry if I'm causing some kind of problem there."

"Reika doesn't like anyone. Please don't take it personally."

Skye does not look convinced. "Okay. If you say so, but let's make sure we find each other later today and read the journal," Skye says. The bell rings and we quickly gather up our stuff so we're not late for homeroom.

# CHAPTER 13
# IN WHICH NAOKO NISHIZAWA WRITES ABOUT KATE

Love doesn't ask your age or your gender. Love doesn't care. It just wants what it wants.

In my first year at university, I made a friend named Kate. Her name was Katherine, but she asked everyone to call her Kate. She was from London, and whenever she talked, her accent mesmerized me. She said she'd applied to study in Tokyo because London was so boring, and she was desperate to get away from home. I laughed at the idea that a city like London could be boring but, of course, there isn't a place on earth that's so glamorous or exciting that a young person isn't clamouring to get away from it.

Kate said she was recreating herself. In our first semester at school her style was very plain. She wore well ironed blouses tucked into trousers or skirts. She was always cold, and she wore a cardigan on her shoulders like a Hollywood actress from the 1940s. By the new year she had disavowed ironing completely and had moved into her bohemian period. She wore long linen tunics over layered skirts. Sometimes she wore flowers in her hair, which never failed to get the attention of our teachers, who scowled at her appearance. Had she been Japanese, I'm certain they would have spoken to her, but the fact of her Britishness seemed to protect her from the harsh words of our professors. Kate, however, was oblivious to their disapproval. Part of her mission in recreating herself was to let go of other people's opinions of her. She said they were none of her business. Although she came from a very traditional and affluent family and had attended posh boarding schools with famous-sounding names, it was as if she had taken a sword and severed the thick rope that tethered her to that world. Until university, I was the most rebellious person I had ever met, but compared to Kate, I was an obedient rule-follower.

In our English literature class, we'd been assigned an essay, and she went to the teacher and asked to submit a short story instead. She assured him that it would demonstrate a deep understanding of the themes of the novel we were studying. She said his face reddened and he said, "I'm sorry. This is not possible," but she was not satisfied with that answer.

"Really, is it not possible or is it just a new idea? Something you haven't tried before? What could be the harm in giving it a try?"

When she told me later, we laughed and laughed at the professor and his red face. It was unkind of us, of course, but she was correct to point out that this was not an impossible request. In the end, he did a most uncharacteristic thing and made an exception for Kate. The word of her alternate assignment got around, but the thing the professor probably most feared did not happen. No one else in the class asked for such an exception to be made. We wouldn't have dreamed of it.

We would often go to clubs with our classmates. Sometimes we would hear American jazz artists at the Shinjuku Pit Inn, but mostly we went dancing. I was forever sneaking out of the house, but the old floors creaked so loudly, the only conclusion I could make is that my parents had decided to look the other way.

One night, in our second year, I'd snuck out of the house and walked over to the boarding house where Kate lived. Most of the other residents were young Japanese workers living in Tokyo for the first time. There were many strict rules, and part of the agreement between Kate's parents and the woman who ran the place was that she was to be home by eleven o'clock at night. I walked around the back of the building and saw Kate at her window. She waved and threw down a pair of bright pink stilettos and a small purse. Beside her window was a ladder to be used in the case of fire. It ended about seven feet above the ground. Kate clambered down the ladder, hung from the bottom rung for just a moment and then let go. She landed with a gentle thud, and she pulled this off while wearing what looked very much like a wedding gown.

"You've got some nerve," I said. "How will you get back up?

"Oh, one of the boys will give me a boost, or else I'll make up some story. Don't worry about it." I laughed at the idea of Kate explaining why she had been out late at night in a wedding dress, but there was nothing she could not talk her way out of.

With her purse and shoes in one hand, she grabbed my hand with the other and pulled me down the street towards our train.

When we arrived at the club, we dumped our bags at a table and ran directly onto the dance floor where the DJ played, one after the next, all our favourite songs, as if he'd asked us for a playlist in advance or, in a darker scenario, broken into our houses and apartments to study our music collections. We knew the words to every song, and we shout-sang in unison as we danced and twirled and jumped. Despite all the training I had received in the fine art of caring about what others think, I danced unselfconsciously and with enormous joy.

At the end of a song to which we'd twirled like dervishes,

Kate stepped towards me, placed her hands on my cheeks, and kissed me long and soft. For a moment I was lost. I disappeared inside a kiss with Kenji, the only person who had kissed me this way, but I was shaken out of the past by the awareness that it had never felt like this. I opened my eyes. It was Kate kissing me and I wanted to kiss her and to be kissed by her. I leaned in and pulled her closer as I kissed back and time passed, thirty seconds or seventy years, before she stepped back and smiled at me. She had moved her hands to my shoulders.

"Oh, that was lovely," she said. "Was it lovely for you, Naoko?" She towered over me because of those pink heels she was wearing.

"Yes. Um. Yes. It was lovely, but maybe a little confusing."

"In what way, love?"

"I guess I am wondering what this means."

"I wanted to kiss you. I looked across the floor and you looked so beautiful and free and belonging entirely to yourself, and I wanted to taste that, to feel it on my skin."

"Oh."

"Don't you ever let yourself have something beautiful?" I stared at her, not able to fully comprehend what she was saying. "Let's dance, Naoko." Kate held my hand, but she didn't initiate another kiss that night, or any other. I heard from friends that Kate was dating this person or another, but these relationships never seemed to last for long. She continued to act like the same old Kate, cheerful and friendly, although I joined the group less and less as exams approached.

After my final exam, I stopped by the English department office to check my mailbox one last time before summer. There was a letter. It was from Kate.

Naoko,

At long last, the parental units have called me home to

London. They'll expect me to attend a proper English university and become an adult now, I suppose. Take up my duties, whatever that means. I've had a good run here, longer than I expected if I'm being honest.

Thank you for being my one true friend in Tokyo. You were the only one who didn't expect anything of me. I've enclosed my address should you want to write.

Kate

## CHAPTER 14
# IN WHICH AKARI IS
# NOT FALLING FOR IT

One of my favourite places to sit and think is on the stairs to a Shinto shrine near school. There's a red torii at street level, and a hundred steps leading up to the small shrine. I rarely go all the way up to the shrine itself, but the stairs are quite wide and flanked by trees, so it is always cool here, even in August. Skye and I are sitting about twenty steps from the red gate, and we can hear the cicadas wailing their life and death song all around us. We are quiet for a few minutes after I finish reading the entry about Kate.

"Wow," says Skye.

"Wow what?" I close the journal and place it inside my bag.

"That night in the club when Kate wore that wedding gown and she and Naoko kissed. Wow that!"

"And?" I say.

"I thought it was romantic."

"Romantic?" A young man walks past us on the stairs at exactly this moment and I feel my cheeks heat up with embarrassment. Skye doesn't seem to notice. I wait for him to pass. "Have you not learned anything about consent in school?"

"Okay. I agree that Kate should have checked first, but Naoko wanted that kiss."

"From a person whose highest praise was that Naoko never asked anything of her, she didn't even bother to say good-bye in person. She gave Naoko her address and left it up to Naoko to write to her."

"You're right. That's not so great either," Skye says, digging her paper fan out of the backpack resting on the step below us. She flips it open and fans herself with such vigour that I am certain she will end up making herself warmer. I choose not to share this insight.

"I thought there were signs that Kate was mentally unwell."

"Really?"

"I thought so," I say.

"There's part of me that hopes they met again when they were older and better prepared to love each other." Skye taps her toes together like Dorothy in The Wizard of Oz.

"Of course you do," I say. "You are an unabashed romantic, Skye." We nod our heads in unison and then laugh. Skye knows she's not going to wriggle out of this one. "The reason I don't find this encounter romantic is that there is no sign that Kate saw or understood Naoko. She was just having her own spectacular adventure in Tokyo and Naoko agreed to be one of her secondary characters. It seemed like the only person Kate loved was herself. Wait just a moment—" I pull the journal out and open it up to the entry: "She says 'I wanted to kiss you. I looked across the floor at you and you looked so beautiful and free and belonging entirely to yourself and I wanted to taste that, to feel it on my skin.' Kate is describing something she wants to feel rather than a connection with Naoko."

"You've officially killed my buzz, Akari," says Skye. She closes the fan, folds her arms across her chest, and leans back against the step above us.

"I promise I did not mean to. Kate was not her lobster," I say.

"Her lobster?" Skye asks.

"Seriously? You haven't seen that episode of *Friends*? When one of the characters was meant to be with someone, their friend said that person was their lobster."

"Ah, I like that," Skye says.

"Of course, you do," I shoot Skye a quick smile and say, "Hey. Are you worried that we are doing something ... I don't know ... naughty here?" Skye looks at me with her eyebrows raised. "I'm talking about reading Naoko's journal," I say.

"Nope. Not one bit. We're not putting her entries on the Internet or sharing the journal with other people. If you wanted someone to help you feel guilty, you picked the wrong friend. I'm a banisher of guilt." Skye opens her fan with a quick flick of her right wrist like a flamenco dancer.

"Since the first day of school when you showed up in our homeroom, I have suspected that you'd be the evil one in our little duo," I say. Our laughter bounces off the stairs and the trees and is offered back to us in the most delightful way.

"Hey, my mom wants to know if you want to have dinner at our place after school on Friday night," says Skye.

"I'll ask," I say.

————

I text Skye when I get home.

AKARI
Yes.

SKYE
Yes?

Yes, Skye. It's a yes.

About what?

Dinner. My mom said yes about dinner Friday.

Cool.

Yes. :)

# CHAPTER 15
# IN WHICH SKYE HOSTS A DINNER PARTY

As I unlock the door to the apartment, I'm met by the smell of beef stew simmering in the kitchen. Perhaps this is a consequence of living for four years in a city where people take their food very seriously, but I swear I can make out each of the individual ingredients: the rich smell of the beef, the carrots, the celery, the mushrooms, and the red wine. Yoko normally serves the stew on a bed of creamy mashed potatoes. I've been thinking about this meal all day long. Yup, I am Pavlov's (and also Yoko's) salivating dog.

Yoko's office door is closed which means she's probably working on a translation. It's cool that she works from home, although if I worked from our apartment, I'm pretty sure I'd never get out of my pyjamas. Yoko, however, is the kind of unicorn-person who emerges from her bedroom fully dressed every morning. Before I'm even awake most days, Yoko is showered, dressed, and impeccably accessorized.

In most of my friend's homes, the office belongs to the dad, but at our house, only Yoko has a study. Dad works long hours at the embassy, but when he's at home, at least while I'm awake, he doesn't look at his phone. Back when we still lived in Canada, I overheard some of dad's friends tease him about not working in the evenings. They called him a slacker. He laughed with them at the time but, later, when I asked him about it, he said that as far as he knew, each one of us was given just one life and that if we didn't design the life we wanted to live, other people would be happy to make those decisions for us. A few years ago, he and Yoko created this New Year's Eve ritual where they discuss their values, priorities, and how they want to feel in the new year, and then they made a list of the kinds of actions that will help them create that life for our family.

The truth is that my parents are kind of wonderful.

I drop my bag on my bed, once again made by Yoko, and head to the kitchen. I try to lift the lid off the large red pot, but it's so heavy that I end up dragging it, which creates an alarmingly loud scraping sound. I wait a moment for Yoko to come running to see what's happened, and when she doesn't appear, I dip a wooden spoon into the beef stew. I blow on it a few times and hold it under my nose. It smells like Paris. Finally, I taste it.

"How did I do?" Yoko crosses the kitchen and kisses my cheek.

"Yummm. Yoko, it's perfect."

"Pretty good, right?"

"Great. Shall I set the table?"

"Skye, I want you to set the table forever. Perhaps you'll attend university in Tokyo and live with your dad and me and, at dinner every evening, you'll set the table. Until you are forty."

"At least!"

I set out placemats and utensils for four. I choose the floral dishes we bought in France and some cream-coloured linen napkins that belonged to dad's grandmother. Yoko comes out of the kitchen carrying a large bouquet of pink roses in a square crystal vase and sets it in the centre of the table.

"Too much?" asks Yoko.

"Maybe we could put them on the sideboard so we can, you know, see each other," I say. Yoko slips into one of the chairs, acts out an elaborate scenario in which it's impossible to see the person on the other side of the table, and starts to laugh.

"Good idea. Skye, I'm glad you changed your mind about inviting your friend."

We hear a key in the lock, and I'm relieved that Dad beat Akari to the apartment.

"Hey, gals!" Dad appears in the foyer. "Look who I caught snooping around the entrance downstairs." Akari steps inside the apartment and grins shyly. She's wearing a black shirt with a mandarin collar and cap sleeves, tucked into a pair of khaki trousers.

"Akari, it's so good to meet you," says Yoko, stepping towards Akari. Akari bows and Yoko lowers her head in an exact mirror image.

"Skye, are you taking this in?" says Dad. I nod.

"Thank you, Mrs. MacTavish," says Akari.

"Please call me Yoko. We call this one Duncan. Thank you for gracing us with the most respectful bow this family has ever seen. These two are terrible at it. They're always forgetting to bow to the people we meet, and when they do remember, they look like chickens with their heads bobbing up and down." Yoko demonstrates our awkward attempts at bowing. Akari laughs, covers her mouth with her hand and takes a small step back.

"Easy with the full-out weird, folks. Akari just got here," I say.

"You are absolutely right, Skye. Dinner will be ready in half an hour," says Yoko.

I give Akari a tour of the apartment, then we sit on the soft white carpet in the living room and watch the sun begin to set over Tokyo.

"May I ask what do your parents do?" says Akari.

"Sure. Yoko is an interpreter and translator, and my dad works at the Canadian embassy."

"So does Makoto's mom. Do you think they know each other?"

"Yeah. Probably," I say.

Yoko calls us to dinner. As we sit, Yoko, Akari and I place our napkins in our laps, and Dad tucks his into the front of his light blue button-down.

"Dad! That's so tacky," I say.

"Yoko says I'm not allowed to ruin any more shirts," he places his hand over Yoko's and pats it a couple of times.

"It's true. He's not allowed," she pulls her hand out and pats his. "Bon appetit, girls."

We are quiet as I put a heaping spoonful of mashed potatoes on each plate and cover the potatoes with stew. Akari passes plates to Yoko and dad, and we all tuck into our meal. A chorus of "Mmmmms" rises from around the table.

"Don't stop," says Yoko, laughing.

Dad delivers his not-so-short history of beef bourguignon for Akari's benefit, explaining how the American cook Julia Child rediscovered the French classic and introduced it to America.

"We like our food at the MacTavish household," I say.

"I like your food at the MacTavish household," says Akari.

"Oh. The new girl has made a joke, so she must be comfortable with us now," says Dad.

"Ah! I now see where you get it," Akari says to me, raising an eyebrow.

"Her brilliant sense of humour?" says Dad.

"Her red hair." Dad and I grin at each other. Once you've

seen our hair, there is no mistaking our connection to each other.

Over dessert, blueberries with cream, Dad quizzes Akari about her life. Where does she live? What's her favourite subject in school? Favourite hobby? Political affiliations? We all laugh, and I assure her she doesn't have to answer that. Dad asks what she plans to study at university. "I'm not sure, but I think I'd like to study art," she says. It's the first time I've heard her talk about art, and I'm intrigued.

The buzzer sounds and Dad goes to the intercom to answer it.

We hear the concierge's voice. "Hello, Mr. Ambassador. There is a delivery for you. Would you like me to sign for it?"

"Yes please, Nakayama-san." Dad returns to the table.

"Mr. Ambassador?" Akari asks.

"Yes?" says dad. Akari's eyes widen.

"It's no big deal, Akari," I say, shrugging.

"I am very sorry. When you said that your father worked at the Embassy, I did not realize that ..." Akari looks down at her plate.

"There's no problem here, Akari. It's just a job. Keeps us supplied with beef stew and blueberries," says Dad.

"So, what have you girls been reading lately? I need a lovely new novel," says Yoko, skillfully changing the subject.

After dinner, Akari and I clear the dishes and load the dishwasher. "I feel so embarrassed. Your dad's job is the very definition of a big deal," says Akari.

"He says he was in the right place at the right time and managed not to piss off any of the decision makers. At home he's just my dad. Okay?"

"Okay," says Akari, smiling weakly.

"Was dinner okay? Oh God, you're not a vegetarian, are you? I forgot to ask. It would be just like me to feed beef stew to a vegetarian." I place the glasses in the top rack of the dishwasher.

"I'm not a vegetarian, and dinner was delicious. Your mom is ..."

"Young? Beautiful? Japanese?" I say.

"Yes. Although you already told me she was Japanese," says Akari. "I was going to say that she's a very good cook. I've never been over to a friend's house for dinner."

"Never?" I close the dishwasher and stare at Akari.

"No. Not that I can remember."

"Wow," I say softly, my eyes widening as I pick up a cloth and wipe the counter.

"I know. I inhabit a sad little world." Akari smiles at me.

"That's not even remotely what I mean. I'm just curious about why?"

"It's not very common here. We almost always eat at home with our own family. Sometimes, for a special occasion, my parents give me permission to eat with my friends but then we go out to a restaurant."

"That's interesting," I say and fold the cloth over the faucet.

"Is it?" says Akari. "It doesn't seem very interesting to me." She shoves her hands in her front pockets and leans against the counter.

"Maybe our own lives never seem that interesting to us," I say. Akari nods. "So did your parents give you a hard time about coming for dinner tonight?"

"A little." Akari nods. "They think it's strange since I don't know you very well yet. It's fine, though."

"Okay," I smile and bow my head ever so slightly. "Shall we squeeze in some Naoko time before you go?"

# CHAPTER 16

# IN WHICH NAOKO NISHIZAWA WRITES ABOUT SAKURA

So much has been written about the cherry blossoms.

I can only write about how they make me feel.

Winter is long and hard. In some regions, Japan is buried under snow. Our houses are not well insulated which has always been a mystery to me, given the fact that we are now able to make a toilet that can practically orbit the planet. But our houses are cold, and winter feels like it will never end.

Not how it is … but how it feels.

Completely logical people make me crazy. They say things like, "This is only your perception." As if there are simply things that are … and things that are not. That which is true and that which is false. For this kind of thinker, there is a line that divides the world into yes and no, black and white. "Is it only my perception, then, that you are a jerk?" This is potentially unfair to the linear thinkers among us, but it has been my experience that life is shaped by our perceptions. The nasty person wins one hundred million yen and remains mean and petty. The sweet and lovely soul is paralyzed in a skiing accident but continues to spread love and light.

Our perception creates our reality.

I will try to tell this story without another outburst.

I was saying that it feels as though winter will never end. The wind blows icy off the Pacific, a gift from the Canadian north, and to stand too long in this wind feels like being pierced by many small knives. Otherwise sane people start talking about moving to Okinawa or Hawaii.

And then, when we have almost lost even the memory of warmth, March arrives. These naked cherry trees, all spindly and knotted and awkward, must draw on all their resources to pull energy up from their roots and begin to bloom. This is life itself. At first the blossoms are shy. Students at a high school dance. Wanting not to be seen but also hoping that someone will notice. A few days later, the sakura gain more confidence. They are swollen with beauty.

This is the point at which the Japanese cannot bear it any longer. Like schoolchildren we must be let outdoors. We lay our plastic tarps and our plaid blankets under the trees, and we unpack our baskets and bags filled with food and beer. Seated under the blossoms, we eat and drink and reclaim the world as our own.

We are drunk on blossoms and spring and inexpensive beer.

We are in love with the world and our lives.

We have survived another winter.

Perception is everything.

When night falls, long after we have eaten all the food we brought, we pack up our bags and baskets. We fold our blankets and roll up our tarps. We hunt down rogue beer cans that have rolled into the bushes. We leave the park as we found it, as though no one has been here at all. We blow kisses to the blossoms as we go.

Arigatou gozaimasu. Thank you very much … for coming back. I needed to believe in spring.

You thought the story was over because I said thank you. It is not.

There is a third act of the sakura, and it is, perhaps, the most poignant. When they are at the apex of their beauty, the blossoms begin to blow apart from the inside. I think, perhaps, a thing that beautiful is never meant to last for long, because the centre cannot hold. The blossoms shrivel. They are small and damaged, and then the petals are distributed by the wind. If you stand under a cherry tree at the end of its season, you will experience the most exquisite snowfall. The petals feel like velvet as they fall on your cheeks.

Perhaps I should feel heartbroken, but this is not my perception. I feel gratitude for the extravagant beauty of the blossoms. I remember all the past years that I stood, just like this, under a cherry tree, in a blizzard of dying blossoms, and all those selves are connected to each other, to the person I am now, to the blossoms, and to life itself. The end of the season reminds me that everything has its season. Winter passes, the blossoms arrive and then depart. Like people. We are transient. Just passing through.

# CHAPTER 17
# IN WHICH AKARI PUTS HER FOOT DOWN

It is Monday afternoon, and the day has been so long that the only thing I want to do is to escape up to the fourth-floor art room, where everyone leaves each other alone to work on their own art, and the soundtrack is a perfect mix of pencils moving against paper and the low rumble of the air conditioner. Even though the Buddhist and Shintoist beliefs of my family do not support this kind of thinking, if there is a heaven, I think it must be like the art room. I imagine an endless supply of materials: pencils, paints, paper, and canvases in all the colours, sizes, and textures that you might conceive of. A kiln that always bakes your pieces at exactly the right temperature. Glazes that adhere to the surface perfectly. An art room where you have access to an infinite supply of extraordinary ideas and where you are guaranteed to slip effortlessly into the deep flow of making things.

That is all I want, to get upstairs, but Reika is waiting for me at my locker after physics class. Although we have had challenges in our friendship before, this disagreement about Skye is uncharted territory. Although she has apologized, things are still strained between us.

I ask her about volleyball tryouts. She and Kimi are trying

out for the Varsity team this year, so when they are not in class, eating or sleeping, they are at tryouts, preparing for tryouts, or talking about tryouts. Everyone thinks they will both make the team as they were the two best players on Junior Varsity.

Reika says there are several new girls trying out and they are very strong, but she still thinks she and Kimi are okay. Then she says, 'I wanted to invite you to join us for dinner at an izakaya on Friday night. It's been a long time since the three of us had dinner together and it would be great to talk."

There's a sinking feeling in my stomach. "So, Skye isn't invited?" I say. She shakes her head.

"I think it would be good for just the three of us to get together. I miss seeing you," she says.

I really do not want to have this conversation right now. "I will think about it," I say. It seems like the calm and prudent response, but then I realize I don't need to think about it. Skye doesn't have any other friends, I really like hanging out with her, and we have already made plans to do something together Friday after school. I explain this to Reika and tell her I would be happy to have dinner another day. She frowns and looks away as she tightens her ponytail with both hands, and I can tell that she is not happy about this. It feels like she is waiting for an apology, but I don't have one in me.

She shrugs and says, "See you later."

# CHAPTER 18
# IN WHICH SKYE SHARES THE SKYE MACTAVISH THEORY OF INNER HEROINES

Ms. Barrett is standing at her classroom door as Akari and I enter and drop into our seats, a full minute before the bell rings. Ms. Barrett gives me the thumbs up sign, which I find both endearing and hilarious.

"Last week we reviewed the hero's journey. You'll find that understanding this model will help you in this course, as it's a tool. Like Jungian theory. Or the Bible. Of course, every theory has its flaws. What about the hero's journey? Is there anything about this theory that doesn't make sense to you? Anything that you find puzzling or annoying, even? Anyone?" Ms. Barrett scans the room several times. "Is it too early in the morning for you? Have you not had your coffee yet?" Ms. Barrett places her hands on her hips.

"It is quite early in the morning, Ms. Barrett, and many studies suggest that teenagers are not at their best at this time of day," I say. Akari glares at me which makes me laugh out loud.

"Skye, I'm going to give you that one. I'd like each of you to pair up with another student and discuss your most compelling objection to this theory." Akari and I nod at each other and pull our chairs closer to each other.

"Go ahead," Akari says. "I know you are probably burning with objections."

"Actually, this isn't so much an objection as much as another perspective, maybe. In all the diagrams, the protagonist's journey is normally depicted as a circle, right? Akari gives me a thumbs up. "So, as she moves around the circle, the protagonist encounters all these conflicts and obstacles but what if she were able to look back over her shoulder and see all the previous versions of herself and remember the lessons she's learned that might apply to these challenges?"

"The heroine becomes her own teacher?" Akari says. She's leaning towards me.

"Exactly! Like those painted Russian stacking dolls, she has all her previous selves inside her and she can draw on their wisdom and strength and energy at any time. You know, like sometimes the thing that would be most helpful is the joy of our inner four-year-old. As the protagonist moves through the circle of her adventures, she interacts with new people and situations but also with her past selves. And the story keeps moving ... but in a circle. You know?"

"I love that theory. Let's call it The Skye MacTavish Theory of Inner Heroines." We both laugh which is followed by the recognition that we're the only ones in the room still talking about the hero's journey.

———

After class, we meet up with Reika and Kimi at our lockers. They are comparing bruises.

"What's with the physical harm?" I say.

"Our volleyball coach is brutal. She's always yelling, 'Sacrifice yourselves. Dive for it.' So, we're diving," says Kimi.

"Tell the truth, Kimi. You are inordinately proud of these bruises," says Akari.

"I am, actually." Kimi displays her bruised forearms like the protagonist in a romantic comedy would flash her engagement ring.

"When do you find out who made the team?" I ask.

"Tomorrow," says Kimi. "Whatever happens, the team is going to be fierce this year. There's this new girl, and she spikes like she's possessed by the devil. It's totally cool to watch her do her thing," says Kimi. I wish them both good luck, but Reika avoids looking at me. I wonder if it's cultural. Yoko says that some Japanese people believe it's rude to look directly into people's eyes. But this is an international school, and Reika has met my gaze before, so I don't think that's what's going on. I know Akari told me not to worry about it, that this is just Reika being Reika, but it definitely feels personal.

"I'm sure you and Reika will be chosen for the team. Akari says you're both awesome," I say.

"Hey, how was English class? Akari loves herself some Ms. Barrett," says Kimi. I nod my head.

"Class was intense," says Akari. "Skye shared an alternative to the hero's journey that was really insightful. Like literary scholar level." Reika turns and glares at me with a kind of fierceness that makes it impossible to deny or misunderstand. She hates me with every fibre of her being, but I have no idea why.

———

We're having a laidback evening at home, a kind of fend-for-yourself affair. I warm up a bowl of Hokkaido pumpkin soup in the microwave. This is one of Yoko's favourite comfort foods, so there's always some in the freezer. I sit on the soft rug with my back against the sectional and eat the soup slowly, reminding myself to savour it like the French savour all things.

Dad and Yoko have decided this is the right time to negotiate the placement of nails in walls. Actually, negotiate is Dad's word. Yoko calls it what it is: arguing.

"Yoko, I have no idea how much we'll be charged for the damage to the walls. It could be a million yen. It could be a billion for all I know," he says.

"Dad, puh-lease," I say rolling my eyes.

"Enough! Even if it's a billion yen, we will pay it because this is our home and Skye's home and we deserve to have beautiful art on our walls," says Yoko. She picks up the hammer and a nail from the dining room table, and heads to the closest x-symbol marked on a small piece of masking tape.

Dad drops down onto the sofa beside me. He rests his head against mine and says, "She always wins, doesn't she?" We watch her begin to hang paintings in the places she has already meticulously mapped out.

"She lets you win plenty, Dad." He chuckles and then I laugh. The deep tone of his laughter mixes with the higher tone of my own and this most familiar of sounds makes me feel safe. He tugs gently on my ponytail as he gets up to help Yoko.

While they work, I nap on the sunny spot on the floor for a while and then retrieve my backpack from my room. I've been slacking off these first few weeks and now I have to face the truth: I'm a student in dire need of better organizational systems. Nope, that's not quite it. The problem is that I don't have any organizational systems yet. Just the thought of what Ms. Barrett would say about my procrastination and sloppy notes is enough to motivate me. I open my laptop and enter my classes and room numbers into my schedule, which I then sync to the calendar on my phone. Inside my journal, I've scrawled my upcoming homework assignments and tasks on various pages and on sticky notes stuck to the inside cover; I go through the journal and make a master to-do list where I record everything that's due.

Yoko announces that they're done just as I'm finishing off my math homework and a sleeve of crackers. She pulls me off the sofa and takes me on a tour of the house, as if it's my first visit, to show me their work. The walls are heavy with family portraits, vacation photographs, and paintings given to us by friends, as well as some newer works by a painter Yoko knew in Paris. "You have a gift for creating a home, Yoko," I say, as we return to the living room. I applaud and she bows to me.

It's nine o'clock and I think about going to bed but, after my nap, I'm not very tired. All this talk about Joseph Campbell in Barrett's class has me thinking about stories, and specifically about how long it's been since I wrote one. I open a new page in my journal. Happily, it's a friendly page. It doesn't stare at me blankly but rather says, "Bring your pen here, Skye-child." For the past few days, I've been playing with this idea about a tiny character who lives inside someone's pocket, and I'm determined to write about her, to try to bring her to life.

In the bottom of the pocket of the red velvet jacket there was a tiny woman and she said, "Hello. Can you help, please? It's quite dark in here and a bit musty and I'm afraid I'm unable to do my very best work." And there was no doubt in her mind whatsoever that someone would hear her and respond kindly because that was the world that she lived in, that she loved and that she had co-created. People always imagined goddesses to be tall, large, powerful women and there were those, true enough. There were also goddesses who looked like regular human women. Women with bad perms and bags under their eyes from not getting enough sleep, and women who carried handbags that were inspired by the Queen of England. There were also tiny goddesses that moved about the world unseen, in the saucers of good china cups and in the bottoms of red velvet pockets such as this one. As it turned out, the tiny ones were the most powerful and had the best insights into goddess and human nature. She wasn't smug about it either. This was simply the truth. In that precise non-smug moment, four pink fleshy fingers and a thumb descended slowly towards her and then gently turned over, offering her a huge flat palm as an elevator. She stepped aboard and tapped the thumb lightly twice so there could be no confusion as to her intention. Up please. The hand rose up towards the top of the pocket and golden light welcomed the tiny pocket goddess.

I read my words over a couple of times and reflect on how this tiny pocket goddess has already won my heart. Why is she here? I find myself hoping that she's made her way out of that pocket to help me.

# CHAPTER 19
# IN WHICH AKARI IS IN HER USUAL SPOT

At the end of the day on Friday, Skye finds me in the workspace at the back of the art room. Her face is red and blotchy with the heat, and she blurts out that she's looked for me in all the usual places, including my locker and the library. Kimi said she hadn't seen me since art class, so Skye climbed the four flights of stairs to the art room, and this had given her lots of time to wonder why there aren't any elevators in this school.

"You've been on the heroine's journey," I say, and this makes her laugh. "This is my usual spot."

"What?" says Skye.

"You said you looked in all the usual spots. This is my usual spot." Entering the art room always feels to me like walking into a forest or a temple. The room is lighter than the classrooms on the floors below, and pieces of art hang from the walls and the ceiling. Even the soft hiccup of the air conditioner is comforting.

"It's cool ... and calm. I can see why you like it here." I sit on a stool with one foot tucked under me and Skye perches on a stool across the table.

"It is calm now but, during art class, when there are twelve of us fighting for space and materials, one would not describe it as peaceful." Skye nods.

"It's good news that Kimi and Reika both made the volleyball team, right?" says Skye. I nod but don't look up from my work.

"May I ask what you're working on?" says Skye, pointing at the drawing in my sketchbook. I set down my pencil and look up.

"I am not exactly sure yet. So far, it is like a graphic novel, but shorter."

"What's it about?" she says.

I sigh, although not on purpose. "Okay but please try not to judge." Skye nods. "It's about this girl whose superpower is to rescue people who jump in front of trains. I honestly don't know if that is a good superpower to have. The story is a new one, and the premise is somewhat overwhelming." Skye nods her head and waits. "Japan has a very high suicide rate, especially in young people. A girl from our school died by suicide last year and she was an amazing person. The government has started to create programs to help, but not enough people talk about this until it is too late."

"Is it okay that we're talking about this now?"

"Oh. Yes, it's fine." Then I realize that Skye is asking me if I'm okay. "I am fine. I mean I know I complain about school and my parents sometimes, but nothing bad has ever happened to me. Oh, I'm saying this all wrong. What I mean to say is that I am not suicidal. I have never thought about ending my life." I feel itchy and sweaty at the same time.

"Honestly, I didn't mean to pry, Akari, but I'm happy you're okay. What's your protagonist's name?"

"Chiyo."

"A thousand somethings?" says Skye.

"One meaning would be a thousand generations," I say.

"Or a thousand worlds." I pick up the pencil and start to shade in a train.

"Like eternal?" Skye asks. I nod. Skye is not completely fluent in Japanese but I see her improving every day, and she makes connections quickly. "Cool. Hey, is it overly complicated to have her stop the train? Wouldn't it be easier if she just stopped the people before they jumped in front of the train?"

I have had the same thought myself. I explain that, technically, it would be easier because Chiyo wouldn't need superhuman strength, but the problem is that what is easier is not always what is truest. "I read this article about one of the only people to survive jumping off the Golden Gate Bridge in California, and he said that as soon as he jumped, he knew that he'd made a terrible mistake, and that everything that was wrong in his life was totally fixable," I say. "When he hit the water and realized he had survived the impact, he started praying to God to let him live."

"Sorry. I don't understand how that's connected to Chiyo," says Skye, shaking her head. She walks around the table and pulls up a stool beside me.

"I'm probably not explaining it very well. You are the first person I have talked to about this. Chiyo lets them jump and then, when they realize how much they want to live, she swoops in and saves them."

"Ah, like their life flashes before their eyes and they realize it's a good life and they're not ready to leave yet?" I nod my head. "Yes. I like that. May I take a closer look?" I push the sketchbook over to Skye. My drawing shows a train screeching to a stop at a platform. I've drawn the front of the train with a face that is grimacing with the effort of stopping the train. There are people on the platform, and they are pointing up and exclaiming, "Oh no!" and "Look, it's Chiyo!" My superhero carries a startled-looking young man under one arm while she holds the train back with the other. The drawing is in black charcoal pencil except for Chiyo's hair which is blazing red.

"Weird, right?" I ask in a voice I recognize as quieter than usual.

"No! This is AWESOME!" Skye is smiling maniacally like she did that first day in homeroom. "You're really good. Why didn't you say so?"

"Um, you have met me before, right?" I say.

"Sure, but when I asked about your art you said something like, 'I just like to doodle. I'm not very good yet.'"

"That's true. I'm not very good yet," I say.

"Girl, you are totally talented. Like I bet you could get this published. Have you made many of these graphic stories? Is this manga?" says Skye.

"It's all manga, but I struggle with calling what I do manga because I do not want my work associated with artists who draw their fictional, anatomically impossible girlfriend and then use their stories to degrade her at every opportunity. Some manga is more like cartoon pornography."

"Maybe you need a different word for what you're doing?" says Skye.

"That is an interesting idea. To answer your question, yes, I draw a lot of comics. Reika and Kimi describe me as obsessed. But I need to get more serious if I'm going to get a good grade in art class."

"Serious in what way?" says Skye.

"Our art class is very intense. In Grade Eleven, we start keeping notes about our work, including how we get inspired, our creative process, and what materials we are using. We are required to record what goes well and how we failed because artists are meant to learn from our mistakes. By the middle of junior year, we need to identify a theme, idea, or question we intend to explore through our work."

"It looks like you have already found your theme," says Skye pointing to the illustrations of Chiyo.

"This? No, this is just something I am playing around with."

The art teacher emerges from her office and asks me to turn off the air conditioner and lights when we leave.

"Seriously?" says Skye. "She's leaving us alone in the art room?"

"Yes. It's very common for art students to stay late if they're working on a piece," I say.

"Cool! No way does that happen anywhere else. Wisconsin, maybe. Since everyone else has gone home, do you want to read here?" Skye says. I nod and Skye pulls Naoko's journal out of her bag and places it on the table. "Hello, Naoko Nishizawa. Hola. Bonjour. Konichiwa."

"Skye, please just open it already," I say.

# CHAPTER 20
# IN WHICH NAOKO NISHIZAWA WRITES ABOUT MASUMI'S PAINTING

Masumi and I sat on the concrete steps at the front of her gallery, drinking green tea and eating brownies from a light pink cardboard box. It was August and Masumi fanned herself with a large yellow paper fan she'd painted to look like a wedge of lemon. Every few minutes she waved the fan in my direction, and I closed my eyes and breathed as deeply as I was able in the oppressive heat.

We'd known each other since high school. Unlike me, Masumi did not allow her parents to spend millions of yen on university tuition before pursuing her art. Right after high school she moved into a tiny apartment that she shared with her boyfriend, a guitarist in a rock band, and his immense collection of manga comics, unsteady stacks of which lined every wall. While the boyfriend didn't last long, painting proved to be her one true love.

"You really like it?" he said.

"I do," she said. Even with the door closed, we heard every word. I turned to rest my back against the railing so I could see Masumi and also watch the couple inside her gallery through the window.

The woman walked right up to the painting. Her husband stood behind her with his hands in his pockets.

"There's something wonderful about the softness of the colour. The pinks make me think of summer days and childhood. Cotton candy. We definitely made the right choice to come at five o'clock. The light is perfect," the woman said.

"I'll have to take your word on it, Junko. There wasn't much cotton candy in my childhood."

"And the girl's hands. They're so expressive." She touched the top of her left hand lightly, like a memory.

"Those hands are way too big for her body. Monster-hands. Like a cartoon character."

"Perhaps she made them large for emphasis."

"To emphasize that she can't paint." He chuckled.

"Shh!" The woman glanced towards the steps where we were sitting. Masumi rolled her eyes at me.

Like a Buddhist monk, she woke early each morning to work. She needed very little to survive. Her apartment was above the gallery and studio and contained the barest of necessities: a few articles of clothing, two plates, two bowls, two glasses, one pot and a rice cooker. She said she'd had to strip her life bare to make space for the images that appeared in her mind. The more stuff she got rid of, the more vivid her inner world became. I worried that I may someday arrive to find that she had vanished entirely, leaving only a folded-up futon and one last, miraculous painting as the only evidence of her existence.

She was far more disciplined than I. More prolific as well. Each time I visited, stacks of new canvases lined the back wall of her studio space. She moved quickly through different phases, so one might find a series of aliens with fuzzy pink antennae stacked beside newer canvases of small woodland animals dressed in kimono. This made it difficult for her to retain clients, because she seldom replicated the work with which they first fell in love. This wasn't some artistic pose for Masumi. She painted what she saw and, when she saw something new, she followed it with the same single-mindedness with which Alice pursued her white rabbit.

"Why are you being such an asshole about this?" the woman asked.

"I'm simply stating a preference. I'm still allowed to have those, right?" he responded.

She walked to the back of the studio, the hardwood floor creaking under her high heels. As she passed him, her shoulder grazed his arm just above his elbow.

"My favourite thing is the feeling I get when I look at it. The love between the girl and her dog. I'm sure they'll be soul-mates until one of them dies," she said, from the back of the studio.

I knew this painting. A young girl with bobbed brown hair and a striped, pink shirt wrapped her arms around a dog. The first time I saw this canvas in Masumi's gallery, something fluttered inside me and dislodged itself.

My affection for this particular dog surprised me, for I had never been a dog person. It had always been cats for me. When I saw this painting, however, I recognized immediately that this girl and this dog had each found their best friend. A cat cannot be a best friend. A cat can be a boss or an aloof companion, but I have never witnessed a cat demonstrate love and need in the same way that people and dogs do.

There was a spot in the bottom left corner of the painting that was still white, as though the painting was not yet complete, and there was something strangely Dali-esque and perfect about the girl's large right hand. With her light grey eyes, pink cheeks and unwavering fidelity to that dog, she took me hostage, and I was struck with a desire to own the painting. That was not even a remote possibility.

"We don't have the money right now," said the husband. His wife returned to the centre of the gallery and stared up at him.

"We absolutely do have the money. In the same way that we have the money for you to golf every weekend," she said.

"That's different," he said.

"Wanting it to be different does not make it different. You work. I work. You golf. I'm buying this painting."

"And just exactly where would we put it?" He pointed at the painting.

"I think I'll hang it at my office, so you don't have to look at it."

"You don't get to decide where our painting goes," he said.

"You must be kidding, Riki. You don't even like it," she said.

"I really don't."

The small bell jangled as Masumi opened the door. The sun was setting, and mosquitoes flew around my ankles, buzzing, asking their air traffic controller for permission to land. On the other side of the room, Masumi and the woman appeared to close the sale; Masumi lifted the painting off the wall and set it on the counter.

A few moments later, the couple emerged from the gallery and descended the stairs beside me; I reached down and grabbed the box to prevent the brownies from being impaled by the woman's heels. She led the way, her head held high like the queen of some long-forgotten island state. The man followed. They walked in a silence that wrapped itself around them like a fog.

I carried the glasses and the box of brownies into the shop where Masumi was wrapping the painting in thick brown paper.

"So, they bought it?" I placed the box and glasses on the counter.

Masumi picked up the wrapped painting and handed it to me.

"It is for you."

"Masumi! It's too much."

"It's yours. I could not let that couple take this painting."

# CHAPTER 21

# IN WHICH AKARI GETS A SURPRISE (BUT NOT A GOOD ONE)

My mother is sitting in the kitchen when I get home from having dinner with Skye. She is just sitting there, which seems strange to me because she never just sits anywhere. She is always moving, always doing something.

"Sit down," she says. It's an order rather than an invitation. "Reika called here looking for you." I sit.

"She said you had plans with Reika and Kimi." The edge of mom's voice is hard.

"Reika invited me, but I told her I'd already made plans with Skye."

"Reika was hoping that you would change your mind. You had dinner with Skye's family last weekend. Why wouldn't you make time for your friends?" I recognize that we are suddenly standing on a steep and dangerous precipice.

"Mom," I say quietly, "Skye is also my friend."

"You have been with Reika and Kimi since we put you in that school. What is going on, Akari?"

"Nothing. Honestly, I'm fine with Reika and Kimi. Perhaps Reika feels a little jealous of my friendship with Skye."

"You've only known this Canadian girl for a few weeks.

Why would you pick her over friends you've had since kindergarten?"

"I haven't picked anyone."

"Perhaps this girl, Skye, made you choose her."

"Mom, she didn't even know Reika invited me for dinner."

"Perhaps you think you are making things better with this explanation, but you are making them worse. It seems that you are losing sight of your priorities. You are away from home too much; you are out with Skye too often. I don't see you doing your homework. I don't hear you playing your violin. Things must change, starting immediately."

"What does that mean?" I could feel the panic creeping into my voice.

"It means that you are grounded. No more going out with Skye."

———

I forgot to text Skye, but she messaged me.

SKYE

Do you want to come over here on Friday?

Or we could do something in Yokohama!

AKARI

I should have messaged earlier. I can't.

What's going on?

I'm grounded.

What? Why?

Reika invited me for dinner Friday, and I didn't accept because you and I had plans.

And?

That's it. That is the whole situation.

How does that get you grounded?

My mom's worried that I am losing sight of
my priorities. A direct quote.

That's totally crazy.

Nope. Wrong response.

I'm really sorry, Akari.

This is not even remotely your fault.

My mother cannot allow anything to come
between me and my perfect GPA.

I'd suck at being your mother's kid.

Perhaps not. She would ensure that you
received intensive training. :)

Is everything okay with you?

Yeah. I'm just bummed about seeing you less.

Plus, this will make reading Naoko's journal
trickier. We've got to get serious about finding
her.

I know. The situation is not ideal but it's
temporary.

How do you know? Have you been grounded
before?

No. But I need to believe that it won't last
long.

# CHAPTER 22
# IN WHICH SKYE REMEMBERS

When I emerge from my bedroom, Yoko is on the sectional, sipping her coffee from her favourite yellow mug and reading a novel. We both have doctor's appointments this morning. Yoko is wearing linen trousers, a blouse, and a scarf at her neck, while I, in direct response to learning that the temperature is already thirty degrees Celsius, am wearing short khaki shorts and a white sleeveless T-shirt.

We get off the train at Kamiyacho Station, emerge from the underground into the hot August sun, and turn left onto the sidewalk beside a busy Tokyo highway. After a few minutes of walking up a fairly steep incline, Yoko turns to me. "Oops. I forgot to tell you about the hill."

"Great." I sigh and reach into my pocket for an elastic to pull back my hair which, due to the humidity, is big and wild in a way that defies the laws of physics. At least it's off my neck now. As we turn the corner, a large orange tower comes into view.

"Hey, we can see this from our apartment," I say.

"Tokyo Tower. It was inspired by the Eiffel Tower," says Yoko.

"Sure. But why is it orange?"

"I think it's for safety regulations," says Yoko.

I take a photo and Instagram it with the caption, *Orange? Seriously?*

We continue up the hill in silence. I can feel my face getting redder with heat and exertion, while Yoko hasn't even broken a sweat, although she has removed her scarf and tied it around the handle of her bag. Inside the waiting room of the doctor's office, the vigour of the air conditioning is much lower than I was hoping for, but the receptionist calls me almost immediately. She pronounces my name "Ski" which makes Yoko smile. She pats my leg twice.

The doctor is unexpected. A British woman in her late thirties, Dr. Devi stands up to welcome me as I enter her office. She asks about my family's move to Tokyo, where we've lived before, and if I have any medical concerns or questions. While I'm talking, she measures my height, weighs me, and takes my blood pressure. I keep waiting for Dr. Devi to mention my weight, because all doctors, everywhere in the world, always tell me I need to lose weight, but if Dr. Devi thinks so, she keeps this to herself.

"How's your new school?" says Dr. Devi.

"Good, actually," I say.

"Have you made some new friends?" says Dr. Devi.

"Yeah. A girl named Akari. I like her a lot. Until recently, I would have said that Akari's friends Reika and Kimi were my friends as well, but now I'm not so sure." Dr. Devi nods.

"How is everything on a scale from one to ten? With ten being amazing," says Dr. Devi.

"If you'd asked me that question yesterday morning, I would have said eight. Now, I feel like it's closer to six," I say.

"Did something happen?" said Dr. Devi. She makes a note in my file.

"My friend Akari got grounded. I think it's my fault."

"How so?"

"Her mother thinks she's spending too much time with me and neglecting what's important," I say.

"Is she?" Dr. Devi is direct, and I like that quality in a person.

"I'm not sure. I've only known her a few weeks."

"But her mother thinks she has. Our perceptions are very powerful," says Dr. Devi. I agree. "Anything else?"

"Yeah. My mom and I were walking up the hill just now and I saw the tower and it reminded me of Paris."

"Good memories?" she asks.

"Complicated. After school one day I was hanging out with these girls I mentioned, and they asked about Paris. Like if I missed it. And I do, mostly, but it felt weird to say that. Like ungrateful and complainey. Plus, it's weird to miss a place that wasn't actually my home."

Dr. Devi glances at her notes. "You lived there for four years." She leans closer. Her breath smells like peppermints. "You moved to Paris as a child, and you left as a young person. Why would it be weird to miss the place you lived and went to school and had friends? The place where you had your whole life?" I start to cry. I kind of can't believe it, but I'm crying in the office of this woman I met just a few minutes ago. In one skillful move, Dr. Devi locates a box of tissues and deposits them right beside my hand, as if they'd been there all along. I pull out a couple of tissues which make this strangely loud scraping sound as I tug them from the box. You don't expect tissues which are supposed to be soft and moist to be capable of such a loud sound, and the incongruousness of this makes me smile for a moment. I blow my nose.

"Skye, these big changes are hard. It's okay to feel sad. If you don't allow yourself to feel this sadness, it will pop up in other, less predictable, less healthy ways," says Dr. Devi.

"Are you sure you're not a psychiatrist? I saw a psychiatrist when I first moved to Paris and she said almost the exact same thing to me," I say.

"Yes, I'm quite certain. Medical schools don't tend to mess about with these matters. Are you able to talk with your parents about how you feel?" Dr. Devi holds out a small white garbage bin from under her desk, which makes me think I'm not the first patient to cry in her office. I toss my tissues in and pull a couple more from the mint green box.

"I know that I can talk to them, that they want me to—"

"What's the but, Skye?"

"But I really don't want to bother them. They're both busy and they have a lot of things to worry about. I don't want to add to that," I say, looking down at my red Converse.

"You're not a bother. You're their child," said Dr. Devi. "Please promise me that you'll discuss how you're feeling with your parents." I nod. I hope that doesn't count as a lie because I haven't actually said yes out loud, and because I try really hard not to lie. I almost always think it's better to tell the truth, but there's no way I'm talking to my parents about the stuff with Akari or Claire right now.

I sit in the waiting room while Yoko sees Dr. Devi. The humidity makes my legs stick to the beige leather sofa so that each time I move one of my legs, the sofa makes a little sucking sound. In the play area across the room, a little boy plays carefully with a colourful plastic kitchen set. He offers his father a yellow plate with three plastic hamburgers and his father laughs as he picks up one of the tiny burgers between his forefinger and his thumb. At the back of the play area, a large window reveals the bottom of Tokyo Tower, the ugly orange underbelly that reminds me of Paris and what I've left behind.

I must look sad when Yoko returns. She sits, turns in towards me, and wraps both arms around me to give me a strange but comforting sideways hug. She kisses my hot cheek.

"I'm sorry it's hard, my love." I close my eyes and try to wish it all away, but it turns out not to work like that.

———

When we get home, I decide to write to Claire. I'm not being fair to her. I begin a new email.

Dear Claire,

I'm sorry I haven't written, although it isn't strictly true that I haven't written. I wrote to you on the first day of school, right after I received your letter about how you stood up to your grandmother. That letter is still in my drafts. I don't know why I haven't sent it because I really want to.

This morning, I went to the doctor. Don't worry, there's nothing wrong. It was just a checkup. The doctor I saw was this really kind and super-smart woman named Dr. Devi and she asked about my new school and how things were in Paris, and I wanted to talk to her, but I was worried she would tell Yoko and Dad or something. I'm not sure what I was afraid of. You know those horror films where someone kills their spouse and then walls the body up behind a brick wall in their house? That's how I feel sometimes. Like there are parts of my life that I've hidden behind a brick wall and the longer those things remain hidden, the more difficult it is to acknowledge, or tend to, or share those things with other people.

You asked if I had made any friends. There's this girl named Akari, and I know you would really like her. She's smart and a really good artist which is an amazing combination in a human. We found this journal that belongs to a woman named Naoko Nishizawa, and we're reading the entries looking for clues so we can get the journal back to her. And I love the woman who wrote the journal. She had so many adventures and all these relationships that she calls 'impossible loves.' But of course, there's a BIG part of me that hopes she will find one love that's real. One person for whom she is their Everything. You know me.

I want to say that you'll meet Akari when you visit me in Tokyo but I'm guessing you're pretty mad right now and that a visit is becoming less likely.

You deserve better than a friend who never writes. I know that's true. But I have a pit in my throat, and that pit has grown a tree, and someone has carved three words into the trunk. Skye deserves love. I deserve to be loved and I wanted that person to be you. I get that you're allowed to NOT love me in the same way that I love you. I really do get that. But it feels like something inside of me is broken now and I can't make myself be your friend when the thing I want is more.

Claire, we both know I'm not going to send this letter either. Although I don't want you to hate me, I do want you to hate me just enough that I can stop being in love with you. I don't know what that amount of hate is and I'm really afraid to find out.

Your
Skye

————

"Did you bring the journal?" says Akari. The lunch bell has just rung and we're standing at her locker.

"Maybe we need a code name. Like Junko Antoinette," I say.

"Fine. Did you bring Junko Antoinette with you?" says Akari, raising her eyebrows.

"Okay. Maybe our code name needs some work. Of course I have it," I say.

"Let's grab a picnic table instead of eating in the cafeteria," she says. I know that things are off between Akari and Reika right now, but if Akari knows why, she's decided not to talk about it. She leads the way, taking the stairs two at a time.

We meet in the cafeteria where Akari asks if I want a brownie (um, is this a trick question?) and I pour us two glasses of water. I catch her attention and wave at her as she lines up to pay. She's polite with the cashier and bows at exactly the right angle, to show exactly the right amount of respect. I'm learning that your bow must reflect the position and age of the person to whom you are bowing in relation to your own age and status. If the bow is not low enough, you show a lack of respect for that person. This is particularly important when meeting a person older than yourself. Almost as tragic is a too-low bow which makes the bower seem ignorant or ill-mannered. Or worse still, the person to whom you were bowing might think you were making fun of them or their position in life. Apparently, I've been bowing too deeply. Yesterday, I popped down to the Lawson's convenience store on the ground floor of our apartment building, and I bowed to the young woman at the counter. As she straightened up, I noticed a slightly quizzical look on her face. For the briefest moment, her eyebrows formed two small tents. Then the look was gone, but I knew I'd overdone it.

Akari doesn't make these kinds of mistakes. She is attentive and precise.

"Seriously? One brownie?," I say as we make our way to a picnic table outside.

"I thought we would share," says Akari.

"It's like we haven't met. Hello. My name is Skye. I have never shared a brownie in my life."

"Oh. Sorry. Let me go back and get you one," Akari turns back to the café.

"No!" I grab her arm. "I'm so sorry. I am, without question, the most selfish person in the world. You offer to share your brownie with me, and I turn into the Incredible Hulk. I once took this personality test online, and it said that my personality was turbulent," I say.

"I do not think you are," says Akari. We sit down at the picnic table.

"Turbulent?"

"The most selfish person in the world."

"You are too nice," I say.

"I am really not," says Akari as she cuts the brownie in two.

"Prove it!"

"I am Hello Kitty on the outside and Batman on the inside. Maybe Wolverine."

"So, still a good person?" I say.

"Good, yes. Just not particularly nice," says Akari.

"You haven't accepted my apology yet."

"Hello Kitty says of course we accept your apology. Batman says you should get your own brownie." I stand up. Akari places her hand on my forearm. "I am kidding. Wow! Some people just cannot take a joke." Using her chopsticks, she places one half of her brownie on the lid of my bento box.

# CHAPTER 23
# IN WHICH NAOKO NISHIZAWA WRITES ABOUT THE OPERA

Not everyone loves the opera. Some people cannot possibly sit still for three and a half hours. Not even in a comfortable, red velvet upholstered chair. There are those that believe an evening at the opera is too self-indulgent, too frivolous, too overwrought for a serious person. A person of substance.

Fine.

There's a saying in English that goes something like, "It ain't over till the fat lady sings." The fat lady being referred to is an opera singer, a soprano, who would often sing the final aria at the end of an opera, usually as she was dying. I once heard of an aria that lasted more than twenty minutes. The saying was invented by an American journalist writing about a conversation about American football. The opera, like love and other sports, is not over until the fat lady has sung her last sad song.

My father took my mother and me to see an opera when I was about eleven. Still small, a bit shy with strangers, and terrified of men with facial hair, but starting to become the person I am now. (Which is to say curious and overflowing with opinions.) My mother was so happy to be taken out for the evening. She'd gone to the hair stylist earlier that afternoon and came back looking exactly the same, but something had happened on the inside, some marvellous transformation. She shook her head every few minutes to feel the swish of her blunt cut bob as it grazed her ear lobes. She chose a simple black dress that landed just above her knees and featured a low backline. She added her long string of pearls and a pair of sparkly earrings that dangled from her ears and, when she looked at her reflection in the hallway mirror, she smiled.

I have no memory of what I wore that night. Something my mother chose for me. She has always been a woman of impeccable taste.

My father was running late, and my mother kept going to the window to see if he'd arrived.

He was already shouting when he walked through the front door. "Hurry up. Can't you see we're late. Why don't you have your coats on?" As my mother headed up the stairs to grab her coat, my father said, "Is that what you are wearing?"

"I'm getting my coat. I'll be right down."

"I asked if that is what you plan to wear to the opera."

"Are you referring to my dress?"

"Yes," he said. There was a strange light behind his eyes.

"That was my intention."

"It is unsuitable. Please change." My mother ran up the rest of the stairs. My father and I stood silent and frozen, one metre from each other, while a dark symphony of slamming drawers and dropped shoes filled the house. When my mother returned, she wore a black dress with a small white cotton collar. The dress was cinched at the waist and although she normally wore a slim belt with this dress, tonight she did not. This dress hung down to the middle of her calf and her high heels were gone, replaced by flat shoes that laced up. The pearls were gone. The flash at her earlobes was gone. She could have attended a funeral in this dress.

My mother shoved my coat in my direction as she strode by me. She walked right up to my father and stopped just centimetres from his face. They stared at each other in this way for a minute that felt like a century.

"Shall we go?" my father said.

The car ride was silent. My parents normally chatted in the car. My mother would ask my father about his boring job and pretend to care about his answers. She would then criticize the old woman who lived next door because the neighbour did not keep the sidewalk in front of her house clean and everyone, my mother would assert, knew that this was a serious responsibility. They would speak of upcoming events and social obligations with loathing, but from which they benefited, nonetheless. Although I disliked these conversations, I would have given anything to hear them talk about nothing on the night of the opera. But they did not. My mother asked me a few questions about school, and I tried to answer these questions perfectly. However, she was not in the mood to be easily pleased or won over. When we arrived at the opera, my mother asked for her ticket, and excused herself to go to the bathroom.

"There's no need to wait for me," she said. "I will be along."

'When?' I thought. 'When will you be along?' "I will be along" was without question the most imprecise thing my mother had said in my lifetime. The parents of Yukiko, a friend from school, had just gotten divorced. Yukiko lived with her mother now and spent every second weekend with her father in a tiny apartment far from her house. She had to take the train over an hour to get there. The apartment was so small, Yukiko said, that she did not have her own room, but slept in the living room, and sometimes, when she woke up on Sunday mornings, her father, smelling of beer, was letting himself into the apartment. Was this how it began?

My father led me into the orchestra section of the theatre.

We stopped several times so my father could say hello to men from his office or old friends from the university. He entered a row near the front of the orchestra and sat in the third seat, so I took the aisle seat to let my parents sit together.

"I think, just this once, it would be a good idea for you to sit between us." I scrambled into the seat beside him, afraid that he might change his mind.

The lights were lowered in the theatre. A bell rang somewhere, distantly, reminding the women in the bathrooms that their husbands and small daughters were waiting at their seats. Holding their breath. My father looked at his watch and then rubbed his wrist.

The opera began.

At the bottom of the stage ran Japanese subtitles to the Italian dialogue and song lyrics, but this seemed an unnecessary arrangement. Our seats vibrated with the voices of Count and Rosina, the Countess, Figaro, and Susanna. Susanna was as strong as the men. Clever, independent, and fierce. Rosina was strong too but softer. I wasn't sure if she should forgive her husband for his affairs as it didn't seem like that great a deal for her. But the woman playing Rosina had blonde hair and breasts like Mount Fuji. I had never seen a woman like this.

Many Japanese women are small. That's how we're made. Small shoulders, small feet, small wrists. Our bodies are birdlike, and well into adulthood, many women have the flat chest and slim hips of a child. When we eat too much we go directly to apples. Small and round. Shiny apples with our skin pulled tight. It is still a rare occurrence to see a fat Japanese woman and rarer still to encounter a Japanese woman that one would call voluptuous. We are not a country of opera singers.

My mother coughed. I wasn't sure how long she'd been sitting there, but she nodded, which was her code for a smile. After she almost-smiled at me, we turned to watch Rosina with her curls and her dimples and her large breasts and we imagined falling down into the magical space between them. Down the rabbit hole. I glanced at my father who seemed to be having the same dream of falling.

Despite her size, Rosina moved like a ballet dancer, light and graceful, her skirts rustling along the stage floor. The sound of her skirts reminded me of the swish of my mother's hair earlier that evening. I had brushed my fingers along the tips of her hair, setting her bob into motion. Back and forth. Back and forth to Mozart.

At the end of the performance, the male opera singers bowed, and the women curtsied. The first few rows of the theatre were particularly overcome by Rosina's charms.

"Bravo," my father said.

In the car ride home, my father talked about his job and my mother talked about the lazy old woman next door and I wondered if I wished hard enough before I went to sleep, if I hoped and hoped and closed my eyes very tight without peeking, if I might wake up the next morning with blonde hair and the breasts of Rosina. Just that. The rest of my body was fine. And I wondered if perhaps I might also wish my way into her forgiving disposition. The ability to forgive seemed quite important if you were born a woman.

# CHAPTER 24
## IN WHICH AKARI CAN RELATE

Skye and I are quiet for a long time after we read the journal entry about the opera. Skye says how much she identifies with Rosina, a well-equipped soprano in a nation of small women, but my thoughts keep returning to the beginning of the scene, when Naoko's father humiliates her mother because he judges her outfit to be provocative. I wonder if Skye's mind doesn't land there because her own parents are ridiculously kind to each other and to her. It's not that I'm jealous of her family. I like them very much. But there are things Skye doesn't understand because she has never experienced them. Perhaps that is true about everyone.

My heart is heavy because I can imagine this exchange occurring between my own parents. I'm quite certain that something like this has happened in the past. My mother would probably punish my father by giving him the silent treatment for a week but, ultimately, if he told her to change her clothes, I believe she would. Then it occurs to me that I am the daughter of a man who would tell his wife to change her clothes if he thought she was not projecting the right image to the world. This makes me the daughter of a woman who would do whatever her husband told her to do. I wonder what this means about me, and I feel a lump forming in my throat. Perhaps this is why my mother wants me to do well in school and attend a great university ... so that I can have a stable, well-paying career and never have to depend on anyone else financially. Maybe a woman who makes her own money wears what she wants. I gasp.

"What?" says Skye.

"An epiphany," I say, and explain what I'm thinking.

"Of course." She looks up from packing up her bento box. "A woman with her own money has more power over her life. She can wear what she wants, live where she wants, vote for whomever she wants ..."

"But shouldn't that also be true for women who work as full-time parents?" I say.

"Yes," Skye says. "But it's not always true."

"Maybe I'm too hard on my mother," I say.

"What?" Skye nose wrinkles up. "You're grounded right now, and you have not said one critical word about either of your parents so no, I don't think you're being too hard on your mother."

"But it's possible that this is why she is hard on me. Perhaps I will conduct a little experiment at home and try to understand things from her perspective, be a better daughter."

"Or you could just talk to her about this stuff," says Skye.

"Let's not be rash," I say.

———

As soon as I've collected my books from my locker, I leave. I don't say goodbye to anyone. I arrive home just before five o'clock and my mom is in the kitchen, so I stop in and say hello. She smiles and then frowns, perhaps to counteract the happiness that was about to flood her body. I tell her I'm going to go practice my violin and then I will help her make dinner. She nods.

The window is open in my room, which is on the Tokyo Bay side of the house, and I feel a cool breeze, the kind of breeze that normally signals the end of summer. Skye will be so excited. The white linen curtain bows and curtsies as I gently remove the violin from its case, settle into my chair and play for forty-five minutes. The weird thing is that it feels good to practice this way, to slow down and enjoy the sensation of moving the bow against the strings, and to analyze why I'm making these particular errors. It feels good not to be in a hurry to be somewhere else with someone else.

I help mom with dinner, although she's already done most of the preparation for our ramen. Dinner at our house happens in two shifts. I eat between six and seven o'clock, and my mom eats later with my dad. He gets home after nine o'clock, or sometimes later depending on what is happening at his office. Some of my friends' families don't eat dinner until their fathers get home from work, but my mother thinks it's not good for me to eat so close to bedtime. She always cooks an elaborate dinner, and sometimes I'm not in the mood for a big meal, so I make myself a sandwich or fry an egg, but today, I'm determined to be a better daughter.

"I'm going to have the ramen if that's okay." My mother prepares a bowl for me. Unexpectedly, she makes herself a bowl as well and joins me at the table. For a while we slurp without talking.

"Nice to hear you practicing the violin. Your father pays a lot of money for your lessons."

I ignore the second part of her comment. "It was nice to play the violin. There was a cool breeze coming off the water," I say.

"Yes. I noticed it today as well."

"The ramen is good, mom. Thanks." She nods and offers a small, tight smile.

After a few minutes she asks, "Are you feeling alright?"

"I feel fine. Why do you ask?" I say.

"I don't know. You seem different today."

"Everything is fine. The ramen is delicious. Thank you for the meal."

When she's done, I pour her a glass of green tea, collect our dishes, wash them up, and head back upstairs to do my homework.

# CHAPTER 25
# IN WHICH SKYE THINKS SHE'S IN TROUBLE

At recess, I find Akari in the art room which is crowded with Grade Eleven and Twelve students working on projects.

"Hey, have you checked your email recently?" I say.

"Not since this morning in homeroom? Why?"

"There's a message for us to see Ms. Barrett at lunch. Here, I'll read it to you." My phone is already in my hand, so I tap on the message at the top of my inbox. "Hello Akari and Skye. Please see me at the beginning of High School lunch about the assignments you submitted on Thursday morning of last week. I'd like to speak to you before class." I drop the phone on the desk and the silicone case makes a whomping sound as it hits the surface.

"Oh!" says Akari. "I wonder what that's about. Did you turn your work in late?"

"Hey. No way. Dropped off before nine o'clock. What about yours?"

"Eight-thirty. As soon as I arrived."

"Show off," I say.

"Slacker," says Akari.

We laugh, but I'm aware that my own laugh isn't quite as plush as normal.

"Oh! You are worried. If you are, then I should also be worried," says Akari.

"Do you want to read each other's assignments?" I say.

"Good idea." Akari reaches into her bag and pulls out her laptop. She opens it, types in the password and places it on the desk in front of me. I do the same and pull up a stool. We sit, shoulder to shoulder, reading our assignments.

"Do you think she's pissed that I wrote from the perspective of a fictional character?" I ask.

"No. It's excellent." Akari looks up from my laptop.

"Too long?"

"It's quite long but I don't believe that is the problem. When have you ever seen a teacher upset about a student writing too much? She said it was an opinion piece. I suspect she finds our arguments too similar."

"Maybe. But yours is much better written," I say.

"Thanks, but that is not true. Your argument is dexterous"

"I don't even know what that means. Are we in trouble?"

"There is no way to be sure until we talk to her. Shall we go to her classroom now, so we don't have to wait until lunch?" As Akari finishes speaking, the bell rings, signalling the end of break. We'll have to wait three and a half hours to speak with Ms. Barrett.

————

During biology class, I stare alternately at the huge clock in the centre of the room and out the window. Everything is so green. In Ottawa, during the very short summer we get each year, the grass turns brown, and everything wilts and looks exactly the same as I feel in that heat. But here, even though the summer is brutally hot, the air is filled with water from a thousand potential rainstorms, and the grass and trees are green like in a French film. Tokyo in September feels tropical, and although I find it beautiful from inside my air-conditioned biology lab, it's probably a fair bet that the tropics aren't for me. Yoko promises that by the third week of September, Tokyo will be the loveliest city on earth, and Yoko has never lied to me.

Does Ms. Barrett really think we cheated? That we discussed the assignment and used the same ideas? I acknowledge that I have a deep desire for Ms. Barrett to like me. Who am I kidding? I want everyone to like me.

———

"Hello, girls. Thanks for coming in."

Akari bows her head slightly.

"Sure," I say.

"As I said in my message, I'd like to speak to you about last week's assignment."

"We didn't do it," I say.

"Of course you did. I have both of your assignments right here." Ms. Barrett is holding the paper copies of our work in her hand. She shakes them a little and I suddenly imagine them as cheerleading pom-poms.

"I mean we didn't cheat," I say.

"What Skye is trying to say is that even though there are some similarities in our papers, we did not discuss the assignment with each other," says Akari.

"Did you think I was accusing you of plagiarism?" says Ms. Barrett.

"Yeah," I say.

"It crossed our minds," says Akari.

"A thousand apologies. I'm afraid I'd forgotten what fear a

mysterious message from a teacher could strike into the hearts of teenagers. I've read through the assignments and you two were the only students who took the assignment seriously and provided a thoughtful response. I'm going to be a bit tough on the class as a whole this afternoon, but I want you to know that you both did exceedingly good work. Whatever I say to the class, just ignore it and keep doing exactly what you're doing."

"So, we're not in trouble?" says Skye.

"Goodness, no. I simply wanted to thank you for your diligence and for your fine minds. Carry on."

———

A few hours later, I find Akari working in the art room, and I pull up a stool beside her. "There's a cool new boy in history class," I say.

"Oh yeah?" Akari doesn't look up from her sketchbook.

"His name is Hero. He grew up in San Francisco. Super smart."

"Did he tell you about his journey?" says Akari.

"What journey?" I say.

"The hero's journey. Really, Skye? Nothing? That was a perfect joke!" She laughs and I smile reluctantly. "Seriously, though, I am curious about why you were so worried when we were summoned by Ms. Barrett this morning?" asks Akari.

"It's not very characteristic of me, is it?" I say.

"No. It isn't."

"I guess I want her to like me. To like both of us," I say.

"She already likes me just fine," says Akari.

"I see you've decided to let your pointy bits show."

"Yup. You're in behind the curtain now, Skye. You can see the Puppet Master and all the strings."

"Hey, my mom asked if you want to come over for

dinner. We could read a few Naoko entries and start our research. Compile what we know about her ... get our spy on."

Akari looks up. "It seems that I need to deliver a short Public Service Announcement." She pauses for a moment. "I am still very much grounded," says Akari.

"What if I got Yoko to call your mom and ask? It would be much harder for her to say no to Yoko. She's a very persuasive person."

"Thank you for kind your offer but no, definitely not. My mother's head would explode," Akari says.

"It's so unfair that you're grounded when you didn't do anything wrong."

"Skye, I understand your frustration, but I need you to leave it alone. The situation with my parents is complicated," Akari says. She sounds tired.

"Okay. Do you want me to go?" I ask. I can feel a lump forming in my throat.

"There is no need to leave. Thank you for asking me for dinner. Please thank Yoko as well," Akari says. I nod, unsure of what to say. I'm the least diplomatic person in my family. Yoko wins by a million light years and Dad has to be diplomatic. It is, quite literally, his job. What would Yoko do here? She would change the subject.

"Which one has been your favourite journal entry so far?" I say.

"Perhaps the one about Masumi's painting. We haven't talked about that entry yet, but I have been thinking a great deal about the painting with the girl in the pink shirt and her dog, so I decided to draw it." Akari flips back a few pages in her sketchbook and opens it to sketches of a girl and her dog in several different styles: animé, pointillism, and realistic.

"Wow!"

"Skye, you say 'wow' a lot for a very intelligent person," says Akari.

"One has got nothing to do with the other. I am a curious person who frequently experiences awe at the world around me. Thus, the wow. You know what the great Federico Fellini always said."

"No. What did the great Federico Fellini always say?" Akari says.

"You have to live spherically and in many directions. Never lose your childish enthusiasm and things will come your way."

"Spherically and in many directions. Hmmm," says Akari.

I look back at the illustrations of the girl and her dog in her sketchbook. "Your art is amazing, Akari. Like SO good. Like I'm actually mad at myself right now for not having the right words to describe how talented you are." She frowns. "Hey, why are you acting like that's a bad thing?" Akari closes her sketchbook and looks down at the table.

"I am not accustomed to this kind of praise," she says.

"How can that be true? Do you just not show anyone your work?" I say.

"Yes. That is correct."

"I think that's really sad," I say.

"Why? It's not like I owe the world my art."

"Don't you?" I say.

"No. I do not." Akari gets up, packs her backpack, and slings it over one shoulder.

"Wait. What's happening? I thought we were just kidding around," I say. I stand up and notice that the lump in my throat is back. Why do I always make such a mess of everything?

"I am not very good at that," says Akari.

"Akari, I'm really sorry. I pushed too hard. You absolutely don't owe your art to anyone. I just get so excited about what you're making."

"Thank you." She puts her bag back on the table. "Shall we read the next Naoko entry then? I'm assuming that is your real motive for finding me this afternoon." She smiles.

"Never lose your childish enthusiasm and things will come your way," I say.

# CHAPTER 26
# IN WHICH NAOKO NISHIZAWA WRITES ABOUT THE TYPHOON

The afternoon the typhoon arrived I was visiting a friend at her apartment. For two days, the news had been full of dire reports. "The storm of the century," it was called. I'd heard this story too many times before and, of course, I love the rain. But my friend stood at her window and said, "It's very bad out there." Her anxiety for my well-being became too great to bear, so I kissed her goodbye and walked to the metro.

"The storm is grave, Miss. We are about to stop the trains. Please hurry. Thank you very much. Thank you." The car was crowded. Women held white plastic bags heavy with groceries. Salary men who had been urged by their bosses to go directly home sat in wet suit jackets clutching black briefcases. As the train moved from its subterranean passage to the tracks above the ground, all of the passengers turned to the windows.

The sky was grey. As if colour had been demoted. Skipped town with sun's wife. Gone. The trees swayed like drunken dancers; all inhibitions lost. The trees closest to the tracks bowed to the train, reached out, touched it with their branches. People moved away from the windows.

And so it was after five when I arrived at my own station in

Hiro-o. "Attention. We will close the station in a few minutes. Please move towards the exits quickly and calmly."

Darkness fell like a net. The mist of the early afternoon re-committed to its job as rain.

A woman in a yellow dress splashed down the sidewalk in pursuit of a taxi.

At an intersection, a young couple held hands and waited for green. The man in a black coat and the woman in cream leaned into each other under a canopy of merged umbrellas. Beyond them, the wet streets glistened in puddles of light.

As I walked through the park, my clear umbrella offered an unobstructed view of the other umbrella people as they scuttled for the dry safety of their homes. A gust of wind flipped my umbrella inside out. I imagined this is what would happen if an ostrich tried to fly.

Black clouds rolled in, and the wind began to roar. I felt myself coming to life. I longed to walk in the storm in my bare feet with my face turned towards heaven. I shall not drown. For I love the rain too much and the rain loves me.

# CHAPTER 27
# IN WHICH AKARI FINDS THE FIRST CLUE

"Wow. It sounds so romantic," Skye says.

"Do you think so?" I ask. She nods immediately. I sigh. "I hope we do find Naoko Nishizawa so that there will be one person in this entire country who understands you."

"You get me," Skye says. "You're not like me, necessarily, but you get me." She holds up a hand for a high five and I connect my hand with hers in a very satisfying way. She's right, of course. I have felt that I understood her since that first day of school when I looked up and saw a girl who looked just like Chiyo.

"Some of the typhoons that come through this area are incredibly violent. We are particularly vulnerable in Tokyo and Yokohama due to our location on the water."

"Yoko told me that sometimes school is cancelled. Like a typhoon day."

I nod. "The trains are often cancelled as well. It is interesting, though. When the meteorologists predict a huge storm, we often get just a thunderstorm. Then, at other times, a small storm is predicted but it quickly transforms into a typhoon."

"What's the takeaway?" Skye says. "Never trust a meteorologist?"

We laugh, and then I realize we've got our first solid clue. "Hey! Naoko names her home station as Hiro-o." I flip back to the entry and there it is. Suddenly I feel cool hands on my shoulders and I sit up straight, slamming the journal closed at the same time.

"Relax, Akari. It's just me." I recognize Kimi's voice. She gives me an awkward hug from behind and I pat her hands. I turn around on my stool and find that Reika is standing beside her. "We just finished practice, so we thought we'd come say hello."

"Why don't you both sit. Everyone else has gone home," Skye says. The tables in the art room are large and not designed for conversation. I can tell this is going to be awkward until Skye slides around the corner leaving a stool free on either side of me. Kimi takes the stool that Skye has just vacated and Reika straddles the stool to my right.

"It's great to see you both," says Skye. "How's volleyball going?" Skye and Kimi chat about volleyball and school and then Kimi asks Skye how her transition to life in Japan is going. They're both sunny and cheerful while Reika and I are essentially mannequins at this point, and my stomach feels sick about the distance between us. I turn to her and say, "Do you have time to talk after this?"

"Sure. Starbucks?" she says. I nod.

# CHAPTER 28
# IN WHICH SKYE SENDS
# A MESSAGE

There's no one in the art room when I meet Akari before class. She's assured me that art students rarely get to school (or anywhere) early, so we'll have the room to ourselves to read another entry from Naoko's journal. Golden light streams through the windows and creates small pools on the floor, making the room feel a bit magical, as if anything were possible here. All the stools are pushed under the tables, the work surfaces are clean, and all the materials are neatly stacked on the counters.

"Hey!" Akari dashes into the room, backlit by sunlight in a way that makes the top of her head glow like a halo. This makes me smile.

"Hey. Did you remember the journal?" I say. Akari drops onto the stool beside me. She's out of breath and I realize I've never seen her move this quickly before. I've kind of assumed she wasn't that sporty with all the art-making and the violin-playing but when she ran across the room, she moved like an athlete. I'm reminded of these lines from Walt Whitman: "Do I contradict myself? Very well then, I contradict myself, (I am large, I contain multitudes.)" We contain multitudes. I like this about us.

Akari holds her backpack between her knees but doesn't make a move to take the journal out of her bag. She's panting a little.

"You okay?" I ask.

"Yes, but something happened last night," Akari stops for a moment. I nod and she continues, "I'm not entirely sure who to talk to about it." There's something slightly wild in her eyes.

"Do you want to talk about it?" I ask.

She nods. "Yes. I need to."

"Then go for it. I'm right here," I say. For the briefest of moments, Akari places her hand on top of my hands that are folded and resting on the table.

"Thank you." She sighs, places her bag on the table, and straightens her back. "You know that I had coffee with Reika last night?" I nod. "I explained what happened with my mom, how she grounded me for not accepting the dinner invitation from Reika and Kimi, and for what she perceived as losing sight of my priorities. Reika feels very guilty about this."

"Did she do it on purpose? Like did she call your mother with the intention of getting you in trouble?" I'm speaking quickly now. "I realize this is not strictly my business and I've been trying really hard to stay out of this which, as you know, does not come naturally to me, and I realize this is going to sound a little dramatic, but this question has haunted me," I say.

"I don't know. I did not ask her. It doesn't really matter, right?" Akari says.

"You're a much better person than I am, Akari. Continue."

"I could tell that Reika genuinely felt bad and then she started to cry, and I knew there must be something else happening because I have seen Reika cry exactly once, the day that Fiona's family moved back to Australia. Reika is just not a crier." I nod but not in a hostile way, which was definitely where I was headed a few moments earlier. "She could not stop crying and I began to ask myself if I had been too hard on her ..."

"That's ridiculous," I say, and Akari nods.

"Yes. I came to the same conclusion. I was trying to comfort her even though I was officially the wronged party and, when she could not stop crying, I finally just asked her what was going on."

"Good decision," I say.

"Skye, this next part is not meant to be funny so please do not laugh." I nod and try to think of something serious to get me in the right head space. Climate change. Corrupt political leaders. Virginia Woolf drowning herself with her pockets filled with rocks. That third image does it. "Reika was crying so hard she couldn't talk, so she took a notebook out of her bag and wrote 'I love you.'" I start to see where this is headed. Akari continues, "I tried to reassure her. I told her I love her too and that this was just a small misunderstanding, and then I said we have been friends for a long time so we will get through this."

"But that's not exactly what she was saying," I say. Akari's eyes fill up with tears.

"No. It wasn't." Akari drops her head and lets the tears come freely. Like Reika, Akari doesn't strike me as a crier, but here she is and here I am. I'm the person she's chosen to tell this story to. I pat her back gently. "You'll both be okay."

"I know. I just feel so bad for Reika. I think she has been feeling this way for a long time, but she couldn't tell me. I don't care that she is bi or gay or however she identifies, I just feel sad that this has been so painful for her."

"Is there a chance you might feel something for her?" I ask. I'm not sure why but my heart flutters as I ask her this question. As if something's at stake. Akari shakes her head.

"No. I do not really feel attracted to anyone. I mean I haven't yet. Is that weird?"

"I don't think I'm qualified to be your sex therapist, and I'm definitely not an expert on what is and is not weird." Akari laughs and pulls a handkerchief out of a pocket at the front of her bag. She begins wiping away her tears. "How did you leave things?" I ask.

"I told her that I love her as a friend and that what she shared does not change anything for me. I also said that I'd like all four of us to hang out if that's possible, and that I understand if she cannot be as close to me for a while," says Akari. She sets down her handkerchief.

"Wow," I say.

"Was it okay? What I said?" asks Akari.

"Like really, really good. Like possibly a perfect response." Akari starts to cry again. Big silent tears roll down her cheeks. I pick up the handkerchief from the table and hand it to her. She dabs at the lovely drops.

"Thanks for listening, Skye. I couldn't hold it in." I nod and pat her back again. She turns and looks at me. "The good news is that Reika called my mother last night and clarified that I never had dinner plans with Reika and Kimi. She also said that you are actually a very nice person and that she had been unfair in her description of you to my mother." I laugh. "This means that I am no longer grounded, my friend." We high five.

"Wow. This has been a lot of emotions to experience before the morning bell rings," I say. And then the bell rings.

————

It's been a big day, so I'm thinking about a nap as I enter my bedroom after school. On my pillow (the bed made once again by Yoko. Damn!) is another light blue envelope.

Claire.

It's been a month since I received her last letter and although I've written twice, they are both sitting in my drafts. I feel sick with guilt and longing. Claire has been my closest friend for four years and she deserves better than a series of unsent letters. Here she is writing to me again, which makes me feel even worse. I tear open the envelope.

Skye,

I've thought a lot about how to start this letter. I would have preferred to begin with an amusing anecdote about my adventures in chemistry class or a quote I think you'll love from a book that I'm reading, but I don't have the heart for it.

I know you're probably busy at your new school and getting accustomed to living in Japan and I'm guessing that you're becoming friends with new people, but I've heard almost nothing from you, and you've been gone for two months.

Did I do something to hurt you or upset you? If so, please tell me what I've done. I promise that I'll try to fix it if I can.

The options are either:

1. You're hurt.

or

2. That you no longer care about me.

The first option is bad, but the second possibility is so terrible to me that I don't even want to consider it. The evidence, however, suggests that I should.

Are we even still friends?

Please let me know that you're okay. Please let me know that we're okay.

Claire

P.S. I've been trying to figure out the best way to tell you this. I've started dating someone. He's new at school this year and he's from London.

P.P.S. I know I sound angry in this letter but mostly I'm just worried and I miss you.

I drop the letter. There's a flutter and although I've had the feeling recently, I can't place it exactly. There's the news that Claire has met someone. Then there's a roaring in my ears like being at sea.

I know I should pause between the stimulus and my response. I can hear Yoko's voice suggesting that I read a book or have a snack or hug a tree or do absolutely anything rather than what I actually do, which is to open a new email to Claire.

Claire,

You're absolutely right. I have been a terrible friend. A terrible, heartbroken friend who couldn't get her crap together to write you.

You win. You win true love, and you are officially off the hook where I'm concerned.

Please don't contact me again.

Skye

Before my brain has a chance to understand what I've written, or to intervene on my behalf, I hit send. Panic arrives instantly, like it's been injected into my blood stream. I make myself stay in my chair and read the message I've just sent, even though I'm wriggly with discomfort and feel like I'm coming out of my skin. The message to Claire is devastating. It's so mean and so small. I've acted like a wounded animal might, you know, if animals could use laptops. My face feels warm and, when I place my hands on my cheeks, I'm shocked by how hot they are. My body knows I'm a bad person.

In an unsent letter I wrote to Claire a couple of weeks ago, I said something about wanting her to hate me just enough that I could stop being in love with her, and although I never would have planned it this way, the message I've just sent will accomplish that goal. I file the message to Claire, block her email address and then block her on social media.

There's a small voice inside me that says, *You can undo this. Write to her now. Or better yet, call her and apologize. Explain how overwhelmed you've been feeling. She'll understand.* I close my laptop harder than I intend to, change into my pyjamas, and draw the curtains. It's only eight o'clock but I can't stand to be awake with my thoughts, and the person I've become.

## CHAPTER 29
# IN WHICH AKARI ASKS THE WRONG QUESTIONS

I t's early in the morning and I can't sleep.

It's just me and the cicadas awake at this hour.

At my desk, I open my sketchbook and flip to the last page on which I drew Chiyo. When she showed up in my mind in August, I knew exactly what she looked like, which was eerily like Skye, and I knew what her superpower was, but I didn't fully understand her why. In the top right-hand corner of the page, I write:

Did Chiyo lose someone to suicide? Is this what motivates her? I should know this. Was it a boyfriend? A girlfriend? Or a friend? Does it even matter if the person she loved was a romantic partner or a friend? To what extent is love simply love?

I place my pencil on the desk and look at these words. Reika telling me she loves me has raised more questions than it has answered. Did I do something to make her believe I was in love with her? Should I have acted differently towards her? Am I responsible for the pain Reika is feeling? I believe Skye would say these are the wrong questions. She would say that no one is at fault. I believe she would tell me that people fall in love all the time. I long to think more like Skye does, to let things go like a leaf on a stream, but I lack both the lightness and the training.

Someone else is awake. I close my sketchbook and pad down the stairs in my bare feet. My mother is in the kitchen. She raises one eyebrow. "I know, right. So early! Mom, since I'm up now, I think I'd like to have a full breakfast with you this morning. Is that okay?"

"Natto, too?" she smiles mischievously.

"Let's not lose our minds," I say. "Everything but the natto. How can I help?"

———

Part of me still cannot believe that my parents gave me permission to go to Skye's house for a sleepover on the week-end. I'm left off balance by their kindness.

After dinner, Skye tells her parents that we need to get some homework done.

"It's Friday night, my wee lass. Why don't the two of you take a break from all that?" says Skye's dad. Yoko stands, places her hands on the back of her chair and gives us a sideways nod in the direction of the bedrooms, a gesture that seems to say, *Quick, make your escape now while you can,* so Skye and I excuse ourselves and head towards Skye's room.

"Duncan, I'm pretty sure homework is still code for 'we just want to hang out,'" says Yoko.

"Thank the gods I have you, dear, to translate our teenage daughter," says Skye's dad. I hear them laughing as Skye closes the door to her room, and we explode with laughter. The laughing slows to giggling then passes, leaving me pleasantly light-headed. Our backpacks are on the bench at the end of Skye's bed. Mine is black and Skye's is orange and whenever we leave our bags leaned against each other like this, they look like Halloween decorations. I reach into my bag, pull out Naoko's journal and pass it to Skye, who is already seated on the floor with her back against the side of the bed. I retrieve my bag and sit facing Skye and Skye's slippers which look like stuffed animals. Two fluffy brown dogs with big droopy ears.

"I keep expecting your slippers to bark at me," I say.

"So where shall we start?" says Skye. She caresses the journal with the tips of her fingers. I reach into my backpack and pull out two hard-cover black journals. I pass one to Skye. I've wrapped it with a red ribbon and tied a bow in the centre of the cover.

"What's this?"

"I purchased journals so we can keep track of what we learn," I say.

"Very *Harriet the Spy*," says Skye, grabbing some pillows off the bed. She passes me two and I lay them on the rug.

"Harriet the what?"

"*Harriet the Spy*. A seriously cool kids' book about this girl who investigates mysteries. She writes everything down in this little notebook she carries. I think you'd like it."

"Okay then, Harriet! Go ahead and open Naoko's journal," I say. Skye opens the journal to the front page. Between the cover and the first page Skye finds a laminated piece of paper with the words "From the desk of Akari" printed at the top. Below that, in my small and ridiculously careful handwriting, I've written my name and email address. I've also made an index of all thirty-eight of the entries in Naoko's journal, as well as the title and page numbers of each entry.

"There were page numbers?" says Skye.

"Not exactly," I say. Skye passes the index to me and starts flipping through the pages of the journal.

"You wrote page numbers in the journal?" says Skye.

"Yes, but in pencil. We can erase them as soon as we find her."

"You are some kind of organizational mastermind," says Skye.

"What can I say? I have a strong preference for order."

"This is so cool. Thank you for my journal, and for all this time and energy you're spending to help me find Naoko, wherever she is," says Skye.

"Listen, Skye, I feel terrible about everything that has happened, with Reika being so mean to you and then my parents grounding me ..."

"None of that was your fault," says Skye, waving off my apology. "How are things with Reika? I get it if that's too private to talk about."

"Better," I say. "Definitely still a little awkward but I think that is to be expected. I'm trying to find this balance between being her friend and also recognizing that I am the cause of her pain. Does that make sense?" Skye nods. "It's a surreal place to live. This is going to sound strange, but I feel the weight of it. You know, the weight of her love for me. I feel it here." I place my hand on my chest, and then my eyes are brimming over with tears.

Skye places her hand on my shoulder. "What does it feel like?"

"Heavy ... but not in a bad way. I love Reika but the quality of that love is not romantic. It would be so much easier if I did feel that way because we've known each other forever and she is one of my closest friends."

"But the heart wants what it wants," says Skye. She looks down at her hands for a moment.

"Yes. I think that is true. I'm not upset that Reika told me. It's just that knowing how she feels is making me think about things in a new way. No, that is not quite right. What she told me is *helping* me think about things in a new way."

"You're a good friend, Akari."

"As are you, Skye."

"You know my friend, Claire?" I shake my head. "Of course you do. Claire from Paris. I talk about her all the time," says Skye.

"You've never mentioned her," I say.

"Wow. Could that be true?" I nod. "Well, that's super weird because she was, is, my best friend. I got this letter from her and she's dating someone, and it feels so strange, you know, because neither of us has dated before."

I nod my head again. I do know. "Do you like the person she's dating?"

"I don't know them." Skye is looking at me, but I have this feeling that she is looking right past me, and, for a few moments, she seems very far away. She shakes her head gently, picks up the index from where I have laid it on the rug, and looks up. "Can you believe we have read only six of her entries?" It's strange that Skye has changed the subject so abruptly, but perhaps she is not ready to talk about her friend with me.

"I feel like I am beginning to know Naoko," I say.

"Me too," says Skye. "I thought maybe we could put together a board with all the information we know about her. You know, sort of like criminal detectives on TV."

"Where would we put it?" I say.

"That's exactly where my plan fell apart. A board is too conspicuous. Not nearly stealthy enough. One of our mothers would definitely find it."

"That is where the journals will be helpful. They're small and we will always have them with us," I say.

"Okay. I'll record what we know," says Skye.

### What we know about Naoko Nishizawa

- Name: Naoko Nishizawa
- Year of birth: Unknown
- Neighbourhood as an adult: Hiro-o???
- Neighbourhood as a child: Unknown
- University: University of Tokyo
- Secondary School: Name unknown. (Japanese school where students wore uniforms)
- Profession: Writer
- Friends and known associates: Masumi, a painter
- Hobbies: drinking at bars, cello concerts, picnics under the sakura, attending the opera, collecting paintings of girls with dogs.

When Skye finishes writing she passes the journal to me. "Not so very much to go on," I say.

"Are you serious? We have her name and a neighbourhood," says Skye.

"Her name?" I laugh. "I have an idea. Why don't you do an Internet search?" Skye crawls over and grabs her laptop out of her bag.

"Wait. In English or Japanese?" says Skye.

"Either."

Using English characters, Skye types Naoko Nishizawa into the window of the search engine. "There are ten pages of results!" she yells.

I roll up onto my knees and look over the top of Skye's laptop. "There will be even more results when we search in Japanese," I say.

"How do you know that? Have you been all Harriet the Spy without me?"

"I have not been even a bit Harriet the Spy without you.

What is a common girl's name in Canada? For someone Yoko's age?"

"I don't know. Jennifer?" says Skye.

"Good. What is a common last name?" I say.

"Smith."

"Jennifer Smith. Finding Naoko Nishizawa here is like finding Jennifer Smith in Canada."

"Really? Naoko Nishizawa sounds so exotic, though!"

"Jennifer Smith sounds exotic to me."

Skye laughs. "Come on, Akari. That can't be true. What are we talking? Like hundreds of Naoko Nishizawa?"

"Many more. Also, there are at least two different spellings of Naoko. There is the spelling we've been using and Nahoko with an H. I would estimate that there are thousands of Naoko Nishizawas."

"Whoa! We really don't have much to go on. I was thinking that we could just call up directory assistance and ask for the number of a Naoko Nishizawa in Hiro-o."

"We could call them, but you need the person's name and address," I say.

"But if we had her address, we could just take the journal to her house. You know ... once we'd finished reading it. I want to find out how things end," says Skye.

"People here guard their privacy carefully."

"Then she shouldn't have left her journal in this bag!" says Skye, rolling her eyes.

"Where is your gratitude?" I say. "We may be a private people, but need I remind you that you are living in the safest country on earth. Earthquakes, nuclear disasters, and tsunamis notwithstanding,"

"Okay, that was a little dark, Akari. I AM grateful. Japan is just a little inconvenient at the moment."

"Were you thinking of going door-to-door?" I joke.

"Would that not be okay?" says Skye.

I fall over on the carpet and my head lands on the soft furry head of one of Skye's dog slippers. "It would be so wildly inappropriate, Skye, that I am not sure if I can even explain it to you." I say, sitting up.

"Why? What's the big deal? I ring the bell and, in my most respectful Japanese. I say, 'Hello. My name is Skye. My lovely friend and I are looking for a woman named Naoko Nishizawa. Do you happen to know her?' See, that's nice, eh?"

"When people move apartments here, they buy a gift for their neighbours on each side of their apartment and the people who live below them."

"What kind of gift?" says Skye.

"Hand towels, perhaps, or a nice edible gift that conveys the following: 'Hello. We have just moved in next door. We're nice people who can be trusted and we will be quiet and respectful neighbours.' You leave the gift and then you never knock on their door again," I say. Skye raises an eyebrow. "Fine. Here are the two situations in which you might knock on the door. One. 'I'm very sorry but your mother seems to have fainted on the path to your home.' Two. 'Please accept my apologies for this disruption but your house seems to be on fire.' That is the whole list."

"Wow. If that's really how people feel, I must be breaking rules left, right, and centre. Like the cultural equivalent of tramping through someone's flower garden," says Skye.

"Yes," I say.

"Yes? You're not even going to try to soften that a bit ... or pretend otherwise?" says Skye, throwing a pillow at me.

"I break the rules as well ... but it's particularly bad when I do it because I am expected to know better."

"Yuck. Sorry," says Skye, and I shrug. "So, no door-to-door search for Naoko Nishizawa?" says Skye.

"Definitely not," I say.

"Directory assistance is out?"

"They will neither assist us, nor will they direct us."

"And our friend, the Internet?"

"Let's take a look," I say. Skye looks through the English search results while I conduct a Naoko Nishizawa search in Japanese. There's a knock on the door, and Skye's dad sticks his head in the room.

"Girls, Yoko and I were going to choose a film to watch. Care to join us?" We look up from our screens and I notice that the freckles on Skye's face are glowing in the light from her laptop.

"Nah. I think we'll pass. Thanks, Dad," says Skye. He closes the door.

"What's hilarious about that," Skye says, "is now he thinks we really are in here doing our homework." Skye smiles. "Okay, I found a Naoko Nishizawa from the University of Tokyo. She seems like she would be about the right age. Oh."

"Did you find a clue?" I say.

"She studies rice."

"That is probably not our Naoko," I say.

"Probably not. Finding our Naoko Nishizawa will be like finding a needle in a haystack."

"This is an unfamiliar idiom," I say.

"Let me explain. No, it's way too complicated. Let me sum up. Finding our Naoko Nishizawa is going to be like finding one particular grain of rice inside a rice cooker filled with rice."

"That's not a terribly creative analogy but I liked the *Princess Bride* reference," I say.

"Fair enough ... but it conveys the impossibility of the task, doesn't it? The Impossible Whereabouts of Naoko Nishizawa."

# CHAPTER 30
## IN WHICH SKYE MAKES A CONFESSION

O n Saturday morning I wake up before Akari. I've been having the strangest dream about a man who could read the mind of anyone wearing pink clothing. It didn't have to be the whole outfit, either. Pink polka dots, pink socks, pink underwear. The man approached a girl wearing a Hello Kitty T-shirt and told her she would give birth to triplets on Christmas Eve and the girl smiled but she had way too many teeth for a regular mouth and then she began to laugh, and she laughed so loudly that I woke up.

Rays of sunlight draw buttered lines across my sleeping bag because I forgot to close the curtains before we went to sleep. I don't even remember deciding to go to sleep last night. We were in our pyjamas, laughing about the sea of Naoko Nishizawas we'd have to swim through to find our Naoko, and then sleep pulled me under.

We were talking about the opera entry, and I suggested that perhaps Naoko's impossible love had been those huge, opera-singer sized breasts. Maybe eleven-year-old Naoko had hoped for them but didn't get them. Akari asked how I could be sure. She said perhaps Naoko grew into her breasts.

I'd given my bed to Akari who said she couldn't take it but, in the end, she had to because I'd already taken possession of the sleeping bag and was wearing it around my shoulders like a big fluffy cape.

When I sit up, I see three black journals on the bench at the bottom of the bed. I grab one and, opening it, realize it is Akari's. Part of me, the part that's most like Yoko, says, *Close that journal right now. Put it back. It's not yours.* I recognize this as the best possible action to take, and I'm aware that the Yoko-voice in my head never lets me down, but the part of me that is most Skye-like says, *Go ahead. Just a little peek. What would it hurt?*

Akari has already been using this journal, and it's clear that everything she encounters is a potential canvas. Folded neatly between the pages of the journal are napkins and scrap paper and the back of a paper placemat from McDonalds. Before meeting Akari, I might have thought of these drawings as doodles but now I know they're way more than that. She can't stop herself from creating art. This is how she sorts information, makes sense of the world, expresses herself. For Akari, meaning happens at the place where her pencil meets the paper.

Akari has been illustrating Naoko's entries, bringing them to life. There are four drawings from the opera entry. On one page, she's drawn Naoko's mother tossing her hair, Naoko's mother walking up the stairs to change her dress, and Naoko seated between her parents at the opera. On the opposite page, Akari has drawn the Countess and her great, abundant bosom laced into a frilly confection of a dress. The journal entry that seems to have captured Akari's imagination, however, is the girl in the pink striped shirt with her dog. In addition to the pencil drawings I saw in Akari's sketchbook in the art room, she has created eight new drawings. In each, Akari has drawn both the girl and the dog with such kind faces that I can see what kindred spirits they are. They are the very best of friends. Not-so-impossible loves.

Akari yawns and rolls over, so I quickly close her journal and put it back on the bench. When she gets up to go to the bathroom, I grab a pair of shorts and a T-shirt from my closet and get dressed. I unplug my phone from its charger and stick the phone in my back pocket. Then I put Naoko's journal and my new one in my backpack. When Akari emerges from the bathroom, I tell her to get dressed because I have an idea that involves breakfast in Hiro-o.

———

"You remember that I have to be home by noon, right?" Akari says. We're seated in a booth for four at the most American-looking diner either of us has ever seen. The front page of the mint green menu is filled with photographs of gigantic break-fasts: golden pancakes topped with perfect squares of butter and maple syrup, plates of French toast with icing sugar, and scrambled eggs with bacon. We both order the pancakes with chocolate chips.

"Relax. It's just nine o'clock. That gives us an hour for breakfast and an hour of detective time before you have to catch the train." Akari takes her journal out of her bag. Folded inside the paper pocket at the back of the journal is a map of the neighbourhood of Hiro-o that Akari printed last night.

"So, we're pretty sure this was where Naoko lived as an adult, right?" I say.

"It is the only neighbourhood she has referred to," says Akari, unzipping the front pocket of her backpack and pulling a red sharpie out of her pencil case.

"You are like a stationery store," I say.

"Oh, I AM a stationery store." Akari draws an X where the

station is. "In the entry about the typhoon, she talks about walking through the park to get home."

I grab my phone from the table, where I left it after my pancake photo shoot, and do a quick search for 'parks in Hiro-o' and, of course, there's an entry in Wikipedia. "Okay, listen to this: 'Adjacent to Hiro-o, the district of Minami-Azabu is home to Arisugawa Park, which spans through a large chunk of the town. The park consists of several paths and walkways, a baseball field, soccer field, children's amusement areas, and a man-made waterfall that empties into a pond full of koi and ducks. The park is situated in the close vicinity of Hiro-o Station.'"

"I know that park. It's just a few minutes from the station," says Akari. I raise my eyebrows and she says, "It is, at most, a three-minute walk, Skye. I think it's named after a prince."

I look at my phone. "Named after Prince Taruhito Shinno Arisugawa, son of blah blah blah, yup, this park is where the palace used to be. There's this bronze statue of the prince on horseback at the main entrance. West side is a ravine surrounded by a thick forest. A gentle slope to from north to south. Oh, there's a pond and a waterfall and some play areas. And there's a library on the grounds."

"That's it. Let's go," says Akari, reaching for her wallet, but I grab the bill, slip out of the booth and run to the front counter to pay. When Akari catches up to me, I flash her a big smile.

"Our treat. My dad gave me money for breakfast for both of us," I say. "Lead on, MacDuff."

"I don't know who this MacDuff person is, but I can definitely get us to Arisugawa Park," says Akari. We walk back to the station, turn left on the main intersecting street, and walk for a couple of minutes. At the T-junction, we go left and pass a large, beautiful man in a blue and yellow yukata tied with a wide cotton obi around his impressive middle.

"Sumo wrestler," whispers Akari.

"Cool," I say, "but no way is this a three-minute walk." I'm looking back over my shoulder at the sumo wrestler and bump into Akari who's standing at the entrance to a park. Our park. "Oh. Sorry," I say.

"Skye, you are, at times, a person of very little faith," says Akari.

An older woman at the entrance to the park looks me up and down and makes a disapproving tsk tsk sound. It's the kind of sound that old people seem so fond of making whenever teenagers are around, and I genuinely don't get why they often seem pissed off at us. Most teenagers are perfectly lovely people. I wonder if it's a lack of imagination that makes some elderly people so grumpy. Akari stops and stares at the woman, who then looks away. Then it dawns on me.

"That was because I'm round, right?"

"Yes. Some people here believe that roundness is a weakness in one's character," says Akari.

"What do you think?" I ask. I realize we've never really talked about my being overweight.

"I think it is a weakness in *their* character." I smile at her with every atom of my being. We follow a path that leads to a large pond filled with enormous goldfish. Akari drops her bag under a tree and sits underneath it, and I drop down beside her.

"This park is gorgeous," I say, looking around. "Do you think this could be Naoko's park from the day of the typhoon?"

"It is the only one that makes sense. There's another park on a small side street between the station and the diner, but it is a children's park with swings and other play structures. It's bordered by two streets, but it is out of the way for most people in the neighbourhood. I cannot imagine walking through that park to get home, especially if you were walking home in a typhoon," says Akari.

"I longed to walk in the storm with my face turned towards heaven. I shall not drown," I say.

"Naoko's typhoon entry? How can you remember that in such detail?" says Akari.

"Maybe that's where my mind redirects all the energy I'm not using on navigation. Naoko is fearless." I say.

"And possibly insane," says Akari.

"There's a fine line between fearless and completely crazy," I say. I'm aware that compared to Akari, I ride this line a good deal of the time.

On the path, between the tree where we're resting and the pond, walks a young couple in crisp, matching white linen shirts, followed by a man in plaid shorts, a green shirt, and a matching green hat. He's walking his dog, a small round pug, who puffs his way along, trying to keep up with his person. The dog stops, looks up at us, lifts one of his hind legs like he's taking a position in ballet and then pees on the path. We laugh while the man in the green hat tugs on the dog's leash.

"Speaking of dogs," Akari says as she pulls her journal out of the bag. She opens it and shows me the new illustrations I saw when I looked at her journal this morning. "Ta da!" she says. It's the first time she's been excited to show me her work, and I can feel my face flush red.

"Your drawings of the girl and the dog are amazing," I say.

"Thank you. I am somewhat obsessed. Not with dogs, in general, but with this particular dog and this particular girl. The way that Naoko describes the girl with her arms around the dog in the painting, the embrace itself, feels like a reflection of who they are. How they feel." Akari looks down as if she's said too much.

"Like they are each other's one true thing?" I say. She looks up and smiles.

"Yes. You've captured it exactly, Skye. They are each

other's one true thing." She pulls out her pencil case, chooses a pencil, and begins sketching the pond. The day is heating up and the song of the cicadas are become louder.

"They are contracting and releasing their abdominal muscles," I say.

"Who is?" says Akari.

"The cicadas. I've been learning about them. That's their mating call. Only the males sing, actually. Some of them register over a hundred decibels. I read that the song of the cicada is the loudest song on earth."

"Sometimes I worry that we won't crack this puzzle, that we won't find Naoko," says Akari, looking up from her journal. "But anyone who knows this many random facts about cicadas is more than adequately equipped to track down one woman named Naoko Nishizawa."

"Akari, I have a confession," I say. She nods her head for me to go ahead. "This morning, before you woke up, I looked at the drawings of the girl in the pink shirt and her dog. The ones in your journal."

"Pardon?" Akari says. Her voice is hard and sharp and pointed directly at me.

"I thought it was Naoko's journal when I grabbed it, but the drawings you've been doing are so cool that I couldn't stop myself."

"Yes, you could," Akari says. She snaps the journal closed.

"Could what?" I say. My face is burning.

"You could have stopped yourself. You are physically able to stop yourself from doing stupid things. You can stop yourself from walking into traffic, for example. The fact is that you sometimes choose to do impulsive things, even when you know they are wrong."

"You're right. I should have closed it as soon as I realized it was yours. I'm so sorry," I say.

"Skye, you invaded my privacy, and what makes it worse is that you know I am very private about my work. I am so angry at you right now."

My eyes fill up with tears and the drops fall down my cheeks. I don't want to cry now in the middle of this park, but there's nothing I can do to stop it.

She packs her journal away in her bag and stands up. "I am leaving."

I scramble up off the grass. "Akari, can you forgive me?" I reach out to place my hand on her arm, but Akari flinches, and I drop my hand to my side.

"Please don't ask me that right now, Skye. I know that you are upset but you are the one who caused this problem and there are some things that cannot be fixed with the word sorry."

# CHAPTER 31

# IN WHICH AKARI STARTS TO UNDERSTAND SOME THINGS

As I leave school, I see Kimi walking towards the train station, so I hurry to catch up with her. I am always impressed by her speed, and I remember not to add the thought 'for a short person' because I know she hates that. I notice she's not carrying her backpack.

"No homework?"

"Correct," she smiles broadly. "I've been in the library since four o'clock, so I'm done for the day. Have you been in the art room?" she asks. I nod. "Hey, I noticed that Skye ate lunch alone today. Is everything okay?"

I'm not sure that I want to talk about this but maybe I need to. "She confessed that she looked at my journal without my permission. We had an argument about it," I say.

"Oh," Kimi has known me for most of our lives, so she knows what that means for me.

"Do you have any thoughts you would like to share?"

"Two," she says. "I have exactly two. The first is that you have every right to be angry so, you know, rage on for as long as you need to."

"Thanks," I say. "I am not exactly a rage monster."

"Granted. Thought number two. Skye is a very good

person, and she really cares about you. Oh, I guess that's three thoughts." Kimi gestures in the direction of a bench a few feet away, and we speed up before someone else claims it.

"Yes, on both counts, but I find myself wondering if she can be a very good person when she's so impulsive? She picked up my journal accidentally but then she looked at it. She knew it was wrong, but she did it anyway."

"In no way am I defending her actions, Akari, but we all have something, right? Reika is dealing with her anger and her feelings about you. I want to make other people happy to the extent that I have a hard time understanding and asking for what I want. You ..." I raise my eyebrows. "You worry way too much about being a perfect daughter, so I guess you also struggle to get what you need." We sit in silence for a minute. "Wait. I'm sorry this happened to you," Kimi says. "I should have said that first." I laugh and Kimi smiles and the sun comes out from behind a cloud and seems to shine its light directly on us.

"Look how powerful you are," I say, pointing to the sun. She chuckles. "Thank you, Kimi. Your thoughts are always helpful."

She places her hand on top of mine and squeezes my fingers. "How are you and Reika doing?"

"Good, I think. I'm okay, but I know this is harder for her than it is for me."

"Why?" Kimi says. I search for a motive behind this question, but her face is a calm lake. She's just asking to understand.

"Because she's in love with me. I love her as a friend, as I always have, but I don't have romantic feelings towards her," I say.

"You've been really great to Reika, but I bet this has been super intense for you," says Kimi.

"It has. Yes, intense is the right word. Has it been intense for you?"

"Not really. I've known for years."

"Really?" I pull up my legs and sit cross-legged facing her.

"I don't mean that she told me. I just knew. We spend a lot of time together, Akari. A person notices things." Kimi shifts so that she is also facing me with her legs tucked up under her.

"Oh. I had no idea," I say. "I wonder if that's why Reika had such a strong reaction to Skye when we started to hang out together."

"Yes, my dear, dense friend. That's why."

"I'm starting to understand some things I didn't see before. Do you think we can be friends? All four of us, I mean?"

"It may take some time, but I think we can."

# CHAPTER 32

# IN WHICH SKYE WONDERS IF SHE HAS A BIG PERSONALITY

"Yoko, can I talk to you for a minute?" Yoko and Dad are both reading on the sofa, and they look really comfortable, and it's taken me fifteen minutes to gather up the courage to interrupt them. Yoko smiles at me, and as she pulls her legs up from where they've been resting on Dad's lap, he pats her feet. We head to my room, and I close the door behind us.

"Skye, you look worried." Yoko sits on the end of my bed. I'm pacing.

"I need to apologize to someone, a Japanese person, and I don't know what to say."

"Is the person your age, my age, or older?"

"My age."

"I would simply be honest about what I'd done, why I'd done it, and then I'd try to convey my sincere apologies for the harm that I'd caused them," Yoko says.

"But what if they don't accept the apology?" I can hear the panic rising in my voice.

"Skye, breathe." I sit down beside Yoko and take a few deep breaths, staying longer on the exhale. "Good," she says. "Sometimes people need a bit of time to recover if they've been hurt.

Also, and I'm not trying to scare you, but every once in a while, the person we've hurt is unable to forgive us. All you can do is be honest and sincere and hope for their understanding and forgiveness."

"Yoko, do you think I have a big personality? Like compared to a kid from here," I say.

Yoko laughs. "You do, Skye, and you come by it honestly. When your father and I were first getting to know each other, it was a little challenging for him to be himself and still leave enough space for me." She wraps her arms around me and hugs me for a long time.

———

After dinner, I go to my room and call Akari. I thought about what Yoko said, and I made some notes about what I need to say. My hands shake as I call her.

"Hey. I was going to write you a letter, but it seemed cowardly, so I decided to call."

"Yes."

"Akari, I'm really sorry I looked at your journal. It was an accident, but I should have closed it as soon as I realized it wasn't Naoko's. I should have, but I didn't. I wish there was something I could do to change what action I took but there's not. I know you're really private about your art and I didn't show you the respect you deserve."

"Why did you do it?"

"I don't know for sure. I think you're an amazing artist and I was probably curious about what you were working on. I think that's what was going on in my head that morning. Can I ask what you're thinking?"

"I am not sure that you will understand this. I am a private person, but I am also lacking in confidence about my art. Aside from the students in my art class, and Reika and Kimi, who hardly count because I have known them forever, you are the first person to whom I have ever shown my work. You are the first person to whom I wanted to show it."

"Oh. That makes me feel even worse," I say.

"Okay," says Akari.

"I really am sorry. How you feel about your art and about your privacy—that's your business. I also should not have said that you owe the world your art. You don't. You don't owe the world anything."

"Okay."

"Akari, Are you okay?"

"I am getting there."

"Because I'm sort of out there with everything, I just assume other people are too. I know this isn't a fair assumption," I say.

"It is not."

"Yoko confirmed today that I have a big personality."

"Yes, I would say that's accurate." I detect a hint of amusement in Akari's voice.

"You are starting to hate me less, aren't you?"

"Perhaps, but it can never happen again, Skye. If our friendship is going to work, you need to learn how to respect what is not yours."

"I'll try," I say.

"Do. Or do not. There is no try."

"What?" I say.

"It's from *Star Wars. The Empire Strikes Back.* Skye, you are hopeless."

"I will do better. Akari, do you forgive me?"

"I am beginning to."

———

Dear Akari,

Thanks for talking with me earlier. I really appreciate that you are willing to give me another chance. I'm so relieved.

If I hadn't messed up so bad, we probably would have talked longer because, you know, I'm a talker. So, I'm going to write down what I would have said to you and slip it into your locker in the morning and you can respond when you're ready. No pressure.

Would you like to meet soon to read a new entry? It's been a few days and that is, of course, my fault.

I've been thinking a lot about Naoko. I've loved all her journal entries. Reading her words is like listening to a friend. A cool, older friend who trusts me and wants me to know things about life.

The entry about the cherry blossoms filled me with something I can't even describe yet. Something thrilling but also calming at the same time. Does such a word exist? I can't wait to see them in the spring and to experience what Naoko calls the three acts of the sakura.

I think my favourite entry is the one about the opera. There's this insanely beautiful opera house in Paris called the Palais Garnier, and I went there a couple of times with my parents so that's what I imagined when we read the story. On the ceiling there's a circular mural painted by Marc Chagall. The architects and city planners who designed the Palais, and probably even the emperor himself, wanted something "new and fresh" for their new palace. Imagine a world where Chagall is just starting out as a painter. Where he's the next big thing.

When we read the entry about the opera, I experienced so many different emotions. Like when Naoko's father told his wife to change her dress, I felt sick until I realized that she had a lot of power over him and could make him suffer by making him wait at the house and again at the opera. Actually, that sort of made me feel sick too. Things are not always what they seem.

In that entry, Naoko seems like a wise and mature kid but she's also remembering this event many years later so maybe she wasn't as together as she seemed. I felt really sad for her. Her parents are angry with each other, and she's caught in the middle. It was especially heart-breaking when her father said that she should sit between them but just this once. Maybe she had waited a long time for her father to notice her and ask her to sit beside him.

The big question I've been obsessing over is which one of the loves in that entry is the impossible one? The love between the Count and the Countess? Naoko's father and mother? Naoko and her mother? Naoko and her father? Naoko and the woman who played the Countess?

Which one is your favourite?

With warm regards,

Skye

P.S. Thanks for not hating me. It's true that I'm exhausting ... even for me. I can't wait to see you tomorrow at school.

———

Skye,

Thank you for your letter. I am following your lead and will place this note inside your locker.

It was good to see your simultaneously happy but apologetic face at school today.

The journal entry with Masumi is my favourite. If I were her, I would be horrified at the idea that my painting might end up in the House of Marital Strife. When those people get divorced, which is where they are clearly headed, the painting would become an object over which the couple fight for custody ... even though the husband hates it. Despite the love and skill Masumi poured into the painting, it would no longer be art but a symbol of the end of their story. Something to be won or lost. I loved it when Masumi handed the painting to Naoko even though Naoko could not afford to pay for it. It felt as though Masumi was whispering directly in my ear: "There are many things more important than money."

Thank you for your apology. Please know that you don't have to stuff any more notes inside my locker. Please talk to me directly. It will be lovely to read an entry with you soon.

Akari

## CHAPTER 33
# IN WHICH NAOKO NISHIZAWA WRITES ABOUT THE WEDDING PLANNER

P lease don't be alarmed by the presence of this letter in your brown leather bag. Although we've never met, I feel like I know you. Your workplace is close to my home, so I pass it several times a week.

I wonder how you came to work at a business that hosts western-style weddings for Japanese couples. Does one train for this work or was it something that you fell into? Perhaps you were recommended by a friend who knows how reliable you are ... and how patient you are with people.

Through the large window at the front of the shop, I see you seated across the table from the young brides and their mothers. The daughters with their pink cheeks and long hair cut in impeccable layers that fall softly around their faces, and the mothers with their stylish bobs. You, I have noticed, prefer to wear your hair up in a knot on the top of your head and, by the end of the day, a few tendrils of hair have always escaped, giving you the appearance of perfect imperfection. This hairstyle draws attention to your elegant, long neck and lovely earlobes. Your appearance and calm demeanour lead me to believe that you are a bit older than most of the young brides that come into the shop. Perhaps you are in your late twenties. Please forgive my brashness. It is, I'm sorry to say, my nature.

Never having met with a wedding consultant before, I must imagine the topics of conversation you initiate with the young women and their mothers, while the men chat on the other side of the room, where they stand with their hands in their pockets. I imagine you ask the young bride for the date and venue she has in mind. That seems like the logical place to begin because everything else will hinge on these details. After the location and date are secured, you must ask the bride about the matter of her dress; what image does she hope to portray to those in attendance? Will the dress be long or short? Will her shoulders be bare? Is it her intention to dazzle, or will her look be somewhat more subdued? You will, of course, ask these questions in the most subtle way, without any hint of judgement or bias for it is, after all, her day. What colour and style of dress will be worn by her bridesmaids, and how many bridesmaids will there be? Tuxes for the men? Top hats? Too much? What is the floral story the bride would like to tell at her wedding? Something wild and exotic expressed with orchids, or a more classic tale told with pink and red roses? Will she carry flowers and if so, which blooms and how many? Does she wish a photographer to photograph the ceremony? Or video perhaps? Shall we make arrangements for photographs of the bride and groom to be taken in advance to reduce the stress of the day? With members of the family, or just the happy couple? Would the bride prefer an actual ordained minister or an actor who can be obtained for a much more reasonable price? How many people will attend the ceremony? Do you require a car to bring you to the wedding chapel? And then you must move on to the meal. Chicken or traditional Japanese? A wedding cake? Yes? With how many tiers? Is it your wish to have dancing after the meal? A live band or a disc jockey? Ninety minutes or two hours?

At every step of the conversation, you watch her face for signs of discomfort or confusion. You solicit questions which you answer patiently, never allowing even a hint of strain to register on your face. You attend to the mother who twists her pearls between her fingers. She is concerned about the cost of several of the items, and you lean towards her to listen more closely and then explain in detail the high quality of each service that is offered. Each answer is an offering. You never slip into a position of defensiveness, for you know that's where the battle with the mothers is always lost.

You take the bill to the father on a small silver tray. He and his son-in-law are discussing the pitiful season the Yokohama Baystars baseball team is having this year. The father glances at the bill and then makes eye contact with his wife, who nods her head ever so slightly. He signs his name. You bow.

Returning to the bride and her mother, you book their next appointment. The bride enters the date in her calendar. The mother accepts the appointment card you offer. You list the arrangements you will have made by that time.

You walk them to the door. The four of them exit the shop. You follow them out onto the sidewalk. You bow and they bow, you bow and they bow, you bow and they bow. Finally, the groom backs away. You bow as they go. You inhale a long, deep breath and watch the world go by. I am standing across the street from you.

You may not see me there because I look so much like you. It may seem that you are simply peering across the universe at an image of yourself. Our mind sees only what it wants to see. Also, and of paramount importance, the mind does not want a stranger meddling about in it, opening the drawers and pulling out the contents. I confess that this is exactly the kind of person I am, a meddler. I was never any good at leaving things alone. Often, my mother has warned me that I will come to a bad end, but I suspect she is not particularly worried about my wellbeing and far more concerned about what the neighbours might say about her, on account of her strange and inquisitive daughter.

Now I'm getting away from the point of this letter. You looked across the street and I was standing there wanting so much to tell you that I admire you. That I admire the way you guide the conversation lovingly towards its inevitable conclusion so that the bride and her mother float out of the shop as if everything in their lives from this point forward could crumble and disintegrate, but they would be happy to have ordered the wedding of their dreams in such a smooth and painless manner. That I admire your thoroughness, your sweet smile, and the kindness in your eyes for each family that enters. That I admire how you manage the men who never wanted anything less than to be at the shop of a wedding consultant on a perfectly fine Saturday afternoon, when they might be golfing or attending a baseball game. I admire your long neck and the escaping tendrils that make you look like a slightly harried angel at the end of the longest day.

You do not wear a ring. You are always the first one inside the shop at ten o'clock in the morning and the last to leave after eight o'clock at night. You never run for the train in anticipation of an evening with a partner or lover.

I know you are unmarried.

I wonder what it must be like for you to sit across that table from the young brides with their pink cheeks and long hair cut in impeccable layers that fall softly around their faces and the mothers with their stylish bobs. Do they ask you about your own wedding? No. Without doubt, this is too familiar a question for the Japanese, and so our formality as a people protects you from this indignity. But do they notice the finger where they think a ring should be? They must. Do they feel pity? Yes, perhaps.

You spend your days helping them plan the happiest day of theirs.

I am writing this letter (which, now that it is almost finished, seems both inappropriate and presumptuous) to tell you that I see you and your rebel wisps of hair, and I admire you greatly, and I think that the world is a large and varied and wonderful place and I hope you will see more of it. I hope that you will leave this job to young women at the start of their careers, women who are just passing through. I hope that when you read this note, you will lock the shop door behind you and walk away and never return. I hope that you will walk out into your own golden sunset. I hope that you will leap into the great golden pond of your dreams.

No one is coming to rescue you. Just you and the woman standing across the street who looks so much like you that you won't see her at all.

# CHAPTER 34

# IN WHICH SKYE IS
# SUCH A DRAMA QUEEN

t's the end of the day, and Akari and I meet on a bench under an awning attached to the elementary building of our school. Some little kids play tag at one end of the playground, and a group of high school students shoot hoops at the other. Reika and Kimi are the only girls in the group, and when Reika shoots, she jumps straight up into the air like an elevator. As she releases the ball, she looks like ballet.

Akari pulls her backpack onto her lap and unzips it. She reaches into the back section, pulls out Naoko's journal and passes it to me, as it's my turn to keep it. I bring the journal up to my face and rest it against my right cheek.

"Hello, Naoko," I whisper.

"Please put that away before someone sees you," says Akari, but I've already opened the journal.

"Hey, this isn't Naoko's. Oh. Sorry." I close the journal and pass it back to Akari. She opens it and flips to the most recent illustration.

"No. It's okay, Skye. I wanted to show you," she says. There's a new drawing of two women staring at each other across a busy street.

"You drew the woman who works at the wedding shop? We just read that a few hours ago," I say.

Akari nods, closes the journal, returns it to her bag, and passes me Naoko's journal. "Maybe we should label these journals," she says.

"You think? Hey, when we were walking to the park the other day, we passed a wedding shop, close to the station. It looked kind of old, like maybe it could be the one from the entry, so I was thinking of checking it out after school tomorrow. You want to join me?"

"I would like to, but I cannot," Akari says.

"You're not still grounded, right?"

"I am not."

"Then why?"

"As I have explained, my mother is worried that I'm losing sight of my priorities. School. Violin. School." We laugh. "She still wants me to come home right after school every day."

"Every day? How is that different from being grounded? That's like prison."

"Prison might be a slight exaggeration," says Akari.

"Okay. House arrest. Why aren't you more upset?"

"I am upset. But she is my mother."

"And?"

"Well ... she gets to decide. That is her job," says Akari.

"Is this one of those things I don't understand because I'm not from here?" I ask.

"Yes. I think so." Akari sighs and looks out at the basketball court.

"But I have a Japanese mother," I say.

"Yes and no," said Akari.

"Seriously? Yoko only thinks she's from Japan? Like she looks in the mirror and sees a Japanese person but actually she's a middle-aged white woman from Montreal?"

"You are such a drama queen, Skye. I meant that Yoko has lived away from Japan for twenty years, and she is married to a Canadian. She probably doesn't feel the kind of pressure that my mom feels to raise a perfect daughter," says Akari.

"While it's true that she's not trying to raise a perfect daughter, she was raised here so she definitely felt that pressure as a kid. She did not have an easy time of it. There are things—"

"My point is that the pressure Yoko felt doesn't get passed along to you." It's the first time Akari has ever interrupted me. "From my mother's perspective, if I fail, she fails."

"I get it. It's a lot of pressure," I say.

"Her friends with children at elite universities tell her I should be spending at least three hours a day on homework, and she is concerned because she doesn't see that happening."

"But it's just the beginning of the year."

"That is not relevant. She says I should be revising my notes from class every day," says Akari. "So rather than waiting for me to earn bad grades, she is being proactive now."

"So, this is a preventative measure?"

"Yup. It is always a preventative measure."

"And you're still spending a lot of time with me, so maybe she thinks I'm some kind of bad influence."

"Not exactly. She just doesn't want anything to get in the way."

"Of what?"

"I don't know. Whatever. Yale, McGill, University of Tokyo. Pick a prestigious university," says Akari.

"Do you want to go to a school like Yale?" I ask.

"I am not certain. Perhaps." Akari leans back against the bench and closes her eyes.

"Oh. I didn't know, but it shouldn't surprise me. You ARE super-smart."

"Hm." Akari opens one eye and squints at me.

"Come on, Akari. You have to admit that you are a big-brained human."

"I do fine," says Akari, looking at her feet.

"Listen, I am asking this next question with extra caution and respect, as I know this is a delicate subject for you, but you mentioned art school the first time you had dinner at my house. Is that a possibility?" I say.

Akari smiles. "I'm not sure. I think about it a lot."

"Honestly, that's where I imagine you after high school. With your own little studio space with the sun pouring in through huge windows, and all these super-cool, edgy friends who dress in black and go to gallery openings."

"Now you are making fun of me," says Akari.

"I'm really not."

"The truth is that it doesn't matter what I think. There is no conceivable scenario in which my parents pay for art school."

"Sorry." I want to say that sucks and it's not fair, but I know that's not helpful right now.

"It is what it is, but that's why I cannot go with you to the wedding shop. Please be careful."

"Meaning?" I say.

"Try not to do anything stupid or impulsive," Akari says.

"Stupid, eh? Ouch!"

"Promise me," says Akari. I nod. Reika and Kimi have finished their game and they run over and join us on our bench. Things have felt a bit stiff since Reika told Akari how she feels about her, but I can see that everyone is trying. These girls have known each other forever, they don't need me hanging around when they are trying to salvage their friendship. I excuse myself and go home.

On the train ride home, I think about the stuff Akari said to me at the playground. About me being impulsive and not getting the situation with her family. It totally got to me even though she's right. I know I'm way too much, but somehow, I think no one will notice. It's so ridiculous, thinking I can hide by being cheerful all the time. It never works. Okay, it works for a while and then it doesn't work. No one is that cheerful.

There's all this stuff building up inside of me. Claire. My friendship with Akari. I mess up so often that it feels like I'm just one bad day away from being completely alone.

I'm not ready to talk to Yoko or my dad, so I book an appointment with the school counsellor for the next day at lunch, and I even go sit in the waiting room and everything, but I feel like I'm going to be sick, so I bail and go to the bathroom. I send an email to the counsellor saying I was sick so I couldn't make the appointment, and that's mostly true, but not entirely.

There's this feeling in my chest, a kind of pressure, and it's there all the time now, like an elephant is sleeping on my chest, but it gets worse when I think of my fight with Akari or the way I left things with Claire. I want to write or call Claire and explain about the email I sent. I want to apologize for not being a better friend, and wish her good luck with her new partner, but I don't really mean it. Just the part about her new partner. I am genuinely sorry for being such a crappy friend.

And I don't want to screw things up with Akari but I'm afraid I'm going to because that's what I do.

There doesn't seem to be a way forward. I need my pocket goddess, that character I created a while ago, to save me. I realize the pocket goddess needs a name and decide to call her Calliope. Callie for short.

Callie, I need an intervention of some kind, and possibly a new personality.

―――――

It's not difficult to retrace my steps back to the wedding shop. I don't know if this strong feeling of familiarity with the shop comes from having seen it on the morning of our pancake feast, or from Naoko's journal entry, but I feel sure this is the place Naoko described. I stand across the street from the shop, in the same place Naoko must have stood watching the wedding planner. The shop is small, with a table and chairs on the left side and a grouping of comfortable chairs on the other. The walls are lined with magazine racks loaded with bridal magazines and bookshelves that house dried flowers, fabric swatches, and figurines I guess might be displayed on the top of a wedding cake. The words "Your Happy Day" are painted on the window.

This is a quiet time in Hiro-o. Many of the restaurants are closed for the break between lunch and dinner, and I feel sure that the two women in the shop aren't clients. One has long hair she wears down like the young brides in Naoko's entry, and the other woman wears her hair up in a tidy bun.

Feeling every bit like Harriet the Spy about to solve a case, I cross the street and stand directly in front of the shop. The women who work there seem younger than the woman in Naoko's journal entry; I'm pretty good at guessing people's ages and they look like they are both in their early twenties. They chat with each other in a relaxed way as they work. The woman with the long hair does paperwork at the table while the other woman arranges the magazines. The other woman has a sharp bob that swings with every movement. A large truck roars by and the women look up and see me on the other side of the large window. The long-haired woman at the table gives me a nod, and the other woman walks to the door and opens it.

"Hello. Would you like to come in?" I enter the cool interior. The long-haired woman is now standing.

"Would you like to sit down?" I sit, and the two wedding planners take seats opposite me at the table.

"How can we help you?" says the woman with the bob.

"You plan weddings?" I ask.

"Yes, we do." The long-haired woman smiles.

"Okay. Oh, it's not for me. I'm not the one getting married." The wedding planners say nothing. "Because I'm too young to get married. But I'd like to get married. Someday. You know, if I meet the right person." The women nod patiently.

"How can we help you today?" the woman with the bob says again.

"I'm looking for a woman who works here." I detect a slight frown just under the surface of the long-haired woman's mask of pleasantness.

"There are just the two of us, and my mother who looks after the finances," says the woman with the bob. They are younger than the wedding planner Naoko described, and unless Naoko was very wrong, the woman she observed in the shop had no husband or children, so the mother of this woman is not the person I'm looking for. As I'm thinking, the women exchange a glance.

"Sumimasen. I am very sorry to have disturbed your work," I say. As I push my chair away from the table, the legs screech against the floor.

"Just a moment," says the woman with the bob. She walks to the back of the shop, opens the door to a back office, and disappears for a few moments, before returning with her mother, who wears a red and white polka dot dress and large hoop earrings.

"Hello. My daughter said that you were looking for someone who worked here. May I ask for the person's name?"

"I know this is highly unusual, but I don't know her name. I know only that she used to work here, and that she had long hair that she wore in a knot on top of her head, and that she had a long and elegant neck," I say.

"You are describing Suzuki-san. Her name was Rika. We started working here about the same time. I am sorry to say that she has not worked here for many years."

"Thank you. Thank you very much. I'm very sorry to have bothered you." I bow and begin to back towards the door.

"How do you know Suzuki-san?" says the woman in the red dress.

"Actually, I don't know her. We have a common friend," I say.

"If you see her, please tell her hello from me. I think of her often, as she was a lovely person, and colleague."

"May I ask you one more question?"

"Yes." She smiles at me as if she were in the habit of saying yes, as if yes gave her great pleasure.

"Do you remember why she left?" I ask.

"Perhaps I shouldn't say." She looks at her daughter who nods. "It was a matter of some mystery. I remember she received a letter, and she gave her notice shortly thereafter."

"Thank you again. Please forgive the forwardness of my questions."

"Where are you from?" asks the woman in the red dress.

"Canada."

"Ah, Canada. We hear it is a very nice country. But cold." The three women follow me onto the sidewalk, where they bow and bow again as I walk backwards and then turn and hurry towards the train station.

———

I text Akari from the train.

I found her.

Who? (For the record, I feel like we do this a lot.)

The wedding planner.

She still works there?

No but the bookkeeper recognized her from the description.

You showed her the journal?

Of course not. I described her.

Amazing!

Right? Her name is Rika Suzuki.

Where is she now?

The woman at the shop didn't know. Rika left a long time ago.

I cannot believe you just went in there and asked them these questions.

The younger women were suspicious, but the older woman wanted to talk.

I am both impressed and relieved you did not get into any trouble!

As soon as I said I was from Canada, they relaxed. I should have told them earlier. Oh! The older woman said Rika quit shortly after receiving a letter.

Naoko's letter?

I think so.

Ah! My brain just exploded.

I know!

# CHAPTER 35

# IN WHICH AKARI OBSESSES OVER A PAINTING OF A GIRL AND A DOG

The art room is the one place where I consistently feel calm and peaceful. Perhaps that's not entirely true, as I've also felt very much myself in Skye's living room, with the light flooding in through the enormous windows, but I have only been there a few times. The art room, on the other hand, is like a home to me, and I have probably climbed the four flights of stairs to make art here two thousand times over the past six years. Most people who feel like I do about the art room would call this their happy place and perhaps this is strange, but whenever I'm about to call this my happy place, I stop myself, because I have this story that happiness isn't my thing. I don't really trust that happiness is real or that it will stay. I wish I could believe in happiness the way Skye does.

I guess what I have with this place is a love affair.

Oscar Wu packs up his materials and leaves, so I end up having the space all to myself. I connect my phone's Bluetooth and play a new playlist through the classroom speakers.

During math class, I had an idea for a new illustration of Masumi's painting of the girl and her dog, and I'm finishing a pencil drawing using only numbers. One stripe of the girl's sweater is made up of tiny sevens and the next stripe features only fives. I am an enormous fan of prime numbers.

Earlier today, Ms. Racine, the art teacher, talked about the theme we will be asked to declare for our final art exhibition. Some students said they already knew their theme, but Ms. Racine encouraged us not to decide too early; she challenged us to keep creating and writing about our process in our investigative workbooks. We have until second semester to choose a theme.

The art students knew this talk was coming because we were very close to last year's seniors, but I have no idea what my theme is. What I know for certain is that I am currently obsessed with the painting of the girl and her dog from Naoko's journal. I have been sketching the painting in different styles for a couple of weeks and, a few nights ago, I had this surreal dream about one of my drawings as a triptych. In the centre panel, I saw a painting of the girl and her dog. On one side there was a panel of just the girl, and on the other side, there was a panel of just the dog. Although I couldn't see how the panels were hinged together so the work could be displayed open or folded shut like triptychs in churches, the image of the work itself was clear. This is how it happens for me; these images simply appear, often late at night or early in the morning. I try to keep a sketchbook close by so that I can capture them before they fade and slip out of my grasp.

Before school this morning I spent some time brainstorming ideas for building the triptych, and as I considered the physics of the problem, an entirely different thought came to me. I have learned through experience that I need to write things down no matter how strange or random they seem. The thought was, "To make the ordinary extraordinary. To elevate." I don't know what it means. Is it about my art? Is it about me at all or about somebody else? Skye maybe? I turn up the volume on my phone.

After I finish my prime numbers sketch, I decide to work on the middle panel of the triptych. I have a strong feeling that after I paint the centre section, I will know how to paint the panels on either side. I place my canvas on an easel and begin sketching in pencil.

"I didn't realize that people still listened to the Red Hot Chili Peppers!" My pencil flies out of my hand and clatters across the floor. Ms. Barrett retrieves it from where it has rolled to a stop at her feet. She comes to the table where I'm working and places the pencil in the seam of my sketchbook. "A thousand apologies. I didn't mean to scare you, Akari." My brain is still trying to process seeing Ms. Barrett on the fourth floor of our school.

"It's fine. Are you looking for Ms. Racine? She left a while ago."

"I'll catch her tomorrow, then." Ms. Barrett pulls up a stool and sits down beside me. "May I see what you're working on?"

I swallow and nod.

"Only if you'd like to show me," says Ms. Barrett. The interesting thing is that I do want to show her, so I open my sketchbook and show her my series of drawings, *The Girl and her Dog*. Ms. Barrett looks at each page without comment. "And this one?" Ms. Barrett points at the pencil drawing I've been working on today.

"The same image but with prime numbers," I say.

"How fascinating," Ms. Barrett holds up the sketchbook. "Did the girl and her dog pose for you at some point?"

"No. The drawings were inspired by a story," I say. "An obscure Japanese writer. I can't remember her name."

"May I look at your other work?" I hand her the sketchbook. Ms. Barrett examines each new page carefully. When she reaches the drawings of Chiyo saving the jumpers, she asks me to tell her about them. She nods her head gently at first and then more vigorously.

"Akari, do you consider this manga?"

"Honestly, I'm not sure. I've read manga my whole life and I'm strongly influenced by the illustration style of many manga artists, but the stories that interest me as a storyteller are quite different. There's a style called shôjo manga, and I wondered, for a while, if that's what I was creating, but really the term shôjo just means they are written for girls, and there is nothing about my stories which is specific to girls or to boys. They are human stories."

"You are creating something new, then?" says Ms. Barrett.

"I guess. Yes."

"This is very exciting," says Ms. Barrett.

"Is it?" I say.

"There's something very compelling about this story. It's the first time I've encountered a manga that I would like to read. It is, as you said, a human story. Is there a genre known as human manga?" says Ms. Barrett.

"No. I don't think so." I laugh.

Ms. Barrett slides the sketchbook back to me. "Perhaps there should be. Akari, one of my friends works at Immersive Tokyo. We had dinner a few nights ago and she said they are always looking for artists to create illustrations for their blog posts and books. She said, and I quote, they are looking for fresh, young artists. Would you mind if I spoke with her about your work? I have no idea if it will go anywhere. If she's interested, she would contact you directly."

"But why would they be interested?" I'm too shocked not to be completely honest.

"I'm not sure if they will be, but I am interested, and I have learned to trust my own judgment. Your work is beautifully done, Akari. Your protagonist Chiyo saves the lives of people who have lost hope, people who think there is nothing worth living for. As you describe it, this is a new, more inclusive kind of manga and, if I might add, a new way of looking at the heroic journey." Ms. Barrett raises one eyebrow and waits.

"Yes," I say. "Thank you very much." I bow my head and my teacher does the same.

"Good, then. It's settled," says Ms. Barrett. "May I take some photographs of your work?" I nod and, with her phone, Ms. Barrett takes a few photos of *The Girl and Her Dog* and of Chiyo. She walks to the doorway and turns back towards me. "That Chili Peppers song is a kind of anthem for your Chiyo. 'Can't stop the spirits when they need you. This life is more than just a read through.'" She smiles and disappears down the stairs. This is the moment that I become absolutely convinced that Ms. Barrett is Mary Poppins.

# CHAPTER 36
# IN WHICH NAOKO NISHIZAWA WRITES ABOUT THE BARTENDER WHO WAS A SURFER

After my mother finally despaired of my meeting an appropriate match, I moved from my parents' home to my own small apartment in Hiro-o.

All the most interesting Tokyo neighbourhoods had become so expensive, but a writer must have a view, a decadent view, from which to watch the world and extract her stories.

About this time, I made the acquaintance of the bartender who was really a surfer. I was twenty-seven. He was forty-one.

He had kind eyes and long black hair that he wore pulled back in a ponytail. When he was not working or sleeping, he was outdoors, and his skin was tanned brown like chestnuts. There were small kind creases at the outside corners of his eyes.

People who believe that all Japanese are shy are not really paying attention.

"A surfer?" I said. "How interesting."

"Do you think so?"

"Oh, I know so."

My father did precisely what was expected of him every day of his small life, and one week after he retired, he dropped dead. Of what? The shock of doing nothing? A great black sea that extended in every direction. Having to spend all that time with my mother?

If I had been born a man, I would have made a terrible husband. I suspect that I take after my mother in this respect.

When the surfer passed my drink across the counter (and I always thought of him that way, as the surfer, because in his soul he was not a bartender) he touched me. It is not that he tried to touch me. This was not a caress. He was the kind of person to whom it had never occurred that it would be a problem to touch the hand of another person. Those who are afraid of germs are also afraid of life.

"What do you do?" he asked.

"Nothing, really. But I'm thinking of becoming a writer."

"But if you do nothing, what will you write about?"

"My apologies for my shocking lack of clarity. I DO all kinds of things, but I have not yet had a job."

"Yes, but are you very sure you want one?"

"I recently left my mother's home, and I am receiving not-so-subtle messages from the universe that it is now time to make my own way. Clear my own path through the rainforest. Once I read a novel and the protagonist claimed our job should help us create the life we want. I don't remember the name of the novel or the author or the character, but I won't forget that advice."

"I'd like to take you surfing sometime."

"Do you think that will help?"

"It couldn't hurt."

Love requires constant costume changes.

From my window, I watched the surfer park a small blue pickup truck in front of my building. He opened the door, got out of the truck, and hopped up on the hood. His feet dangled off the front. I waved. He waved, lay back on the windshield, and closed his eyes. Stretched out like a cat.

"I hate to disturb you," I said. He leaped off the truck as I approached.

"Nothing disturbs me." He bowed.

"Nothing?" I returned the bow.

"Nothing."

"Isn't that delightful?"

"You are a surprisingly direct woman."

"I'll always choose a sword to get the job done and leave the clean-up to the diplomats. Where are we going?"

"Onjuku Beach. Good waves today." He drove without looking at me. His shoulders were relaxed.

"Really? How can you be certain?"

"I called a friend," he said.

"How did you manage to get the day off?"

"I work part-time. Just enough to pay for rent, food, and surfing."

"You've got some kind of big love affair with surfing."

"Yes." He was looking straight ahead, and he smiled.

"Tell me the story of you and surfing."

"Words sort of let me down. I'd rather show you."

"Words never let me down. They are among my closest friends."

"Thus the thinking about becoming a writer."

"I know. It's ridiculous."

"I don't see why."

"It's much harder than I thought. My degree was in literature, but when I started to write, I had to unlearn everything I had learned in four years of study. I am trying to discover how to actually tell a story. They don't teach you that in school."

"What would you like to write?"

"I'd like to rewrite the fairy tales and put the princes in towers and make them wait to be rescued. Then I'll give the princesses weeks and months to devise schemes and plots. I'll teach them that as a woman, you are not a thing, and you must not let others treat you like one. You can belong only to yourself. Finally, I'll give them swords and see what happens."

"Ah. The swords again."

"Nervous?"

"Intrigued. So, are you writing?"

"I write things in my journal."

"True things or fiction?" he said.

"Is there a difference?"

"What do I know? I'm a surfer. I'm interested in what you think."

"The edges are blurry. Stories are some of my favourite places. When I first create a fictional world, I often find it preferable to my own, so I go there and live for a while, but the gossiping neighbours always show up at some point. I realize that they always will."

"Yes. The gossiping neighbours. The only thing to do is to love them," he said.

"I adore other people right up until I don't."

The surfer drove with both hands on the wheel. We stopped at a convenience store for lemon tea and rice crackers with peanuts. He opened the door for me.

"I'm suddenly quite tired. Do you mind if I sleep for a bit?" I fell asleep almost immediately.

I knew I was dreaming, the way that I always know, but the scene was so wonderful, so I waded further and further into it. Lost myself.

I was sitting on a white sofa holding a baby with pink cheeks and large dark eyes and the baby touched my face with its plump fingers and gurgled in some secret language. I leaned my head towards the baby and kissed its nose, its forehead, its cheeks. The baby made a joyful sound, somewhere between singing and laughter. "Naoko, I'm home." The surfer appeared in the door wearing a black wet suit still slick with water. He crossed the room, water pouring off him onto the bamboo floor, and kissed me on the mouth. He tasted of seawater.

When I woke, I could see rays of sunlight dancing on the surface of the sea.

"I am so very sorry. I know that we are almost there and that you have probably been looking forward to this surfing trip all week, but would you please take me home?"

"Of course. Are you sick?"

"A kind of sickness."

"Can I get you something? Water?"

"Nothing."

"What are you afraid of?"

"Everything. Old age, blindness, not being able to do as I please."

"Darling, everything is going to be okay."

"How can you be sure?"

"My life's work is joy. Nothing lovely is ever truly lost."

The surfer and I remained friends. He was always happy to see me at the bar and seemed to forget that there had been, for forty-eight hours, the slight shimmer of something small with pink cheeks and plump fingers.

As a child, my best friend was always a boy. I should have known.

# CHAPTER 37

# IN WHICH SKYE HAS HER WORST IDEA THUS FAR

Our lemon squares remain uneaten, nestled beside each other on the pale pink plate with scalloped edges on our table at the back of The Delightful Café. Because we always bump into people we know at Starbucks, it's become impossible to read Naoko's journal in secret, so Akari suggested this place as an alternative. When I first heard the name, I burst out laughing. Like a good ending to a novel, it is both unexpected and inevitable that we find ourselves reading Naoko's journal in a place called The Delightful Café. Also, it's just so freaking adorable. It is Japanese cuteness, or kawaii, in the form of a coffee shop.

As Akari finishes reading the entry about the bartender, I drop my hands onto the table and let my head fall on top of my hands with such force that the little plate clatters against our coffee mugs. The person at the counter looks up in our direction.

"Too much?" I say.

"This depends on your definition of too much. You seem to have scared the barista, though," says Akari.

I sit up straight. "What in the world is wrong with Naoko?" I say.

"What do you mean?" says Akari.

"This surfer is such a deeply good guy that I want to date him."

"He was forty-one. That was a number of years ago."

"As Naoko writes, Love doesn't ask your age or your gender."

"Love might not ask, but your parents will," says Akari. I high five her as a reward for her wit.

"But really ... why does she not love him?" I say.

"Maybe she's not ready," Akari picks up a fork and sinks it into one of the lemon bars.

"I don't get that," I say. "Seriously. I don't."

"I know," says Akari. "But that doesn't make it any less true. Most people don't have that thing you have."

"What thing?"

"Your enduring belief in a happy ending, in combination with that outrageous courage gene. You have the heart of a lion."

I close my eyes. "That might be the best compliment anyone has ever given me. The heart of a lion," I say.

"But when someone has a lion's heart, it may be more difficult to understand when other people aren't ready to love or to do whatever it is they are afraid of."

"It seems that we're not just talking about Naoko now?"

"Perhaps," says Akari. An older woman sits down at a table close to us and Akari nods at the woman and drops her voice. "Listen, I've been thinking lately that perhaps Naoko Nishizawa is not the kind of person who will let herself be found," says Akari.

I gasp. I've never even had the thought that Naoko might not want to be found. "But we have to get her journal back to her ... you know, so it doesn't fall into the wrong hands," I say.

Akari laughs. "Like the hands of two curious teenagers?"

"Exactly," I say.

"Admit it, Skye. You are dying to know if Naoko found her happy ending."

"Guilty. I want to know that a BIG love is possible. Naoko might be the coolest person on the planet so if true love is possible for anyone, it must be possible for her."

"And you want to meet her," says Akari.

"I do want to meet her, to talk with her about her mother, and her first love who died, and why she didn't tell the surfer about her dream or, I don't know, at least have a second date with him."

"Skye, I worry that this is becoming an obsession for you."

"It's just that I feel like she has the answers."

"What answers?" says Akari.

"I'm not sure." I rub my hands together in a small circular motion. "You're really not curious about how her story turns out?"

"I would like to return the journal to her. That is the right thing to do," says Akari.

I smile. "Have we learned anything new about her?" I open my journal and flip back several pages to where I listed, the night of our last sleepover, what we knew about Naoko Nishizawa. Akari reaches into her pocket and retrieves a tiny golden buddha holding a Hello Kitty doll. It looks like it's meant to be attached to the bottom of an ancient cellphone. Akari picks up the silver string that acts as a bookmark in my journal and ties the buddha securely to the end. She then closes the journal to make sure that she's left enough space for the bookmark to still work.

"Is that okay? I thought it might help us keep better track of the journals," Akari says.

"Cool! Sagaciousness!" I say.

"What does that mean?"

"Showing a sagacious grasp of the identical journal problem, she purchased small charms so each owner could easily and quickly identify her own journal. Smart with good judgment. It's an SAT word and a compliment."

"Thank you," says Akari.

"Did you get one for your journal?" I ask. Akari places her journal on the table. At the end of the silver string she has tied a small ninja in black, drawing a sword from behind his back. "So, I'm the kawaii Buddha ... wise and round and complacent ... and you are the lean, stealthy ninja, destroying your enemies."

"As a matter of fact, yes," Akari says.

"Okay. I accept that," I say.

"Hey, have you been doing any writing?" says Akari. I'm surprised at this question but also very happy that she's asked.

"Remember that day I went to the wedding shop?" I say. Akari nods. "I sat on a bench outside the station and watched people. It's one of my favourite things, actually, just watching people go about their regular lives. I've been noticing more similarities between Paris and Tokyo."

"I am trying to imagine what those might be," said Akari.

"People in both cities are well-dressed. There are rules governing what side of the sidewalk you walk on, how you behave in the metro. There is a sense of decorum to be upheld. Formality. Dressing well for other people. Anyway, I was watching all these people outside the station, and I started to write things down. You know how everyone here is always so worried about what everyone else thinks? I've noticed that when people are dropping off their kids or their wife or whatever, the car stops, the person jumps out and the car drives away. Really efficient."

"Courtesy towards others," says Akari.

"Sure. So, I was watching as this car pulled up and a man

got out of the passenger seat. He was wearing a suit, and he had an injury of some kind, so he was limping, and he was kind of slow as he crossed the intersection but then he looked back at his wife and waved, and she waved back. And I don't know why exactly but I got this big lump in my throat and tears in my eyes. So, I wrote it down. He was just this regular middle-aged man, but he looked really kind, and there was this connection between him and his wife. Like this string that couldn't be broken. So even though he'd been taught not to take any action that might stop traffic or inconvenience anyone, he took a moment to wave at his wife."

"A possible love," says Akari.

"Yes. Sorry. There I go ... on about Naoko again."

"Do you know that you say sorry more frequently than is required?" I shrug. "I think the encounter between the man and the woman sounds lovely," says Akari. "This journal entry you wrote sounds very much like a tiny love letter to ordinary people. Does that sound familiar?" She rests her fingers on the cover of Naoko's journal.

"Cool connection, Akari. I'll take it. A few weeks ago, I wrote a weird little piece about a tiny pocket goddess, like a goddess so small she fits in your pocket."

"Is she a superhero?" says Akari. She leans towards me, and her eyes are shining.

"Maybe," I say.

"Perhaps I could illustrate her for you!" says Akari.

"Oh. That would be so cool. Hey, were you planning to go to Reika and Kimi's volleyball game tomorrow?"

"I'm thinking about it."

"This bartender who was really a surfer, he worked at a bar in Hiro-o. We could try to track him down right after school!"

Akari slams her hand down on the table. "Skye, this is your worst idea thus far. We don't know which bar it is. This bartender was forty-one, perhaps twenty years ago, so he probably does not work at a bar anymore. Plus, our parents are definitely not going to give us permission to go inside a bar," says Akari.

"Okay. You're right," I say.

"Really?"

"Definitely. What about this? After school tomorrow, we just go to Hiro-o and look at a couple of places that might have been there twenty years ago. Obviously, we won't go in. That would be reckless," I say. Akari raises her eyebrows at me. "We'll look for clues and then come up with a plan for our next step. That sounds good, right?" Akari nods cautiously. "We can use the volleyball game as a cover, and you would be home by eight o'clock. We wouldn't be doing anything wrong."

"I would be missing Kimi and Reika's game," Akari says. "Most of me knows that this is a terrible idea, but a little part of me really wants to say yes."

"And who's in charge today?" I say.

"The ninja part."

————

It's four-thirty in the afternoon as we arrive at Hiro-o Station. In order not to be identified as students of our particular high school, we've changed out of our school uniforms which are now stuffed inside our backpacks. No, that's not quite true. My uniform is stuffed inside my bag, while Akari's is folded neatly into these tiny perfect blocks of clothing. I've already done some reconnaissance in Hiro-o, and I think there are two bars that are likely candidates to have a bartender who was really a surfer. I explain to Akari that I've developed a complex set of criteria including the likelihood that the bar was here twenty years ago, and whether the bar seemed cool enough for Naoko to have frequented. When she raises her eyebrows, I point at my stomach and say, "The gut doesn't lie."

The first bar is between the station and the park near where we think Naoko may have lived. I acknowledge this is a lot of ifs. The second bar is between the station and the diner.

"You are kind of quiet this afternoon," says Akari.

"Even I am a little out of my depth here," I say.

"It's not too late to go back to school and watch the volleyball game."

"I think we're getting close to finding Naoko."

"Your spidey-sense?"

I smile at Akari, but I don't feel nearly as gleeful as I normally would on such an expedition. There's no denying that this afternoon's spy mission is sketchy at best. At long last, I seem to be growing a conscience, and she's named Akari.

We walk from the cool semi-darkness of the metro into the bleached-out late-summer sunlight. I lead the way to the first bar.

"What now?" says Akari, as we stand across the street. I signal for her to stay where she is, but she shakes her head and follows me across the street and into the darkness of the bar near the park. We stand just inside the door squinting. The place is small with just eight or ten tables; there's a small stage on one side of the room and the bar is on the other. The wooden walls have been painted black, making the bar seem even smaller. Even from the doorway, we can smell beer mixed with sweat and cigarettes. There's someone standing at the bar.

"I've got this," I whisper.

We approach the bar, but the bartender is washing glasses in a small sink and doesn't even look up as he says, "We're not open for business. Happy Hour begins at five o'clock."

"Oh. Okay. Well, actually, we just wanted to ask you a quick question if it's not too much trouble," I say. The guy's head snaps up and we can now see his eyes, which were hidden by the brim of his baseball cap.

"You're too young to be in here," he says.

"It looks like you are too," I say.

"I'm twenty-one."

"So, you're half an hour older than us," I say.

"Skye, let's go," says Akari.

"One quick question and then we'll go." I address the bartender.

"One. And then you've got to leave because I could get in a lot of trouble if the owner stops by. This is not some Roppongi club. Everyone knows each other in this neighbourhood."

"Are you a surfer?" I say.

"What?"

"Are you a surfer? Do you surf?"

"Sure. Who doesn't?" he says.

"Do you know a woman named Naoko Nishizawa?"

"He's far too young," whispers Akari, pulling on my arm.

"That's two questions, and I've never heard of her. Now, it's time for you two to go." The bartender walks out from behind the bar. He's wearing jeans and a Peanuts T-shirt, and he dries his hands on a red and white checked hand towel that he then drapes over his shoulder.

"We're going," I say. We take a few steps towards the door. "Is there an older guy who works here?"

"Just the owner," he says.

"Does he surf?"

"He's about six hundred years old so no, I don't think he surfs. Look, if you really want a beer, you can buy it at the combini."

"We're very sorry to have bothered you," says Akari.

"Thanks. I'm not sure Red here is sorry," he says, pointing at me. Akari bows to the young bartender and then yanks me out by the arm. We spill out onto the sidewalk and back into the light. Akari's pulling me along and it's not until we cross the main street and can no longer see the bar that she lets go of my arm.

"Skye, the way you talked to him was rash, ill-advised, irresponsible," says Akari.

"I didn't like his attitude."

"We were the ones breaking the law. Have I not explained with sufficient clarity that you need to be twenty years old to enter a bar here?"

"You have. It's just that he was on a big power trip. He's only a year older himself. Can we sit down for a minute? You're walking really quickly," I say. We sit on the same bench where I made my notes about the sweet man waving to his wife. I pull my water bottle out of my bag, take a few long sips, and offer it to Akari, who shakes her head.

"Okay, Skye. Here's the deal. These things that seem perfectly normal to you ... well, they are not. That guy was not kidding around. He could get fired or worse. We could get taken to the koban. The police officer would have to call our parents. If they thought we had broken the law or if we were not respectful, they could hold us."

"But we didn't do anything wrong. Not really," I say.

"Ahhh! Skye, we broke the law. How are you not getting this?" Akari sits back against the bench and closes her eyes. She starts breathing heavily.

"Hey. Are you okay?"

"I think I'm having a panic attack, so just let me breathe." She inhales and exhales loudly.

"Place the emphasis on the exhale," I say. I've read that it's the exhale that brings down the blood pressure. Akari doesn't look at me, but she balls up her right hand and punches my leg.

"Okay, Akari. Message received. Is there anything I can do for you?" I say.

"Just give me a minute," says Akari, as she continues her deep breathing.

"Sorry. I know I'm impulsive. I feel weirdly desperate to find Naoko."

"Shhhhh," says Akari. "I seriously need you to stop talking." I sit back on the bench with my shoulder touching Akari's shoulder. After a couple of minutes, Akari turns to face me.

"Please say that you forgive me," I say.

"Here is the situation, Skye: I cannot go inside another bar. Not even if it will help us find Naoko. It is a truly terrible idea, and I should never have followed you into that place," says Akari. Her voice is calm but determined.

"You know I would have come on my own, right?" I say.

"Unfortunately, yes," says Akari. Now she's smiling.

"I have an idea," I say. Akari groans. "No, really. This will work. You stay right here and keep breathing, and I'll be back in ten minutes."

"Skye, you need to be careful and respectful. Channel your inner Akari!"

"Consider it done," I say.

I walk down the street and around the corner until the second bar comes into view. It has windows on three sides and light floods the place. People sit at small round tables. There are some old men inside but also some well-dressed middle-aged women with shopping bags piled on a chair. This bar definitely seems more promising as a Naoko kind of place. There's a guy standing at a counter at the other end of the bar, and I'm determined to talk with him and also to keep my promise to Akari. Instead of entering the building, I walk down the sidewalk beside the bar and then turn right onto the small pathway between the bar and the building next door. When I reach the back of the building, I peer in the window and see a man who looks about my dad's age. Maybe a little older. He's wearing a long apron. I drop to the ground and fish around in the bottom of my bag for my notebook. I tear out a page and write the name "Naoko Nishizawa" in kanji. I kind of wish I'd asked Akari to write it, but it's too late to go back now. I drop the notebook back in my bag and stand at the window waiting for the bartender to notice me. When he finally sees me, he smiles. Not a creepy old man smile, but a smile of amusement. I hold up my handmade sign against the window and the bartender moves closer to read it. Then he opens the back door and walks out onto the gravel path where I'm standing.

"You don't look like a Naoko Nishizawa," he says.

I don't understand what he means at first. "Oh, right. White girl. Red hair. Sir, I'm very sorry to trouble you but my name is Skye and I'm looking for a woman named Naoko Nishizawa. I could not enter the front door because I am not twenty, and I don't want anyone to get in trouble."

"That was very considerate of you," says the bartender.

"Thank you. You are the only Japanese person who has ever called me considerate. So, you don't know someone named Naoko Nishizawa?"

"I have never met anyone named Naoko Nishizawa," he says.

"Are you, by any chance, a surfer?"

"Yes, I am a surfer. Why do you ask?" I look carefully at this man, and I know he is kind. I don't know if he is our surfer, but I feel that I can trust him. The words come tumbling out of my mouth like tiny Russian gymnasts.

"It's sort of a long story but my friend and I found the journal of someone named Naoko Nishizawa and we are trying to find her in order to return it to her and there's a story, more of an entry, about a bartender who is really a surfer and so we've been trying to find the man in the story so that we can find Naoko."

"That sounds very exciting," he says.

"It is but I've made a terrible mess of things today by going into a bar and making the bartender mad at me. My friend, Akari, she's really stressed, so I promised her that I wouldn't go into any more bars."

"That's a wise friend you have. I am sorry to say that I don't know any Naoko Nishizawas but if you'll leave me your name and email address, I can ask around." I turn over the page I ripped out of my notebook and write down my first name and my email address.

"Thank you for your kindness," I say.

"Thank you for trying to do the right thing. If I hear of anyone by this name, I will send you a message," the man says.

"Domo. Thank you so much. Oh! May I ask for your name, please?"

"My name is Daichi."

"Thank you, Daichi-san."

"You are welcome, Skye-chan."

As I make my way back to the street and walk the length of the building, I look in the windows of the bar. Everyone inside seems very relaxed, as if an enchantment has been cast over them. The three women have stood up, as if to leave, but they're talking and laughing instead of leaving.

Akari is listening to music on her phone, and she jumps a bit when I collapse onto the bench beside her. She pauses the track and pulls off her headphones.

"How did it go?" she asks.

"I met the bartender. He was really nice. Daichi-san. Looked like he could be the right age. He said he didn't know Naoko but I'm not sure. I just had this feeling. I can't really explain it."

"But you didn't go into the bar, right?" Akari asks.

"I promise I didn't. He came out. I gave him my first name and email address. He said he'll let us know if he hears of Naoko. Really, Akari, stop worrying. It was fine and the man was just really, really nice. I really wish it had been him. I'm hungry. Are you hungry?"

"I am starving but I don't have much money with me," says Akari.

"I've got cash. Ramen?" I say.

She smiles widely. We walk back towards the park to a small ramen place Akari knows, and we get a table right away because they've just re-opened for their dinner hours. As we're eating, Akari checks her phone, and a cloud passes over her face.

"I missed a call from my mom."

"No big deal, right? She thinks you're at the game."

"Still, I'm always supposed to pick up." Akari's phone buzzes. "A text from Reika. She says my mom called and asked if I was there." Akari types on her phone. "Reika said I was at the game, but she is very angry that I put her in a position where she had to lie to my mother."

"Sorry, Akari." I'm aware that this is the one millionth time I have apologized to Akari today.

"I know you are, but I'm not cut out for this life of espionage, or for breaking the rules in any way. Next time, you are going to have to do this on your own."

# CHAPTER 38
# IN WHICH AKARI LIES TO HER PARENTS FOR THE SECOND TIME IN A WEEK

T he most interesting aspect of all this dog art I'm making right now is that I have never owned a dog. In fact, I might not be a dog person at all. Also, from a purely philosophical perspective, I am not convinced that a person should or can "own" a dog. It seems unethical for humans to own other living creatures. Many of my neighbours have dogs, but these are tiny, delicate creatures dressed in raincoats and polar fleece and, because most apartment buildings don't allow dogs to walk in the hallways and common spaces, the dog owners push them in a carriage, which you can't accurately call a baby carriage since there are no babies involved, or they carry the dogs in their arms. These dogs don't have a chance. I wonder if it's humiliating for the dogs or if they consider themselves lucky.

During the weeks I've been sketching Masumi's painting of the girl and her dog, I've concluded that this is not an apartment dog. This is not a Bichon Frise, poodle or pug. I feel certain this is a dog's dog; a dog that could knock a little kid over if they weren't too steady on their feet. When I sketch the girl's arm around her dog, their heads are the same size.

The central panel of the triptych came to me very quickly,

almost as though my hand, the pencil, and canvas were in collusion. The girl and her dog appeared on the canvas as if they were already there in invisible ink and my only job was to shine ultraviolet light on the canvas and exclaim, "Oh, there you are!" Tonight, as I prepare to add colour, I feel that I should be restrained. When painting the stripes on the girl's pink shirt, I leave some of the canvas showing through. I make her cheeks slightly rosy but make no attempt to paint a skin colour. Her hair asks to be painted light brown, and I make a small black slash for each of her eyes. For the dog, I mix a sandy brown, a classic coat of dogness, and he emerges gorgeous and golden, tucked contentedly under the girl's arm. The dog looks down to the bottom right of the canvas while the girl stares out at me as if to say, "Is this not the most amazing dog in the entire history of dogs?" I can't help but agree.

The two other canvases are smaller than the central panel, about two thirds the size. I draw the dog on one canvas and the girl on the other. Their facial expressions are virtually the same as those I've painted in the central panel, but the girl looks wistful without her dog. Without the embrace of its person, the dog looks utterly lost. In each case, they lack the presence and context of their other half. I decide to represent this feeling of absence by painting the outline of each in dark grey but to add no colour or shading to the images. It is not so much a decision as an instinct. When I complete the outlines, I consider the canvases side by side and think of chalk outlines at murder scenes.

Before I leave the art room, I line up the three paintings: the girl and the dog in the centre, the canvas with only the dog on the left, and the outline of only the girl on the right. I'm uncertain if the canvases are done yet, but I am interested in the story they tell together and that is a very good sign.

Ms. Racine emerges from her office. I'm the only student

left, and she walks to the back of the room to look at what I'm working on. "I really like your choice to leave so much negative space in the side panels of the triptych," she says.

"Thank you."

"It looks like you were inspired," she says.

"Yes, I was."

"When did you see it?" Ms. Racine says.

"See what?" I look around the room. Does my teacher know about the journal?

"The exhibit," says Ms. Racine.

"What exhibit are you are referring to?"

"This girl and her dog. You didn't see this painting in Roppongi?"

"No. I must have seen it online somewhere." I hear these words float out into the world and while that was certainly quick thinking on my part, I hate deceiving anyone.

"Really? I'm surprised to hear that. I didn't think the artist was very well known. But this piece caught my attention. The relationship between the girl and the dog is compelling. I felt really ..."

"Moved," I say.

"Yes. That's it exactly, Akari. I felt moved. You've captured that brilliantly in your piece. Please ensure that you include, in your workbook, a description of how you first encountered this painting and how you approached this triptych. I want it to be clear that you were influenced by the artist."

"Of course. May I ask where you saw the painting?"

"The exhibit is in a gallery on the ground floor of a huge complex near Roppongi Station. Maybe it's a conference centre. Oh, the name is not coming to me." I squeeze my bottom lip against my teeth. "Wait. I think I picked up a card. Let me check my bag." She disappears into the office for a few minutes and then reappears with a card that she hands to me.

"It's your lucky day! The exhibit ends on the weekend. Perhaps you'll even get an opportunity to meet the artist."

———

For the second time in a week, I've lied to my parents.

"The good news is that your art teacher told you to see the exhibit. We're simply following orders," says Skye.

"You have an interesting relationship with the truth," I say.

"And if I didn't know you better, I'd think you were being tactful." In Roppongi Station, we ride an escalator that ascends through several stories of marble, glass, and steel. According to its website, the gallery is just a five-minute walk from the closest exit.

"Yoko says we should be very careful," says Skye.

"We are going to an art gallery. What is dangerous about that?"

"She meant Roppongi on a Saturday night. She says not to accept a drink from anyone," says Skye.

"Noted." I check my phone and look up at the grey building to our right. "This is it." The gallery is called "Because" which I find annoyingly pretentious, and Skye finds hilarious. A woman at a desk takes our bags, places them in two white cubbies, and gives each of us a small yellow plastic tag with a number.

"These security precautions are in place in case we are thieves," whispers Skye. "Nefarious art thieves. What an excellent cover."

"That is a terrible cover," I say.

"Perhaps, but this is a LOT of art," Skye says. There are ten smaller sub-chambers off the main foyer, five to our right and five to our left. I begin with the first room to our right and Skye heads straight up the centre of the gallery; I see her looking left and right as she goes. As I look at the paintings, I think about each of these artists. Who were they? What did they hope to say through their art? Did they feel successful? After just a few minutes, I hear Skye whispering aggressively in my direction. "I found it!" I follow the sound of her voice to the other end of the gallery. We stand in front of the painting.

"Akari, your painting looks eerily like this one. It's like you copied it, but that's not possible, right?" Goosebumps spring up all over my arms as I take in the similarities between this painting and mine. I read the card mounted below the painting.

"It's called *Love No. 2*. The artist is listed as M. Obi. M. Obi? Masumi Obi?," says Skye. My heart is pounding.

"It seems likely, right? Also, this work is called *Love No. 2* which makes me think that the painting Masumi gave to Naoko must have been *Love No. 1*.'

"We're so close. I can feel it! Let's find someone who can give us more information," says Skye.

"Skye, soft like a feather, right?" I say, repeating something I heard an elementary teacher at our school say to a hyperactive first grader.

"Yup," she says. We approach a woman in a navy-blue suit. "Hello. I'm wondering if you would please tell us about the artist of the painting, *Love No. 2*?" Skye uses her most respectful tone, and the woman seems surprised.

"I apologize but I do not work here. I am attending a conference upstairs."

"My sincere apologies for bothering you," Skye says. We bow our way backwards out of that conversation.

"That could have happened to anyone," I say. "You are doing a great job." Skye gives me her first-day-of-school smile. We walk around to the entrance of the exhibit and find a man in a slightly shiny black suit and thick, black-framed glasses.

"Good evening. Do you work here?" says Skye.

"I do. How may I help you this evening?"

"My friend and I are wondering about one of the artists. Is it suitable if we show you?"

"I will do my best to be of service to you." He and I bow to each other.

"Sorry. I forgot. Bowing," says Skye as she bows.

When we reach the painting, I say, "If it wouldn't be too much trouble, we would like to inquire if the given name of this artist might be Masumi?"

"Yes. That is correct. She is Masumi Obi." The young man looks pleased to provide us with this news.

"We thought perhaps she would be here this evening since this is the closing," I say.

"No. She is not present. I apologize for the inconvenience," he says.

"Thank you. If it is possible, could we please obtain her contact information?" I say. I know I am pushing it here. The man inhales slightly through his teeth.

"I am very sorry to inform you that we do not give out the contact information of our artists. This is for their protection."

I see Skye roll her eyes ever so slightly.

"Yes, of course. We understand," I say. "Perhaps, then, we could leave her a message?" Skye winks at me.

"Certainly. There is some paper at the front of the gallery." We accompany the man back to the desk where he provides me with a slip of paper and a pen. In my best handwriting, I write my full name, email address and cell phone number and, at the top of the small note, I write, "Regarding *Love No. 2*."

"We will pass this message along to Obi-san at the earliest opportunity."

"Thank you very much. You have been very kind," I say. We bow as we back away and then return to the painting. Skye stares at it and then moves closer. "He was very friendly," she says.

"No. He was just being polite," I say.

"He likes you," says Skye.

"Dating must be very confusing for Canadians if you constantly mistake politeness for attraction."

"Whatever," Skye says.

"Do you try to set up all your friends?" I ask. Skye ignores me and takes one step closer to the painting.

"But seriously, don't you think it's weird how similar the paintings are?" Skye says.

"I will admit that it's slightly unnerving," I say.

"Yours is better."

"That is absurd, Skye MacTavish," I say.

"The eyes of the girl. You made them kinder." Skye pulls her phone out of her pocket, backs up a few steps and takes a photograph of the painting. The whirring electric click of her phone echoes through the gallery.

"Put that away." Now it's my turn to whisper aggressively.

"You didn't think we were going to leave without taking a photo, did you? You're a terrible spy," says Skye. She mutes her phone and shoots a couple more photos of the painting before sliding her phone back into her pocket.

"You're right. I'm far too committed to staying out of trouble," I say.

"A spy lives for trouble," says Skye.

"You know what? My painting is pretty good. I got the eyes right, didn't I?"

"Show-off!"

As we pick up our bags from the bag check and head outside, Skye says, "Well, that lovely man said he'll give her the message, so I believe he will." I hope Skye's optimism is well-founded.

My family has just finished dinner and I am putting the leftover vegetables in a plastic container when my phone explodes in my pocket. My parents look up from their conversation. I hit "Accept" on my phone and run upstairs to my bedroom.

"Hello. I am calling for Akari."

"Speaking."

"This is Kazuki Hoshikawa calling from Because Gallery. We talked yesterday about a painting. *Love No. 2*."

"Yes. Thank you for calling." I sit down on the edge of my bed.

"I spoke with Ms. Obi's agent who has informed me that Ms. Obi is volunteering at an orphanage in the Himalayas for the next few weeks."

"The Himalayas?" I say.

"Yes. The Himalayas."

"In India?"

"Possibly. Or Nepal, Bhutan, China, or Pakistan."

"Oh," I say.

"I have asked Ms. Obi's agent to have her contact you when she returns."

"Thank you very much," I say.

"Also, I have just emailed you the information regarding this painting should you be interested in purchasing it."

"I am very sorry if we misled you in any way. We cannot afford to buy a painting. We are still in high school," I say.

"Yes, of course. I understand. But *Love No. 2* is being sold at a very reasonable price."

"Thank you very much for your attention to this matter, Hoshikawa-san" I say.

"It is our pleasure to be of service. Best wishes reaching Obi-san."

I hear him hang up and then I check my email. There are several unread messages in my inbox, but the most recent message is from Hoshikawa-san. I forward the message to Skye and include a short message.

Skye,

Hoshikawa-san from the gallery called to tell us that Masumi Obi is volunteering at an orphanage in the Himalayas for the next few weeks. He confirmed that the Himalayas are, indeed located in five countries. He has asked her agent to have her contact us when she gets back.

I am forwarding you the information for purchasing the painting. It is listed at 40,000 Yen so I think they must be missing a o in the price because that seems unbelievably affordable.

There was absolutely no romance in the call. Nothing of the sort. Sorry to disappoint you.

For the briefest of moments in the gallery, I believed that Masumi Obi might lead us to Naoko as soon as this weekend, but now I feel quite frustrated at the delay. I am certain that you would say something like, "Hey, Akari. That despair is not a good look on you." Nonetheless ...

Akari

P.S. For the record, I was not made for the spy life.

# CHAPTER 39

# IN WHICH NAOKO NISHIZAWA WRITES ABOUT HOW SHE FELL IN LOVE WITH HER MOTHER

As a teenager, I couldn't wait to move out of my mother's home.

It's odd that I should put it that way, since my father was the one who went to an office every day to earn money to pay our family's bills. Technically, then, it was his home, but I always thought of the home as hers. It was her domain.

As a small child, the only time I saw my father was if I was still awake when he got home from work, and on Sundays when he was not required to be at the office. His life was very mysterious to me. He dressed in black suits and went off to another part of the city for his job. It seemed to me that all the people in his life away from us were men like him. They carried black briefcases and gave the impression that they were very important people doing very important things. A young girl cannot conceive of her father as a mid-level bureaucrat who moves papers from one pile to another for a living. She shouldn't. We want to believe that our parents are heroes.

My mother, however, was formidable.

I was, in the most literal sense, her job. It was understood that she was responsible for me which meant that she must ensure that I was thin, had good manners, and did well in school. Although it's not my intention to diminish her enthusiasm for, and commitment to, the first two tasks, her primary focus was doing whatever was necessary to help me earn top grades. She believed that these grades were the key to securing a place at a good university, a large and ancient wooden door that would swing open, leading to a suitable marriage and lovely children for whom I would be responsible, and the system would reset itself like some gigantic beeping machine in a science fiction movie.

It has taken me thirty years to understand that this was simply the time and place she was born into.

Then the sixties exploded with movements like Woodstock and "Make Love, Not War," and then the Americans and Russians put people on the moon, and women all over the world decided that we should be equal and that we could be free.

My mother never got that memo.

Every day my father went to work, and my mother cleaned the house and made balanced meals and lectured me about being more responsible. She said, "You shame our family when you bring home these grades." And perhaps the failing was with me, but not for the reason she thought. All that shame and guilt talk worked on my friends who lived in constant fear of shaming their families. One friend pulled her hair out before each test, and especially on the days she had to take home a less than perfect score. Her mother took her to a hair salon and asked for a shorter cut, thinking that would deter her daughter from pulling out her hair in handfuls. The young woman assigned to cut my friend's hair had just graduated from her training program so perhaps she had never seen the scalp of a guilty, hair-pulling daughter, but when she saw the bloody patches on the girl's head, she shrieked and ran from the room.

The old man who owned the shop cut my friend's hair without further incident.

My mother said I was a hedonist. She was not wrong. If it came to choosing between pleasure and work, I would choose pleasure every time.

What I learned from my mother had nothing at all to do with what she believed in and everything to do with the strength of her will. I was a curious daydreamer. A voracious reader. A quirky child who interviewed herself in the bathroom mirror. I was not a great intellectual and I had no intentions of becoming one. Although she did not have much to work with in her quest to produce the perfect daughter, my mother cajoled me from one assignment to the next, from one grade to the next until I was in my final year of high school, and my grades were decent enough that my father could call in a favour and I was admitted to the university. They sat at my graduation ceremony with straight backs. I am still not certain if it was pride or something else.

It was her will, not mine, that got me through high school.

Then my boyfriend died.

My parents accompanied me to the funeral. We kneeled near the back because my mother was concerned the ritual might be too much for me. Japanese funerals are very intimate. You are faced with the body of the person. You must face that they are dead. She was right; it was too much. I felt a sob rising in my throat and then from some place lower. From the deep place where we feel loss. From the place where there are no words, only sounds and darkness. She placed her hand on my arm and said, "Silence."

My mother and I never spoke of him again.

When I graduated from university and there was still no young man, my mother began to see that my will was gathering strength and speed like a typhoon travelling over the Pacific

Ocean from the Philippines to Japan. We did not fight. I did not rage and scream, "I will not marry." I simply did not.

After a while she stopped speaking of marriage and grandchildren and the house got quiet. I felt a deep sense of peace, and I knew she did not, but I decided that was acceptable.

It was about this time that my father started to plan his retirement. He would bring home books he thought I might like to read, and he passed me sections of the newspaper and talked to me about politics. I wasn't particularly interested in politics, but I enjoyed listening to my father speak passionately. I had become, in not marrying, the son he always wanted.

Then my father died.

My mother and I were alone. She cooked and cleaned but, for the first time, I felt guilty and began to help her. She gave me terrible jobs like cutting the onions and then ridiculed the haphazard way in which I accomplished the task, laughing at my onion-tears. She loved to boss me around and I let her, once again, become responsible for my education.

One night, several months after my father died, I heard a cry from her room. I found my mother crouched inside her closet, folded up like a beach chair. She was dressed in her pale pink nightgown over which she wore my father's black suit jacket. On her feet she wore an old pair of my father's slippers and she rocked back and forth. When she saw me, she reached up to close the closet door, but I took her hand and pulled her up so that we were standing face to face. She looked at me as though I were a stranger. She was deep inside an earlier time, and I had been pulled into the great black hole of the unborn where my own children live. I pulled her up, led her to the bed and pushed her gently into a sitting position so that I could remove the slippers. She rolled over on the mattress but when I tried to remove my father's jacket, she pulled it closer to her. I could see the brown age spots on her hands as she clung to the jacket. I pulled the duvet up over her thin legs and body, over my father's jacket covering her thin shoulders. I got into the bed, rested my head on the pillow where my father's head had rested every night for the past four decades, wrapped my arms around my mother's small body and held her until she was heavy with sleep. Then I slept.

The curse was broken.

When I woke the next morning, my mother was already in the kitchen. "Would you like some breakfast?" The kitchen smelled of pickles and eggs and fresh coffee, and my mother's face was fresh and filled with light. As she turned her head, her hair swung out and I remembered that long-ago night when the three of us went to the opera. "Did you sleep well?" she asked. I confirmed that I had. She said, "I feel like a new person."

For a while, we lived together like roommates, sharing the responsibilities of caring for each other and the house. We both came and went as we pleased, and I watched my mother's social circle grow. She started talking about a trip to Europe, and she bought luggage, because she said she would be too embarrassed to take their old bags. She and three other friends booked a two-week trip to Italy with a tour group. She said all she would have to do was get up each morning and put her luggage on the bus and that the only other challenging task of the day would be deciding what to eat. She said, "I've always wanted to go to Italy," and I said, "Have you?" and she said, "Of course. It's always been my dream."

# CHAPTER 40
# IN WHICH SKYE EMPLOYS THE HELP OF A POCKET GODDESS

t's late and I'm supposed to be in bed but there are some things rumbling around in my mind or my heart or somewhere more tender, so I grab my journal and a pen. This journal, my series of journals, is where I work things out. It's like conducting an internal search and then replacing all the YUCK I find in my life with words that are more descriptive and helpful. True words. When I was in Grade Seven, my therapist recommended journal writing and, over the past four years, the blank page has become a place for gathering and sorting my feelings, and for my creative writing. Sometimes the line between those two endeavours is invisible.

Yoko invited Akari over for dinner tonight. She cooked a Japanese curry that made Dad, Akari and me swoony with delight. As soon as we finished eating, Akari and I washed up the dishes and went to my room to read Naoko's entry about falling in love with her mother. I felt a little bad that Yoko and Dad thought we were doing our homework again. Yoko brought us oatmeal and raisin cookies and two glasses of chocolate milk and suggested that perhaps we'd worked enough for today.

Akari said this might be her new favourite entry. I feel the same. I love how Naoko's mother breaks out of this hard shell of what's been expected of her and starts to become herself, like a full person, maybe for the first time. It's sad that it doesn't happen until after her husband dies, but maybe she couldn't be her whole self while he was alive. I love that she goes off to Italy with her friends, that she realizes this dream, even though Naoko had never heard her mother mention visiting Italy. I think we expect the people who care about us to be able to read our insides. Maybe it's because the voices on the inside are shouting so loudly that we can't imagine this person who loves us doesn't hear them.

Akari said she noticed that I don't talk about my biological mom. She was really quiet and gentle when she brought it up. She's not wrong. Even though I wanted to talk with her about Yoko and my birth mom, I couldn't make myself say the words, so I changed the subject, and Akari seemed to understand. I'm so lucky to have her as a friend.

There was this character I created a while ago: Calliope, the Pocket Goddess. In the piece I wrote, she lived inside the pocket of a velvet jacket, and when someone pulled her out of that pocket, she was free to be one of the most powerful of all the Goddesses. The whole idea of this makes me laugh but there's something compelling about this tiny but powerful wise woman. I decided to write to her.

SKYE MACTAVISH: Dear Calliope, the Pocket
 Goddess, things are kind of intense right now, so I
 thought I'd write to you for guidance. May I call
 you Callie?
CALLIOPE, POCKET GODDESS: Please do. I
 respond to many names. What's on your mind
 today, lovely Skye?
SMT: Callie, I've been thinking about mothers.

CPG: That's a big topic. Can you be a bit more specific?

SMT: I just read this story about a mother, and it made me think about lots of complicated things. Did you know that I have two mothers?

CPG: Yes. I do.

SMT: But my biological mother is dead.

CPG: Yes. I'm sorry about that, Skye.

SMT: It's okay. I don't remember her or anything. The only mother I've ever known is Yoko. She's a good mother.

CPG: She is a very good mother. I notice you still call her Yoko.

SMT: I've always called her Yoko. When I was old enough to understand that my mother had died, my dad and Yoko explained that Yoko never wanted to take the place of my mother. That's why she never asked me to call her mom.

CPG: Why do you think this is on your mind right now?

SMT: I'm not sure. I guess I've been thinking about losing people.

CPG: Who have you lost?

SMT: Well, my mom and Claire. All the friends I had in Ottawa and then the friends I had in Paris. It feels like that's what I do. Like I'm a Professional Loser of People.

CPG: Is that true?

SMT: I'm not sure. It kind of feels true. Claire has a boyfriend now and I think I've made it impossible for her to be my friend again.

CPG: You seem like a loving and generous person, and you are a great friend to Akari.

SMT: Yes. I think that's true.

CPG: But there's something that makes you feel like you don't deserve their love.

SMT: Yes. That's why they leave.

CPG: Your mother didn't want to leave you.

SMT: How can I be sure, Callie?

CPG: You can choose to believe it.

SMT: I'm not sure I can.

CPG: Skye, I'm happy you wrote to me because it means that you are sorting out some big stuff, but you know that I'm you, right? When you write to Calliope, the Pocket Goddess, you are writing to yourself.

SMT: Yeah. I know.

CPG: You need to talk to someone else, love. Someone real. Preferably an adult. You could see a counsellor at your school. Or you could talk to Yoko or your dad.

SMT: I don't want to bother them when they have so much going on.

CPG: Why would it be a bother?

SMT: I'm always such a big, loud mess. I have all these crazy feelings. I want to be more like Yoko. She's orderly. I want to be orderly.

CPG: You deserve to be well. Healthy. Loved.

SMT: Thank you, Callie.

CPG: Will you please talk with someone about how you're feeling.

SMT: I'll try.

CPG: There is no try, Skye.

SMT: I know. "Do or do not." Thanks, Callie.

CPG: I love you, Skye.

# CHAPTER 41

# IN WHICH AKARI
# DRAWS A MOTHER

What kind of mother does one give a super-girl who stops people from killing themselves? Is she a good or a bad mother? Maybe there are no bad mothers at all, just mothers in difficult situations.

It's evening, my parents are asleep, and although I'm in bed, I'm wide awake after spending the evening with Skye's family. After dinner we read a Naoko entry provocatively entitled "How I fell in love with my mother." It made me think about Chiyo and her mother, which means I am thinking about my mother and me. Sometimes it seems like my mother enjoys being angry, but that's probably not true.

When you get a new computer, it comes with a set of default settings that you can simply accept, or you can choose custom ones. Of course, custom settings are more work. It seems like my mother's default settings are for suspicion, cynicism, and strictness. Not enoughness. It must be painful to live that way—to expect bad things, to believe that the world is acting against you. It must be exhausting. Naoko's mother had the same settings as my mother, right up until she didn't. Then she said she was going to Italy, and I knew she had dropped the story about the world being against her. I wondered why

Naoko had never heard about her mother's dream to visit Italy. Perhaps Naoko's mother didn't know how to talk about her dreams or perhaps she thought it would never come true, so there was no point in sharing it. When her husband died, Naoko's mother was finally free. This fact is uncomfortable. I don't know exactly what to do with it.

It seems that each of us can be another person's safe place, and that we can also be their prison.

I get out of bed, retrieve my sketchbook from my bag which is already packed for tomorrow, choose a pencil, and get back under the covers. I open the sketchbook to a new page and draw Chiyo jumping down from a train. She has just saved a girl who hugs her and says, "Thank you for saving my life, Chiyo. I promise to make it a life worth saving." In the crowd on the platform, Chiyo spots her mother, whose mouth is open, forming a large O. In the fourth frame, her mother pushes towards her through the crowd. In the fifth frame, she faces her daughter and whispers, "You did this? You stopped the train?" Chiyo nods. Her mother responds, "I have not been able to see you clearly, Chiyo."

My eyes fill with tears. I am drawing the mother I want. No, that is not quite right. I love my mother. I am drawing a version of her that understands how deeply I love creating art, and who can permit and support this dream, even though her friends and neighbours will think less of me. Even though they will think less of her.

# CHAPTER 42
# IN WHICH NAOKO NISHIZAWA WRITES ABOUT THE SHIP

Truly, I never expected to fall in love with an address.

I'm not a very materialistic person. Reading that phrase back, it sounds like it might not be true. This is where I give you my full permission to choose to believe whatever you like.

My first encounter with the ship occurred when I first moved to Hiro-o. It's a white apartment building that is very narrow at one end, like the bow of a ship. I'm not at all sure why it is this shape. Perhaps the only available parcel of land was a triangle and the architect said, "Yes, of course I can work with that."

On the side of the building next to the road the windows are small and far apart. Like portholes. That side of the building looks like a great white cruise liner rising up beside the street. On the other side of the building, the one that overlooks the park, there are balconies that wrap the building from one end to the other. These are not pretend balconies, those awful terraces wide enough only to stand outside your window. These are real balconies, big enough for tables and chairs and tall, leafy green plants that sprout out of terracotta pots the size of small cars. The balconies are large enough for parties.

The first time I saw the ship, I had just moved into my first apartment: a studio so small that I had to fold the futon my mother gave me in half in order to lay it down on the floor. But I was happy for my folded futon, my tiny cooking space, and my closet made for doll's clothes, because it was mine, and having my name on the lease meant that I would finally figure out a way to survive. For too long I had relied on the generosity of my parents and, later, just my mother. I relied on the habits we had developed as a family. I relied on an ancient story about the children of the affluent not having to work. But I was no longer a child and I had chosen not to marry.

When my mother visited me for the first time, she cried.

"I can't have you living like this."

"But I want to," I said.

"Are you unwell? Has something broken inside your brain?"

"Perhaps, Mother. But I like it."

"You must come home often."

Because we had healed the sore spot between us, I knew she said these things out of love, and I promised her that I would come home often. She said she would like to buy me something. What did I need? I told her I needed nothing, and besides, there was no space. She smiled at my joke even though she didn't want to.

With time, I came to know the people at the noodle shop and the woman who owned the coffee shop and a very kind bartender, and I found that the whole neighbourhood became my living room and my writing space. When it was time to go home, I always felt lucky to have this cosy place to sleep. I called it the womb, but not in front of my mother, who would not have been amused by this wordplay.

In the coffee shop there is a board where people share notices for the community: festivals and lost dogs. One day I saw a small ad for an apartment, and I recognized the address immediately. It was on the big road near the train station. The building with the balconies. The ship. I pulled the pin out of the board and slipped the advertisement into my pocket. I knew I shouldn't, but I did it anyway. If we are being honest, not simply putting forth a story about the person we'd like to be or the way we'd like to be thought of, then we all have stolen things in our pockets. We know better and we do it anyway.

The woman who showed me the apartment reminded me of my mother. She was elegantly dressed. Polite and articulate. She gave away nothing. I explained that I lived nearby, that I had always loved this building. She nodded and unlocked the door. We were on the top floor of the ship so I knew that the apartment would be small, and it was, in fact, not much larger than my current apartment, but the terrace seemed as large as a football field. The apartment was filled with light from the glass doors. We slipped off our shoes, and the woman provided me with a tour that we could, just as easily, have done from the doorway. Tiny kitchen, tiny closet, tiny toilet. Slowly, she made her way to the balcony doors which she unlocked and then slid open. I waited for her to go first.

"It is quite cold," she said.

I stepped onto the terrace. The neighbourhood of Hiro-o stretched out below me, and I could see the tops of people's buildings, spaces I didn't know existed. The wind was cool and filled with secrets.

"Yes," I said. I didn't know how I would afford it, but the answer was yes.

## CHAPTER 43
## IN WHICH AKARI IS TALKED INTO IT

"Let's go to the ship tomorrow after school. Even I know which apartment building she's talking about, and I just moved here," Skye says.

"You're right. It is our best clue yet."

"Clue? Are you kidding? It's way better than a clue. It's a freaking address!" Skye stands and starts waving the journal around her head. I reach up and grab her elbow.

"Sit down. You are making a scene," I say.

"Am I?" Skye looks around the Delightful Café which has become our journal-reading salon. People look away as soon as she meets their gaze. "Oh, I am making a scene. Sorry." She drops back into her chair.

"Listen," I say, "I agree this is very good news, but how can we be sure that she still lives there?"

"There's only one way to find out. Plus, you know that my intuition is my greatest super-power," Skye says. She takes a long sip of her café latté and ends up with a bit of the foam on her top lip. I trace my finger over my own upper lip while raising an eyebrow. Skye laughs and uses a napkin to wipe the foam off her face.

"Perhaps your superpower is impulsivity," I say.

"It can't be a superpower if you don't mean it as a compliment," says Skye. "Okay, so about tomorrow ..."

"No. I absolutely cannot. Are you forgetting about our last little excursion when we went to find the bartender?"

"The surfer. He really is a surfer. Maybe not our surfer but a surfer just the same," Skye says.

"Yes. I acknowledge that you found a surfer," I say. "But ..."

"There were some technical difficulties," says Skye.

"Now your superpower is understatement. It was a disaster. We entered a bar, thereby breaking the law. I had a panic attack on a bench in Hiro-o. We didn't find anything helpful, and Reika is still angry at me for using her game as my alibi with my parents."

"Some people are constantly looking for a reason to be unhappy. Not me. Just the opposite. I don't dispute a single thing you just said; however, you're conveniently leaving out the fact that I went to the second bar myself, out of a deep concern for your anxious state, and that I did not physically enter the second bar," says Skye. I nod, and she beams. "So, let's swing by the ship after school tomorrow and look at the names at the front door. No need for an alibi. You won't be late getting home. We'll just look and see if she lives there, and if by some stroke of good luck, she does, we'll come up with a plan."

"Breezy, right?" I raise an eyebrow at Skye.

"Yup. You in?" Skye says.

"You are extremely persuasive."

# CHAPTER 44
# IN WHICH SKYE GETS IT VERY WRONG

'm waiting on a bench in the little park across from school when I see Akari running towards me. Her hair has grown a bit since I first met her, and it swings as she moves. She slows up just before reaching the bench.

"How did you get out of school so early?" says Akari.

"Packed my bag before class. Didn't go to my locker. Took the stairs two at a time."

"So, you are a little excited?" says Akari.

"Look." I pull a black beret out of the front pocket of my backpack and put it on. Then I tip it so that it sits slightly askew.

"Really?"

"It felt fitting," I say.

"It's still somewhat warm for a beret, though," says Akari. "Not to mention that we are trying to be less conspicuous, right?"

"We are." I reach up, pluck the beret off my head, and stuff it back in my bag. "But it's cool, right?"

"I very sincerely like your beret, Skye."

"Thanks. When will it be cold enough to wear it?"

"December. Probably December. Let us begin the investigation, Harriet." Akari pulls me off the bench and we walk to the station. Our train is packed with kids leaving school, but we're too nervous to make small talk with anyone. When we exit at Hiro-o, a huge pack of kids emerges from the station and then separates like ribbons unfurling into different parts of the neighbourhood. We cross the street and walk towards that great white ship of an apartment building. A blonde boy walks beside us.

"Hey, you go to my school, right? I'm Jeff."

"Yes. I'm Skye," I say. "This is Akari." Akari bows slightly. We're closing in on the ship and Jeff is still walking beside us.

"You know somebody who lives here?" says Jeff.

"Yes, we're meeting a friend. Naoko Nishizawa," I say. I don't look in Akari's direction as I'm pretty sure she's not too happy about me sharing this information.

"Cool. I live here too." He swipes a plastic card over the metal sensor and the door swings open. We pass the board with the names and apartment numbers of the tenants. "The elevator's straight ahead," Jeff says. "Have fun!" He turns into a room filled with mailboxes.

On the board we see that there are three apartments on each floor, except for floors seven and eight, where there is just one tenant listed. Akari runs her finger along the board as she reads. She stops at the third floor. Nishizawa. 3C. We stand completely still and silent. We found her. We found Naoko Nishizawa. We're just minutes away from meeting her, from returning the journal. The noise I want to make is way too loud for this foyer, for this country, so I say nothing, but we're both beaming with happiness. I spot the door to the stairwell and point. It feels more properly spy-esque to take the stairs, so we climb the two flights quickly and emerge into a narrow hallway covered in beige carpet. As we reach the door of 3C, Akari puts her hand on my arm.

"Wait. Let me do the talking. Okay?" I nod my head. Akari is absolutely right. She should be in charge of all introductions and explanations.

"Are you sad that we haven't finished reading the journal?" I say.

"Yes. I am, and I didn't expect to feel that way. What about you?" Akari says.

"Definitely. But the stories we've read, I have them inside me, you know?"

Akari nods.

"I know it's time." I say.

Akari knocks gently on the door. There's no response, and although I push my ear against the wooden door, I can't hear anyone moving inside. Akari knocks again, more loudly. We hear footsteps. Someone is slowly making their way towards the door. I notice that Akari looks pale, and I squeeze her hand.

The door opens and a very small, very old man appears. He's wearing a dark grey suit and glasses with thick black frames, and he stares up at us but does not speak. Akari turns to me with a blank look while my mind works as quickly as it can.

"Good afternoon, Sir," I say in my very best Japanese. "We are sorry to disturb you, but we are looking for your daughter Naoko." The man steps back. He takes off his glasses and puts them back on again. He stares at us and then, without speaking, closes the door. We look at each other.

"Skye, Naoko's father is dead."

"Ahhh." I hit my forehead with the palm of my hand. "How could I have forgotten? I don't know why I seem incapable of slowing down and thinking things through." I look over at Akari whose eyes are large with what I suspect is panic. "Should we stay?" I say.

"Shh. He's on the phone. Let's wait," says Akari. After a few minutes in the warm, stuffy hallway, I sit down on the floor. Akari continues to stand. She's such an Akari.

The bell on the elevator door dings. I get up quickly as a middle-aged woman walks towards us. She's followed by a police officer. The woman strides past us and opens the apartment door with a key. As the officer passes us, he instructs us not to leave.

"What's going on?" I whisper.

"I don't know exactly what's happening right now, but we got this wrong," Akari says. A furrow appears between her eyebrows, a tiny trench I've never seen before.

After a few minutes, the police officer opens the door and steps into the hallway. He has a very serious look on his face. Which is to say he has a serious look on his face for a police officer. "You will follow me to the koban." He leads us onto the elevator, out of the building and down the sidewalk for three blocks, down the main street of Hiro-o with everyone watching and knowing we are in trouble. But for what? I feel my cheeks burning. Inside the tiny office of the koban, the officer pulls a small notebook out of his pocket.

"Names," he says.

Akari tells him our names and, of course, my strange foreign name takes a little longer. The officer records our names in his notebook and then asks for our addresses, phone numbers, and parents' names and phone numbers. When he asks for our parents' phone numbers, I know things have escalated from Bad to Very Bad. I try to get Akari's attention, but she won't look at me. I suspect she doesn't want to make things worse than they are. Then the officer calls Akari's father and asks him to come to the koban. It takes a long time for him to get my father on the phone. Then he sits down at the desk and begins filling out some kind of report using the information he's written in his notebook. We stand at the counter and watch him, until he indicates that we should sit down on the folding chairs in the tiny space between the counter and the door. I place my hand on top of Akari's, but she gently withdraws her hand. This is what she has been worried about all along and I didn't believe her.

Our parents arrive together in our black SUV, because my dad's driver has picked up Akari's parents. With the seven of us in the koban, there's barely enough space to raise an arm.

"Skye, are you okay?" asks my dad.

"I'm fine, Dad." I don't have any idea what's happening or even if I am, in fact, fine but I want to reassure him.

The police officer clears his throat. "According to the complaint, this afternoon at approximately 16:30, these two girls went to the apartment of Nishizawa-san and asked to see his daughter. Is this true?" We nod our heads.

"This was upsetting for Mr. Nishizawa, because his daughter is deceased."

"Dead?" I say. Akari shushes me.

"Mr. Nishizawa is elderly and becomes confused easily. When you asked to speak to her, he thought his daughter was still alive. He called his niece who brought the matter to my attention. Please explain why you asked to see his daughter."

I take out the journal and pass it to Akari.

"We are very sorry for any discomfort we have caused to Nishizawa-san," Akari says. "Some time ago, we found this journal and we wanted to return it to the woman who wrote it. Her name is Naoko Nishizawa. We have been reading the entries in the journal. Although we did not want to violate her privacy, it was the only way to find clues about where she lives. We found the address of this apartment building in the journal and went there after school today. Again, we deeply regret any

236

pain we have caused Nishizawa-san. It was not our intention." Akari passes the journal to the police officer who scans through several pages before setting it on his desk.

Akari's parents and Yoko wear three different shades of disappointment. Akari's mother has tears in her eyes.

"This cannot be the same person," says the officer. "Nishizawa-san's daughter died by drowning as a child. This is the journal of an adult. Why did you go to this particular apartment?" Akari opens the journal on the desk and shows the police officer the entry about Naoko's new apartment. As he reads it, he seems to smile ever so slightly.

My father is losing his patience and steps forward. "Please accept our most sincere apologies for our daughters' behaviour. We will speak with them and ensure that they receive an appropriate consequence for their actions. We can assure you that nothing like this will ever happen again." His Japanese is not brilliant but it's good enough. He bows. The police officer bows. The mothers bow more deeply still.

"I will inform the family that this was a misunderstanding. I will convey profound apologies from both families," says the officer. Our mothers back out of the koban followed by Akari's father and then my dad. Akari and I follow them, and I realize my knees are shaking so hard I'm afraid I might fall down. I take a deep breath and keep going. Akari looks straight ahead as she walks. She is silent and pale, and she wears no expression on her face. It's like someone has taken a whiteboard eraser and wiped away everything that made her Akari. She won't look at me and I know I can't ask her how she's doing or make any kind of scene in front of her parents. My stomach is filled with knots of worry for her. About her.

Our car is parked around the corner and the driver turns on the ignition as soon as he sees us emerge from the koban. My dad hugs me. "I'm so sorry," I say. He kisses the top of my head and then he opens the door of the SUV so that Yoko and I can slide in. He continues to hold the SUV door open for Akari's family.

"Thank you, Ambassador-san. We do not wish to trouble you further. We will take the train," says Akari's father.

———

"She didn't do it on purpose," says my father.

"I know," says Yoko.

My parents are in the living room and I'm on my bed with the door open. When we got home, I explained the entire story of the journal to Dad and Yoko. I gave them the extended dance mix version and left nothing out. Yoko cooked chicken breasts and made a big salad for dinner, but I knew I couldn't eat so I didn't bother putting anything on my plate. My father tried to make small talk at the dining table, but both Yoko and I were silent.

"Why is everyone so angry? It seems rather an over-reaction, doesn't it? Hauling two teenagers into a police station over a silly mistake?" says Dad.

"Akari's parents feel embarrassed," says Yoko. "No. Not embarrassed. They feel humiliated that their daughter was taken to a police station. They are ashamed that her actions caused pain to this elderly man."

"But it was an accident," Dad says.

"True. But if the girls had told us, we could have helped them. They have not been careful enough with other people's feelings. They have been reckless," says Yoko. I feel as though there's a small, sharp rock where my heart should be. The worst part is that I know she's right. Akari has been warning me all along, but I wouldn't listen.

"I'm not sure I see it that way," says Dad.

"In this case, my love, you are outnumbered by a parental score of three to one. We will have to agree to disagree."

# CHAPTER 45
# IN WHICH AKARI
# ATTEMPTS TO EXPLAIN

The house has become unbearable. I feel as though I have lost the right to be in our shared spaces, the living room, dining room, and kitchen. The air crackles with tension and anger. All weekend long, I've helped my mother make the meals, set the table, and clean up afterwards. I am afraid to breathe too loudly just in case the evidence that I am still alive might set one of them off.

My father is normally home on Sundays; it is the one day of the week that he is not required to work. But his boss called after dinner last night and asked him to come in today. He isn't talking to me anyway.

My mother and I eat lunch in silence. She washes the dishes and I dry them and stack them carefully back in the cupboard. A glass slips from my grasp and lands heavily on the shelf, pinging against another glass. My mother sighs. She has been sighing a lot since we got back from the koban.

"Mom, I'd like to explain the whole story to you."

"Yes?" She drops the dishcloth in the sink and sits across from me at the kitchen table. Our table is so small that our knees touch.

"At the beginning of the school year, Skye bought a purse, and this journal was inside it. We found it on the train ride home."

"But why not take it back to the store? They would have contacted the owner," says my mother.

"You are right. We should have returned the journal to the store, but after we read the first entry, we decided to find her on our own by following the clues in the entries. That is what we were doing in Hiro-o on Friday; we thought we had finally found Naoko."

"Your father and I understand that it was not your intention to hurt that man, Akari, but you did. You made many poor decisions: not returning the journal, not telling us or Skye's parents, and conducting these detective missions on your own."

"Everything you have said is true, Mom. I didn't mean to hurt anyone but I'm not perfect."

"That's not true," says my mother.

"Of course, it's true. I'm not perfect. I don't even want to be."

"Akari, do not say such a thing." My mother folds her arms across her chest.

"Mom, is that what's really bothering you? The idea that I am not your perfect daughter?" There's a mug of hot tea on the table and I wrap my hands around it.

"You are confused. Your father and I believe that your friendship with Skye has resulted in you losing your way."

"I can understand why you feel that way, but it's not her fault. I need you to understand that." My mother's expression grows dark. She stands, picks up the cloth she dropped in the sink, and hangs it on the drying rack with great precision. When she speaks her voice is very quiet.

"Akari, this conversation is over. I am trying to be patient with you, but it seems that you are going out of your way to be disrespectful towards me by insisting that I don't understand you. I do understand. I am your mother."

# CHAPTER 46
## IN WHICH SKYE REACHES OUT

SKYE (10:17AM)

Hey! Are you there?

SKYE (10:35AM)

Text me back, please.

SKYE (2:12PM)

I'm sorry for everything.

SKYE (5:41PM)

I've lost the journal.

## CHAPTER 47

# IN WHICH AKARI TEARS HER NAPKIN INTO A HUNDRED PIECES

Skye keeps texting. I finally turn my phone off so my parents won't hear it buzzing and take it away from me.

My father gets home in time for an early dinner and, after we finish, we sit in an uneasy silence at the kitchen table. My mother begins to clear the table and I get up to help her.

"Sit down," instructs my father. I drop back into my chair.

"Your mother says that you spoke with her about the events that led to you being taken to the koban."

"Yes."

"Don't waste your breath on these kinds of explanations. Why you made these choices is irrelevant. All that matters is that you persist in making the wrong choice. You come home late, you lie about where you have been, you trespass in an apartment building when you should have been on your way home. This behaviour began when you became friends with the Canadian girl."

"It's not her fault," I say.

"Finally, something we agree on. It's not entirely her fault. You have chosen again and again to betray your values and your family."

"I understand and I am deeply sorry."

"I believe you are only sorry because you got caught. That is what you're sorry about. Perhaps you are also sorry because you must suspect that your mother and I can no longer allow you to be friends with this girl," my father says.

"Skye."

"I am aware of her name. Your mother says you have some classes together so obviously you will see her in school but there will be no more dinners and sleepovers in Roppongi, no more sneaking around buildings where you have no business being. As soon as school is over, you will get on the train and come home. No exceptions. Do you understand?"

"Yes."

"If you are unable to meet these expectations, we will transfer you to St. Theresa's here in Yokohama. I've already contacted the headmaster and it is not too late to make this happen. Perhaps they will succeed where your mother and I have failed. Do we understand each other?"

"Yes. I understand you," I say.

"Having you in that school all these years has been a substantial financial sacrifice. I was willing to make this sacrifice because I believed this education would give you a better chance in life, so that you could go to any university and be successful. Now, I am no longer certain if we have done the right thing. I do not know if it has been worth all the money. I don't know who you are, Akari."

"I am the same person I have always been."

"Who is that, exactly?"

I look down into my lap. I have torn my paper napkin into a hundred small pieces. I do not answer my father.

"You are excused from the table," he says.

———

AKARI

Hey.

SKYE

Hi. You're still alive. I've been so worried.

Yes. I am still alive.

I lost the journal. I think maybe it's at the koban but I'm not sure we can get it back.

Probably not.

You okay?

Not really.

Are you grounded? I got grounded. By Yoko!

I am beyond grounded. My life is basically over.

My father is furious like I have never seen him before.

He says we can't be friends anymore.

If I break even one rule, he will transfer me to the Catholic girls' school in Yokohama.

Did you explain what happened?

Did you tell them that I was the one that messed up and asked for his daughter?

I apologized.

But did you tell them about the journal? How we were just trying to get it back to Naoko.

I tried to tell my mom. They are not exactly receptive right now.

Why don't you just tell them the truth?

Stand up for yourself.

You said you wanted your insides to match
your outsides.

Are you angry at me right now?

Because none of this would have happened if
it weren't for you.

I know. And I am SO sorry.

Sorry does not repair the damage for me.

I know that too.

I have to go.

———

I can't focus in English class. It's been five days and Skye has
not returned to school. It's not like Skye to miss even one day of
school, let alone a week. Or maybe it is. Sometimes I forget that
I've only known Skye for a couple of months, so maybe this is
perfectly normal for her. No, I know it's not. Skye is just as
much of a nerd as I am, and learning makes her insanely happy.

Where is she?

I feel bad about our last text exchange on Sunday night. I
was still in shock from getting taken to the koban and my father
saying we couldn't be friends. I don't think I was unfair to Skye,
but maybe I should have tried harder to understand how she
was feeling. Honestly, I don't know. By Monday afternoon her
texts had stopped coming and, for a couple of days, that felt like
a relief. Now, Skye is not responding to my messages, and I feel
very worried about her. Perhaps she is just done with me. I
can't really think about that possibility.

As always, Reika and Kimi have been great. I told them
everything ... all about Naoko's journal and our mission to track
her down and return the journal. They weren't mad at all.

"That explains where you've been," said Reika.

"The stories sound so cool, Akari. I hope you find Naoko," said Kimi.

I love these girls so much. I will always love them. But they aren't Skye.

Yesterday, Mrs. Page from Immersive Tokyo emailed me about the Chiyo manga. She wrote that she was "enchanted" with the story and illustrations that Ms. Barrett sent her and asked if we could meet at the Immersive Tokyo office. They have already discussed the story at an editorial meeting and are keen to publish it as a tear-out in the centre of the spring issue of the magazine. This is such an amazing opportunity, but the timing could not be worse. I cannot talk to my parents about this, and I absolutely cannot meet with Mrs. Page behind their backs. I send a quick email to Mrs. Page and say that I will discuss this with my parents and get back to her as soon as possible.

The bell rings and shakes me free from my thoughts. Ms. Barrett calls my name and asks me to stay after class. After the last student leaves, she is even more direct than normal. "Akari, I wanted to ask if Skye is alright. We've received a note from her parents that she is unwell."

"I'm not really sure."

"My apologies. I assumed you'd know." I am completely unable to stop my bottom lip from quivering. I am equally unable to prevent the tears that arrive as I stand at Ms. Barrett's desk. It proves impossible to stop myself from telling Ms. Barrett everything that has happened over the last few weeks.

Ms. Barrett offers me a chair, passes me a box of tissues from her desk, and listens carefully. When I finish speaking, she pauses for a moment, and says, "Akari, it may not feel like this right now, but you will be fine. I am not one of those awful fanatics who thinks everything happens for a reason. No, terrible things sometimes happen to lovely people. But everything I know about you and Skye indicates that you are exactly the kind of young people who will learn from this experience and emerge stronger."

"Thank you, Ms. Barrett."

"Do you know what you need to do next?" she asks.

"Yes. I need to call Skye."

"Very well. Is there anything I can do for you that would be helpful? Appropriately helpful, coming from your English teacher."

"There is one thing," I say.

# CHAPTER 48
# IN WHICH SKYE STAYS
# IN BED

"Skye, you've got to tell me what's happening with you." Dad turns on the overhead light in my room.

I'm exactly where I've been for the last week. Buried under my floral duvet, curtains drawn, air conditioning blasting. As Dad sits on the edge of the bed, I pull the duvet up over my head. Gently he pulls it away from my face.

"It's time for you to talk with me, Skye. It's well past time."

"Okay. I'll try." I sit up.

"Look, Yoko and I, we know you're not sick with the flu like you said, but we wanted to give you some space to feel whatever you were feeling about this business with the koban and your friend, Akari. But now you've missed a week of school, and you're not eating. When was the last time you had a shower?"

"I don't know. Yesterday?"

"Yoko says it was Monday afternoon. That's four days ago."

"Maybe."

"Are you embarrassed, or sad, or ... do you know?"

I lay back down and close my eyes. "Dad, could you please turn off the light? I'll talk to you, but the light is killing me." He gets up and turns off the light switch. "Thanks. I don't know what the big deal is, Dad. I just haven't felt like going to school."

"You're sixteen. School is not an optional activity. It is, in fact, your job. The only one you have. Why aren't you going to school, Skye?"

"I can't." He sits beside me and peels back the duvet again so he can see my face.

"Do you mean you can't, or you won't?" he says.

"I don't know. They feel like the same thing right now."

"Okay. I understand that feeling," he says. Despite my best efforts to hold it in, I start to cry. He wipes away my tears with his fingertips and I let him. "What's going on, Skye-girl?"

"Why don't you ever get mad at me?"

"What do you mean?"

"Why don't you ever yell and scream and tell me I'm a terrible daughter?"

"You're not a terrible daughter. You're a magnificent daughter. You've brought Yoko and me nothing but happiness and laughter for your entire life."

"Yoko is not so thrilled with me right now."

"She was upset about that koban business, and what it might mean for your friendship with Akari, but if you'd spoken with either of us this week, you'd find that all is forgiven. She's as worried as I am."

"Maybe she shouldn't forgive me."

"Why are you talking like this, Skye?"

"Because I'm the one who deserves to be punished. I was the one who was so keen to find Naoko Nishizawa. I dragged Akari into it, talked her into things she wouldn't normally have done, and now her father is furious, and she's grounded and she's not even talking to me anymore and she won't return my texts and here's MY dad and he's not mad at all and he keeps saying that it's okay."

"It is okay. Or it will be."

"I do not feel okay, Dad."

"How do you feel? Can you describe it?"

"I feel like someone turned off the power. Or the sun. And everything's grey and there's no reason to hope for anything better. There's no reason to get out of bed."

Dad pulls me up into a sitting position and wraps his arms around me and my duvet. "You are the reason, wee girl. You are the reason to get out of bed. The possibility that better things are waiting for you."

"I don't believe that," I say.

"This morning I received a message from your friend, Claire, in Paris."

I shake my head. This can't be true.

"Don't be angry with her, Skye. She said she had written to you a number of times and when you finally responded, you asked her not to be in contact with you."

"It's more complicated than that."

"I'm sure it is, but the point is that she is really concerned about you and so are we. Yoko thinks you should talk with a lovely psychologist she knows."

"I can't talk to a stranger."

"Talk to me, then," says Dad.

"I don't want to disappoint you."

"You couldn't. It's not possible," he says.

"You've already been through so much," I say.

"What are you talking about?"

"Mom."

"Oh." Dad is still holding me like a mummy wrapped in my duvet. He rests his forehead against mine for a moment. "It's true that what happened to your mother was not fair, Skye. It wasn't fair to her or to me ... or to you."

"I don't remember her, Dad."

"Of course you don't. You weren't even one year old when she died."

"Do you think it's possible to miss someone you never knew?"

"Yes. And you did know her, even if you don't remember her. You knew her. In the first year of your life, you were almost never more than ten feet away from her. You rubbed noses constantly. She sang to you and told you stories about the adventures we would have together. She gave you butterfly kisses on your stomach, and you'd stretch out your legs and your toes would curl up and you would laugh. You made a sound that was somewhere between a giggle and a sigh. You were so happy together. You did know her, Skye. I'm sorry you don't remember. I should have done a better job telling you about the amazing love affair between you and your mother."

"You have, Dad. You always have." I free my arm from the duvet and place my hand on his arm.

"You think you are the grown-up, don't you, Skye?"

"What do you mean?" I say.

"You think it's your job to make me feel better, to protect me." I nod. "It is not, sweet Skye. It has never been your job to protect me. It is my job to protect you, and to help prepare you to live a gorgeous, full life in the world. That's my job description."

"You've been doing that, Dad," I say.

"What else have you been protecting me from?"

"Nothing."

"Keep going, Skye. What else have you been worried that I would find out?"

"People have always told me how lucky I was to have a father that loves me so much, and a not-at-all-wicked step-mother who is young and cool and not strict. So, I've tried to be grateful and happy and cheerful ... you know, the kid who deserves that life. When I feel sad about … I don't know … sad about Mom or moving or being round or losing Claire, I've tried to make the best of things, tried to make everyone else happy, tried to keep believing in happy endings. Even when things are hard, I keep these things to myself. And I distract myself with projects or a crazy adventure like finding Naoko Nishizawa." My voice breaks as I mention Naoko's name and I'm suddenly aware of my heart pounding violently in my chest. I place my right hand over my heart. "I've been too pushy, and I've made bad choices, and this made things way worse for Akari who has been such a good friend to me. Now everything has fallen apart, and I can't fix it."

"Skye MacTavish, you are one of the bravest people I have ever met. I'd like to ask you to let Yoko and me carry some of this with you."

"Okay," I say. It feels like something has lifted off my chest and taken flight. My shoulders drop and I lean back against my pillows.

"Really?" Dad smiles for the first time in the conversation.

"Yes, really. I'm so tired, Dad."

"Skye, why don't you, Yoko, and I go see this psychologist together? Would that be okay?"

"Yes. Okay."

"I love you, Skye." I'm snuggling under the duvet again and Dad leans down and kisses my forehead. "Tomorrow is a new day," he says.

"Isn't it nice to think that tomorrow is a new day with no mistakes in it yet?" I say.

"Anne of Green Gables?" he says.

"Yup."

"That's my girl."

# CHAPTER 49
# IN WHICH AKARI ATTENDS AN IMPORTANT MEETING

My parents have never been called to a meeting at my school before. They attend parent teacher conferences without fail, and take notes about any suggestions my teachers make. But there haven't been very many suggestions. My teachers say that I'm intelligent, participate well in class, and work diligently to earn the best possible results. I have been, in every way possible, a model student.

"I told you. That friendship has ruined Akari. Now we're being called to school about poor grades," my father says to my mother when I give him the note from Ms. Barrett.

"The English teacher mentions nothing about grades. She says she would like to speak with us about an opportunity. Let's not make assumptions," says my mother. My father frowns.

Ms. Barrett meets with my parents and me at eight o'clock on Monday morning. In her note, she explains that the meeting will not take more than twenty minutes as she does not want to disrupt my parents' day. When we arrive at her classroom, I notice that Ms. Barrett has opted for sensible blue pumps. She is all business today. She is seated on one side of a table and there are three chairs arranged on the other, so we sit opposite her, with my mother in the middle.

"It's so good of you to come on such short notice, and I'm terribly sorry to take you away from other things. As you know, I have been Akari's English teacher for several years, and I have always been extremely impressed with the quality of her ideas, and her work ethic. Yes, I've made no secret of it." My parents look at each other and nod their heads in unison. "Recently, I was in the art room, and Akari was working on something, so I asked to see it. If you are agreeable, I'd like to share this with you." I pass Ms. Barrett my sketchbook and she opens it in front of them.

"This is the hero of the story. Her name is Chiyo; I am told this means a thousand generations. Chiyo has quite an exceptional superpower; you see, she saves the lives of people who have lost hope and have jumped in front of a train. It's extraordinary, isn't it? In fact, I was so taken with both the illustrations and the story that I contacted a friend of mine who works at Immersive Tokyo. It's an English language magazine for foreigners and tourists."

Again, my parents nod their heads.

"You see, I did something I should not have. I sent my friend, Mrs. Page, a photograph of Akari's manga. I apologize for this lapse of judgment, as I can now see that I should have spoken with you first to ensure that you felt comfortable with Akari's work being considered for publication."

"Publication?" says my father.

"Yes. Almost certainly. The editorial team loves Akari's work and would like to print it in the spring issue of their magazine. She'd be paid, of course, and it would be published with her name as long as this is acceptable to the two of you," says Ms. Barrett.

"What do you think? Is it good?" My mother leans in ever so slightly as she asks this question.

"Oh, it is wonderful. I don't ordinarily read manga as the

stories aren't to my liking, but Akari's storytelling is strong and compassionate. I hope she will do more of this work. She has a real gift for it." My father turns the pages of my sketchbook, past the Chiyo story, through the drawings of the girl with her dog. "Your daughter is a very talented person."

And then comes the part I've been waiting for. "Her friendship with Skye has really helped Akari thrive as an artist and as a person. I feel very fortunate to be their teacher."

## CHAPTER 50
# IN WHICH SKYE WRITES IN HER JOURNAL

This afternoon, Yoko, Dad, and I went to see a psychologist that Yoko knows from university. Her father is American, and her mother is Japanese, so she really understands a lot about international kids. Her name is Ms. Hansen, and, towards the end of the conversation, she suggested it might be helpful for me to keep a journal. I told her I already do that.

I felt really nervous about going to her office, but it turned out to look a lot like a living room. And she looks like someone's kind mother.

I cried. A lot. And that made Dad and Yoko cry too. I've been crying pretty much non-stop for the past few days, but Ms. Hansen says crying is good for us, that it's a signal that we have something we need to deal with, and it also releases stress hormones or toxins from the body. I've been releasing toxins like crazy.

She asked about my moms, and no one had ever said it like that before. Moms. Like acknowledging there have been two. My mom who gave birth to me and who died, and Yoko who is my now-mom. I really liked that idea of moms.

She asked how I felt, and I told her the truth, which is that I feel sad a lot of the time, but I don't want other people to know, and that I even try to distract myself from those feelings. She asked me why I don't want other people to know, and I said that I want them to think that I am happy, and then she asked me why I want them to think I am happy, and I said SO THEY WILL LIKE ME. She asked if I had some reason to think people might not like me if I were sometimes sad.

And I said no. I just assumed they wouldn't. And even as I said this, I knew it wasn't true.

She asked if I thought I needed to protect my parents, and I said absolutely yes, then she asked if I understood that it was their job to protect me. I said I was starting to. It's what Dr. Devi said, and then my dad, just a few days ago.

Then she said the most interesting thing. She said I have an opportunity to learn how to be myself and to trust myself.

That's my homework question. She calls it an invitation, and it's what we're going to talk about next time: what's making me sad and how I can be myself.

When we got home from Ms. Hansen's office, I took a nap. When I got up, Yoko and Dad were sitting on one of the sofas and he had his arm around her. She had been crying.

"I'm going to be okay. Really," I say, and I mean it. For the first time since we moved to Japan, I think I'm going to be okay. They both scoot over a little bit and make space for me in between them.

# CHAPTER 51
# IN WHICH AKARI TAKES A STAND

When I get home from school, my mother is waiting for me in the living room. "Mom, you are sitting on the sofa. Is something wrong?"

"I'm fine. Oh, that is a joke." She smiles a very little bit.

"An attempt at one anyway. You don't spend much time sitting there in the middle of the day," I say. She pats the cushion beside her, and I sit down.

"Akari, I want to talk about the meeting with Ms. Barrett. This manga you've drawn about the young woman, Chiyo. It is very good."

"Thank you, Mom."

"Ms. Barrett thinks you should publish it."

"What do you and Dad think?"

"We agree. It is a very fine piece of work. You should have an opportunity to publish it."

"Okay." Wait. Am I hallucinating? Did she just agree to me publishing the Chiyo stories?

"Akari, I am not proud of this but, earlier today, I found myself wondering if we would have given our permission had your teacher not intervened." She looks down at her hands folded in her lap.

"I understand, Mom. I have made some poor decisions recently that have made you and Dad believe I have lost sight of my priorities. It was never my intention to disrespect you."

"What are your priorities, Akari?" I sit down beside my mother and lean back against the sofa cushions.

"School, of course, and the violin. To learn new things, to make art, to listen to cool music, and to hang out with my friends."

"Perhaps, what we want is not so different, then."

"Maybe," I say.

"This is confusing for your father and me, Akari. The way we were raised was so different. Everything was decided for us. Your father and I placed you in an international school so you could have the best education and the best possibilities, but perhaps there's no way for you to have an international education without becoming different. An international person." I could not have expressed this idea better than my mother has. "Your English teacher is a very intelligent person. You are fortunate to have such a teacher." I nod. "She also said your friendship with Skye has been very good for you."

"Yes. It has."

"Tonight, after dinner, I will speak with your father. Perhaps there is room for this friendship as long as you promise to follow some guidelines."

"Mom, I know the wise thing for me to do at this moment is to agree to your plan and hope that Dad says yes, but there's something I need to say." My mother lets me speak, but she looks annoyed when I use the word need. "Skye has missed more than a week of school, and I have not contacted her because you asked me not to be friends with her. But this is not working. In this situation, I don't know how to do both what you want me to do and be true to myself. Does that make sense?" She nods. My mother's face is expressionless, but she is still leaning towards me, and I know she is listening to me. "Skye is my very close friend. I miss her and I am very worried about her. I am going to call her, Mom. With or without your permission." My mother doesn't respond, but she looks out the window for a few moments.

"Go ahead, fix yourself a snack. You are always starving when you get home from school," says my mother, so I head towards the kitchen. My mother is so cool, she could negotiate hostage situations.

# CHAPTER 52
# IN WHICH SKYE WRITES MORE IN HER JOURNAL

'm an incurable romantic. Think of all the clichés you've ever heard about romantics and then apply them to me.

I come by it honestly.

My mother died when I was a baby. My father adored her; they started dating in high school. He thought that he would never get over losing her. Then he met a Japanese woman, a translator who worked at his office, and they became friends. Over many months, they fell in love and eventually got married. Sometimes I want to call Yoko 'Mom', and I'm starting to think my biological mother wouldn't mind. No, I'm positive. Even though I don't remember her, my father and my grand-parents talk about her and how much she loved my dad.

I'm the child of two happy marriages.

I'm a cheerleader for romantic love, and it's worth noting how unlikely it is that I would be a cheerleader for anything else.

Ultimately, I've always believed that a happy relationship completes us as people. I have grown up believing that finding that person was the goal. THE goal.

To love and to be loved in return.

Akari's wired differently. Like if she finds a partner, that will be great, but she doesn't need one. She doesn't try to persuade me that real love doesn't exist or anything, but she always encourages me, in her quietly brilliant way, to challenge and question my obsession with romantic love.

She's not wrong to do so.

Maybe something gets lost in all the planning and the plotting and the wondering if this particular person is "the one." Perhaps it's not possible for people to always know exactly what a relationship is or where it's going. If we try to force love into a particular shape or container, we could damage it before it's even had a chance to begin.

Maybe, when it comes to love, it helps to let go.

Ms. Hansen observed that I have a hard time recognizing the love that's already in my life. Like from my parents and my friends. It's hard to write the word friends right now because I'm afraid that my friendships with both Claire and Akari are over, and that this is my fault.

Ms. Hansen asked me to consider the possibility that we could plant ideas like we plant trees. I thought that was really beautiful. One of the ideas I planted was that perhaps it was not too late to mend my friendship with Claire. I read Ms. Hansen the second letter Claire sent me, and the thing that stood out for Ms. Hansen was how much Claire cares about me. I've been fixated on how mad Claire was, and I've been upset about her dating someone else, but, when I read Ms. Hansen the letter, she heard love.

Then there's Akari. I'm not sure if her parents are going to let us be friends or not, but that doesn't change the fact that I love her.

Ms. Hansen asked if I was ready to discuss the question of how I love Claire. I cried for a few minutes, during which Ms. Hansen didn't interrupt me or try to comfort me. She just let me cry.

"I am in love with her," I said. Ms. Hansen nodded. "She loves me as a friend but she's not in love with me. I don't know if she's attracted to girls. We've never talked about it."

"Skye, I am very sorry the person you are in love with doesn't love you in the same way. That feeling sucks." I looked up at her face and saw that she was completely serious.

"Yes. It does. It sucks," I said.

"You get to feel sad about this. You are allowed to grieve this loss."

"This impossible love," I said. Ms. Hansen probably won't understand why that phrase is so important, but I felt like something slipped into place. Naoko had many impossible loves, but she didn't stop loving.

Ms. Hansen asked who I'd shared this with. No one. She asked if I was ashamed of being attracted to Claire. I'm definitely not ashamed of loving Claire or being attracted to girls, but I explained that I feel like my queerness might be too much for other people, like too much on top of all the other inconvenient and unacceptable things I am. The daughter of a dead mother. Fat. Foreign.

Ms. Hansen said that sounded like an unhelpful thought and, after a few moments, I started laughing really hard. It's not a very helpful thought. In fact, that set of thoughts has been kicking my butt. She said it would be lovely to spend some time talking about how I can be kinder to myself. It feels really good to know that's something a person can learn, that I can learn.

———

After writing in my journal, I realize that I'm hungry. I'm about to head to the kitchen when I notice my messy bed. One pillow is at the foot of the bed and the other is on the floor. A few days ago, in a TV show I was watching, a character said something like "Goodness is not something we are, but something we do," and if that's true, I need to start making my bed. I pull up the sheet and then the duvet and place the pillows at the head of the bed. I smooth out a couple of wrinkles in the duvet. The whole operation takes about sixty seconds. I'm proud of finally doing it and embarrassed about how ridiculously easy it was. I promise myself that I will make my bed every morning before I eat breakfast.

While I'm standing in front of the open fridge, Yoko comes in behind me and wraps her arms around my waist.

"Hello, lovely. Can I make you something?" My impulse is to say that I'm fine, but I'm beginning to think that my impulse-generator might be broken.

"Actually, I would love a grilled cheese sandwich."

"Grilled cheese for the win," she says. I pull up a stool while she gathers the ingredients: bread, mayonnaise, butter, sharp cheddar, pickles. I love the precision with which Yoko works. She assembles everything she needs to make the sandwich, and then, while it's cooking, she puts everything away. My Dad and I are the opposite, pulling things out as we need them, and leaving the kitchen a disaster. The real miracle is that Yoko doesn't get angry about our chaotic ways.

"How's the journaling going?" she says.

"Good, actually. I really like Ms. Hansen. Thanks for introducing us."

"She's my Skye."

"What?" I'm not sure I've heard her correctly.

"My Skye. Before I went to university, I didn't know any foreigners. None at all. But then I met Hana, she was Hana Clark back then. Hana was so different from all my other friends. Her father was American, and her mother was Japanese. She had passports from both countries, she spent summers in Vermont with her dad's parents, she dressed in this cool way, and she was much more confident than I was. Hana is a close friend, and she was my first English teacher."

I laugh. "I get it. She's your Skye ... like the foreign friend I am to Akari. Except that Akari's English is better than mine." We laugh, and Yoko flips the sandwich so that the grilled, golden-brown side is facing up. "Imagining you and Ms. Hansen when you were just a little older than I am now makes me happy." I realize I am feeling happy right now, sitting on this stool while Yoko makes me grilled cheese.

"Speaking of Akari, she's called three times this afternoon. I told her I wasn't sure if you were ready to talk yet, and she understood, but she asked if you were okay." Yoko uses the spatula to transfer my perfect sandwich from the frying pan onto a plate. She cuts the sandwich diagonally, separates the halves, and places a dill pickle between them.

"What did you say?" I asked as she passed me the plate.

"I said you were getting there."

"Yoko, are you free this afternoon to run an errand with me?"

# CHAPTER 53

# IN WHICH AKARI AND HER MOTHER DISCUSS BOOKS

"Yes?" At the sound of knocking, I pull off my headphones. I'm spread out on the tatami mat floor of my bedroom reading *The Catcher in the Rye*. My mother opens the door and stands in the doorway.

"Akari, when your father and I were looking through your sketchbook, there was a series of drawings of a young girl in pink holding a large dog. That image was familiar to me, but I could not remember where I had seen this painting. Finally, I realized that it's not something I've seen but rather something I've read."

"Something you've read?"

"The painting is described in a novel by Emi Yamaguchi. It's taken me all evening to figure this out. This is the novel." My mother passes me a small, well-worn book. I sit down on the bed and flip through the familiar-seeming pages.

"But the description of the painting came from the journal we found. Not a novel."

"Akari, you said the journal belonged to someone named Naoko Nishizawa. The protagonist of this novel is also called Naoko. Just a moment, let me check." I pass the book back to her and she thumbs through it looking for something. "Here it is. Naoko. Naoko Nakayama." She spins her chair around, so we are facing each other.

"Um. I don't understand. The book is fiction? Not a memoir?" I say.

"Emi Yamaguchi has published five novels. Or is it six?" She counts on her fingers. "Yes, six."

"Six novels? Which one was this?" I say.

"38 *Impossible Loves* was her second," she says, "but it might have been written earlier. Let's take a look." She flips to the end of the novel. "In the acknowledgements, she writes: 'These were the first stories of my adult life. By the time I had published my first book, I had abandoned them in the dusty attic of my mind, but my editor asked what else I had written. My mind ran back over these stories like an adult ruffling the hair of a beloved child. I told her that I had written them as a young woman and that they weren't any good. She said she would be the judge of that, so I gave her the notebook in which I had written these 38 Impossible Loves. To her credit, only once did she ask me if these stories were autobiographical. I told her that I could not remember, and she assured me that this kind of amnesia is quite common amongst writers. We decided these stories must be a fiction and published them as such. I have known this character Naoko for so long, I feel as though it is like looking in a mirror.'"

"So, it's about her? Emi?" I say.

"It does seem so." My mom closes the book.

"Have you read it?"

"Of course. I've read all her books. She is one of my favourite writers. This book, though, is quite special for me." She rests her right hand on the cover as if she is taking an oath.

"May I ask why?" My mother and I have never talked about books. Not once. I'm not sure which is the bigger miracle: the revelation about Naoko's journal, or this conversation.

"The life of this young woman, Naoko, was described in powerful short chapters, almost like short stories or vignettes, and I often felt as though I were reading my own thoughts about my mother, and about not being ready to be married." She looks up at me. "I do not mean to imply that I am unhappy with my life."

"I know," I say.

"How could you know?" asks Mom.

"She has written some stories that I can relate to as well."

"I understand." She passes me the novel. "The journal you and Skye found was the first draft of one of my favourite books. That is quite remarkable."

"It is. I'm really sorry we lost it," I say.

My mother places her right index finger on the cover of the novel. "But you see, nothing has been lost." I stare at the small book. "Akari-chan, I appreciate that you wanted to do the right thing in returning the journal to its owner but, as you can see, it was not her only copy. All this time, we have had the published version of the journal you've been reading on our bookshelf." My mother smiles and she looks, to me, like a teenager. "Now, why don't you let Skye know that this story has a happy ending?"

————

Skye,

Yesterday, I talked to Yoko and left a message for you. I hope you are doing better, and I am very, very sorry that I didn't contact you sooner. If you are feeling well enough, I would like to come to your apartment after school tomorrow to share some news. I will be there around five o'clock.

Akari

# CHAPTER 54
# IN WHICH SKYE RECEIVES A VISITOR

'm catching up on my math homework when the doorbell rings. I know it's Akari and my stomach does a little dance. It's weird that I feel nervous, but it's been more than two weeks since we saw each other, in which time I've sort of dropped my basket, so maybe it's not that weird after all. I run to the door and pull it open, and there she is, still in her school uniform, and we're hugging, and I'm not sure if we've ever hugged before.

"Have we ever hugged before?" I say.

"No. I am not exactly a hugger," she says, and this makes me laugh so hard I think I might fall down. Our laughter has stopped the tears I'm pretty sure were on their way when I first saw Akari in the doorway. We both say how good it is to see each other. It feels very adult. She asks if I'm well, and I say yes, which feels true, mostly true anyway, and is certainly true at this moment. I am well.

Then, at the same time, we both say, "I have something to show you." I let Akari go first and, as she takes off her backpack, I pull her into the living room. We collapse onto the carpet. Akari takes a small book out of her bag and presents it to me. She says it is from her mother's collection.

"What's this?" I say.

"Open it. Read the first page." She's wearing the biggest smile I've ever seen on her.

"My first love was also my first impossible love. I'm sure this is the case for most people," I read aloud. "Wow! It's 38 *Impossible Loves*. How is that possible?" I flip to the copyright information and find that it was published fifteen years ago. Akari tells me that her mother saw her drawings of the girl with her dog and recognized the image from a novel written by someone named Emi Yamaguchi.

"But it's not fiction," I say. Akari points out the acknowledgements, and we laugh at Emi's cagey way of answering the question while not answering the question. "Wait, what do you mean your mother saw your drawings of the girl and the dog? You showed her your sketchbook?"

"It was actually Ms. Barrett who showed them, with my permission, and she got my parents to agree to let me publish the Chiyo story with Immersive Tokyo. She also told them what an amazing friend you've been to me. She said that our friendship was important to me as an artist."

"Congratulations," I give her another hug. "I'm so happy for you. People are going to love your Chiyo story. This is almost too much to take in," I say. "Hold on just a minute. I'll be right back," I say as I hop up and head towards my room.

"Are you doing okay? Is this too much?" Akari asks.

"I'm fine. I promise," I yell back. I grab a large envelope from my desk.

Back in the living room, I pass the envelope to Akari. "Open it."

She carefully inserts her thumb under the flap and eases it open. She pulls out Naoko's journal.

"You thought it was lost!" she says. She beams as she opens the journal.

"I know, right? The last place I remembered having it was at the koban, so yesterday I went back. The same officer was there, and he had the journal. Honestly, he seemed happy for us to have it back. This whole situation is sort of blowing my mind. We have the journal, but it's also a published book which means we can now track down Naoko, I mean Emi. We'll finally be able to return her journal. We'll be able to read the rest of the entries in Emi's novel whenever we want.

"Thank you, Skye." Akari holds the journal to her chest, and I notice she has tears in her eyes. "Thank you for going back for the journal, thank you for everything. I've missed you so much. I wanted to contact you when you stopped coming to school but my parents would not permit it. Even though I have never disobeyed them about anything big, I knew they were wrong. I told my mom that it didn't matter if they changed their minds or not, that I was going to call you."

I feel large, hot tears on my cheeks, and I don't even try to wipe them away. I'm learning to let my feelings come when and how they want.

Akari continues, "The strange thing is that my relationship with my parents is actually a little better now. Especially with my mother."

"You stood up to your parents." I say, extending my right hand. She sticks out her right hand and we exchange a strong Canadian handshake. "Did you happen to mention art school?" I ask.

"One thing at a time," she says, as she crosses her legs. "Skye, are you coming back to school? Is it okay to ask this question?"

"I think I'll be back next week," I say. She applauds, and I bow my head and make a small flourish with my hand. "I've been seeing a therapist." She nods, and there's no sign of judgment on her part. I tell her about how sad I felt after the incident with Nishizawa-san and the koban, and how I blamed myself when her parents said we couldn't be friends anymore, but I couldn't talk with my parents because I always try to protect them from the way that I'm feeling. And about how those sadnesses got layered on top of my sadness about my friendship with Claire, because I feel more than just friendship for Claire, but she doesn't feel the same, and all those layers made it impossible for me to keep going.

"Does it feel better? To talk about things?" Akari asks.

"Definitely. I'm learning a lot in therapy. How to tell the truth, how to be kinder to myself, and how to think differently about love. You know? I'm learning that the most important love affair I'm ever going to have is with myself."

"Oh," Akari closes her eyes. "That is such a wonderful thought. If it's okay with you, I'm going to borrow that line for my next Chiyo story." I nod and she repeats what I've just said. "The most important love affair I'll ever have is with myself."

"Perhaps you will become the romantic one," I say.

"That seems highly unlikely," Akari punches me on the arm and smirks. Then she pulls back her hand. "But seriously, Skye, I am sorry that things didn't work out with Claire."

"Thanks. Listen, I know I'm not the first person to experience unrequited love."

"It does not matter that you are not the first one. It matters that this is what you are feeling now. I am very sorry that Claire does not feel in-loveness towards you. If I were a different kind of person, Reika, for example, I would say that is Claire's loss," says Akari.

My eyes fill with tears. "Thank you for saying that even if it was via Reika without her knowledge or consent." We both laugh and then I take a deep breath. "The truth is, it's a little rough right now and I'm still not very good at talking about negative feelings." My right hand rests on the leather sofa and

Akari covers it with one of hers for a couple of moments. The pressure and heat transferred by her palm feels reassuring. "It feels good to tell you. Hey, how are Kimi and Reika?"

"They're good. They send their love," she says, and I raise my right eyebrow at her. "Seriously. Things are good with Reika, and we're finally able to joke around a little, which was hard for a while because I wanted to be really careful with her feelings. I'm sorry that Reika was not kind to you when you first moved here," Akari says.

I shrug. We both know it has nothing to do with me.

"Ms. Barrett says hello. I told her I was coming to see you today."

"Cool! I miss English class," I say.

"I know." Akari flashes me a big grin. "I have been thinking about what you said about the hero's journey. Do you remember this idea about the Russian nesting dolls? How each of us has these smaller stacking dolls inside us, like younger versions of ourselves?" I remember, but I kind of can't believe she remembers. "In class that day, you talked about how the hero of the story can draw on the wisdom and experiences of all of her previous selves. Her past selves become apprentices on her journey."

"I wish I'd expressed it so eloquently, but sure, I remember," I say.

"In your theory of the hero's journey, perhaps the hero has a responsibility to care for all of those previous selves. She must send the smaller heroines love, compassion and support. She never berates them for mistakes they have made, because she recognizes they were doing the best that they could at the time."

"Wow," I say. "So, the kinder she becomes to herself, the easier the journey becomes?"

Akari nods. "Which also makes it easier for the heroine to

help others." She is beaming with pride. We high-five. "Is this too much?" Akari says. "Should I go now?"

"Are you kidding? I was just going to ask if you wanted to order pizza."

"Sure," she says. "Just let me call my mom and make sure that it's okay with her."

———

One week and two more visits to my therapist later, and I'm back at school. Dad is worried that it's too soon, but Yoko says that I'll tell them if that's true. She's right.

It's lunchtime, and Akari and I are seated at one of the picnic tables outside the cafeteria. Reika arrives first, and she bows her head just a bit when she sees me. "Welcome back," she says. Then Kimi comes bounding along, drops her lunch on the table and pulls me off the bench so she can hug me.

"I hear we're hugging now," she says. Akari and Reika laugh.

"Yes, we're hugging. Even Akari," I say.

There's a cool breeze blowing while Reika and Kimi talk about volleyball, and I realize that for the first time since moving to Japan, I'm not too warm. The temperature has cooled down just like everyone said it would. Akari asks Reika about her cello lessons, and Reika says she's got a recital coming up and that she feels nervous. Kimi reminds Reika how good she is and asks if it would help if we went to the recital. I'm surprised when Reika says yes. Then Akari says that it's okay to feel nervous. Akari's love language turns out to be not needing the people she loves to be different than we are.

Kimi turns to me, "I'm really sorry about things with your friend, Claire." Reika and Akari stop talking and look at each other. "What? Am I not supposed to know that?" says Kimi.

"Sorry, Skye," says Akari. "I was telling the girls about seeing you again and it just sort of slipped out. You have my word that I will not share this with anyone else."

"No. It's fine," I say, and it really is. These are Akari's closest friends and now they're becoming my friends, and friends talk to each other about their big stuff. I ask them about volleyball, and Kimi says they're playing the American School on Saturday afternoon. There's a fierceness in her voice that tells me that losing is not an option. I ask Akari if she wants to go, and she says she'll check with her mom. Then I text Yoko to ask if she can drive us, and she texts back right away to say that she'd love to, and her kindness feels overwhelming. I feel over-whelmed a lot lately. I'm filled with gratitude for this ordinary October day, to be eating lunch at this picnic table with these three lovely friends, and to be making plans for the weekend.

"Skye, are you okay?" says Akari.

"Yes. Just a little emotional. Sorry. I missed what you said."

"My mom texted to say I could go to the game and then she reminded me that I shouldn't be using my phone during the school day. Oh, moms!" We laugh, and Kimi collects our trays and takes them inside. Then the bell rings, and the four of us scatter across the campus for our next class. Reika and I walk up to the third floor together, and just before we get to her classroom, she says, "Hey, Skye. Are we okay?"

"Better than okay," I say. She smiles, and I give her a thumbs up, which feels like such a stupid move, and then I remember that I'm learning how to be kind to myself, so I let it go. As I drop into my seat, I resolve that I will video call Claire tonight and apologize for being such a terrible friend to her and, if I can, I'll tell her why.

# CHAPTER 55
# IN WHICH AKARI RECEIVES AN INVITATION

Our invitations arrive on the day Skye returns to school. It is a very good day.

When I showed Skye my mother's copy of Emi Yamaguchi's novel, we realized that we finally had a way to return her journal. We both checked with our parents and then, with their blessings, we wrote an email to Emi's publisher with Skye's provocative heading: REQUEST TO RETURN EMI YAMAGUCHI'S JOURNAL. Even after I insisted that the staff at Emi's publishing house were obligated to read all incoming messages, even those with non-sexy headings, Skye said we could not take any chances, when we'd worked so hard to find her. I conceded the point.

I'm in my room doing homework when I check my email. The invitation is addressed to both of us, but it seems too perfect to be true. Since I can't actually believe what it says, I text Skye, but then I remember she has a therapy appointment this afternoon. I find my mom reading in the living room and I pass her my laptop. She reads the message and laughs.

"Does that mean I can go?"

"Yes. I will discuss it with your father when he gets home, but yes, you can go."

A couple of hours later, Skye calls. "Are you crying?" I say.

"Of course, I'm crying. The question is, why aren't you crying?" Then Yoko calls my mother. They are on the phone for a long time, and I wonder, for the first time, if they will become friends. Just before she hangs up, she says to Yoko, "Isn't this the most perfect ending to this story?" It is, of course, but I've never heard my mother speak in this way. She sounds like Skye.

We have two weeks to get ready.

My mother thinks I should wear a dress. I choose navy trousers with a navy blouse.

Skye decides to wear a red floral dress that Yoko bought her when they lived in Paris, and that she'll carry the vintage bag that brought Naoko's journal into our life. Our parents help us put together a basket of goodies, including a bottle of maple syrup from Skye's father and a new journal I made. It's my mother's idea to wrap the original journal inside a furoshiki cloth as though we were giving Emi a gift.

We decide to get ready at Skye's place since she lives so close. Skye's father volunteers to drive us, but we decide it would be best to arrive on our own. He walks us to the door of the apartment and gives each of us a hug. "Have a great time, Akari and my Skye-girl."

As we're leaving her building, my mind flashes back to the first day of school. So much has changed over these past three months: for Skye, for Reika, and for me and my mother.

I remember I was in a mood that morning, not buying any of the first-day-back propaganda, and I was sitting on the floor drawing Chiyo in my sketchbook. The idea for the comic was brand new and I was still freaked out about Chiyo's superpower. Then I saw Skye and she looked just like the character I had just drawn, right down to the freckles.

"Skye-girl!" I say.

"Yes?" says Skye.

"On the first day of school, just before I saw you in the hall before homeroom, I was drawing Chiyo. The resemblance was so similar, it was as though I based the character on you."

"Except you had never seen me."

"Except I had never seen you. Just now, when we left, your dad called you Skye-girl, and I just realized that Chiyo is, quite literally, a Sky-girl.

"Oh, Akari. That's perfect."

# CHAPTER 56
# IN WHICH SKYE ATTENDS A PARTY WITH HER BEST FRIEND

I t's late Saturday afternoon when we emerge from the station, and the neighbourhood is busy. We're carried along the sidewalk by crowds of shoppers and people making their way home from work. The sun is golden, and we can see Emi Yamaguchi's building like some great ship making its way down the main street in Hiro-o. A police officer is standing near the exit, and I grab Akari's hand. It is the same police officer who detained us for traumatizing the old man who lives on the third floor of the ship. But the officer is smiling today. He bows and explains that Ms. Yamaguchi has asked him to ensure that we arrive without incident. Akari and I look at each other in amazement.

We ride the elevator to the top floor of the building, and it opens into a small foyer that's painted red, and feels like a beating heart. When the officer opens a door, the sound of jazz music spills out all round us. The apartment seems like a garden with windows on both sides. The doors to the balconies are open, and people are standing and sitting in small trios and groups. The officer closes the door behind us and announces, "They are here!" and we freeze, remembering our first brush with the law. People stop their conversations and turn towards us the way a revolving door at an airport opens for the newest traveler. There is applause and then cheering. We look at each other, and Akari is wide-eyed and smiling broadly. Her face reflects the intersection of fear and delight.

A small, slightly round woman in a red dress enters from one of the balconies and bows to us, and we bow more deeply. "Akari?" she asks, and Akari steps forward. The woman takes Akari's hands in hers for a moment. She then turns to me and her bob-length hair swings through the air. "You are Skye, then. The troublemaker?" The woman smiles as she extends her hand.

"Yes. I'm afraid so."

"Welcome! I'm Emi, and you must call me Emi. I am not interested in any of this Yamaguchi-san nonsense." Akari holds out the journal that her mother has wrapped. "Is this what I think this is?" she asks. We smile but stay silent. Emi quickly unfolds the fabric, opens the journal, and runs her fingers along the title. "Naoko Nishizawa. My editor did not like this name, so we changed it."

"We like the name Nishizawa. We will always think of her that way," I say.

"This bag!" Emi is pointing at the bag I bought at the vintage shop. "It belonged to my editor."

"This was where we found the journal. Well, we thought it was a journal," I say.

"After we published 38 *Impossible Loves*, I asked for the original manuscript back, but my editor couldn't find it. She and her staff tore their office apart looking for it. Her home too. Just a moment." Emi crosses the room and returns with a woman dressed in jeans and a black turtleneck. "Girls, this is my editor, Mari Yoshida."

"That bag!" says the editor.

"Skye bought it at a recycle shop," Akari says. "The journal was trapped between the lining and the leather." I open the bag so that Emi and Yoshida-san can see where the journal had been. They peer inside the bag and Emi starts to laugh, then the editor laughs, and soon they are laughing and crying and hugging without embarrassment.

"Oh, Emi. My deepest apologies. Evidently the manuscript has been inside this bag, at the bottom of my closet, for years. About three months ago, I cleaned my apartment and sold the bag at a recycle shop in Shibuya."

"Thank you both for bringing this back to me. It has brought me immeasurable happiness," says Emi.

"This must be your favourite birthday gift," says the editor.

"It's your birthday?" I say.

"Yes. Did I not mention that in the invitation?" says Emi. We shake our heads. "Yes, well, sometimes the details escape me. Today, I am fifty."

"Fifty?" I say.

"Indeed," says Emi. "Fifty glorious years. These stories are from half a life ago."

"We didn't know it was your birthday, but we did bring some gifts," I say, passing Emi the basket of treats we've assembled for her.

Emi peers inside the basket like a little kid. "A new journal?"

"Akari made it for you," I say. "She designed and drew the cover. That's you. As a superhero." A woman with a short black bob and a red cape sits at a table, writing. Entire worlds explode from her pen.

"This is exquisite, Akari. Have you ever designed any novel covers?" says Emi.

"Um no," Akari says.

"If you don't mind, I'm going to show this to the people in the art department at my publishing house."

"I don't mind. Thank you very much." Akari and I look at each other in disbelief.

"Skye, the email that you two sent to my publishing house mentioned that you are a writer."

"I love writing. Recently, it's been mostly journal entries," I say.

"I'd like to invite you to share your work with me and, if you are interested, I'd be happy to give you some feedback. I've always believed that mischievous girls make the very best writers." My cheeks heat up and I am, perhaps for the very first time, speechless. I bow to Emi. "Good, then. It's settled. Girls, there are some people here you might know, but I don't want to ruin the surprise. Please make yourselves at home. There is lots of food, and your mothers have said that you may each have one glass of champagne."

"You spoke with our mothers?" Akari asks.

"Of course. I only *seem* irresponsible." Emi winks and bows and makes her way out to the other balcony.

We scan the room. The first person we recognize is the young bartender who threw us out of the bar in Hiro-o.

A Japanese woman with long braids calls us by name. She's seated on a burgundy velvet sofa with two other women. We go over to her and kneel on the carpet. "My name is Masumi. I am an old friend of Emi's."

"The painter," Akari whispers.

"Yes. I'm a painter. I've been away for a bit ... "

"In the Himalayas!" I say.

"And my agent said one of you had contacted her about *Love No.* 2."

"That was Akari," I say.

"In 38 *Impossible Loves*, there's a story about the very first painting of the girl with her dog. It was called *Love No.* 1 and I gave it to Emi. Did you read that?" We nod. "Would you like to see it?" Masumi leads us back to the red foyer and down a flight of stairs. She opens the door to a massive apartment.

"Is this your place?" I say.

"Oh no. My place is very small. This is Emi's."

"And upstairs too?" I say.

"Yes, that's hers as well. That was her apartment for years and when this apartment came on the market a few years ago she bought it. She calls the upstairs apartment The Garden." We enter an office. "Here it is." Masumi looks towards the painting that hangs above a desk piled with papers and books.

"*Love No. 1*," says Akari, almost at a whisper. Presiding over the beautiful clutter of Emi's apartment, the painting of the small girl with her arms wrapped around her dog radiates warmth. Maybe the painting doesn't need a number at all. Maybe calling it 'Love' is everything a person needs to know. I look at Akari. Her eyes are wide and I grab her hand. She squeezes my fingers and, for a few moments, we stand very still. We take in this painting that Akari, magical person that she is, drew even before she saw its sibling in the gallery.

Masumi says, "I adore Emi, but her life would be simpler if she had less stuff."

"Maybe she doesn't want a simpler life," I say. Akari shoots me a look but I'm practicing being myself.

"That's an excellent point, Skye. She's exceedingly happy with her life. Would you like to have a look around?" Emi's home is the least Japanese space I've ever seen. Huge rugs cover the floors and there are paintings everywhere. Some hang from nails on the wall and others sit on the floor waiting for a space to open up, as if they are waiting at a train station. Sweaters and coats are draped over the backs of chairs, and a surfboard leans precariously against a wall in the hallway.

"It's a wonderful home. Like a treasure chest," I say.

"It's true. She loves beautiful things," says Masumi. She

leaves us for a moment and retrieves, from a table, a large flat package wrapped in caramel-coloured craft paper. "This is for you, Akari. Please go ahead and open it."

Akari takes the package from Masumi and gently peels back the tape and tenderly unwraps what turns out to be a painting. She turns it over and discovers *Love No. 2,* from the exhibit. Akari's mouth hangs open and then large tears begin rolling down her cheeks. "Oh," says Masumi. "I did not expect this reaction."

"Please don't worry. She's just a bit overwhelmed," I say. "She's been painting your girl with the dog for weeks."

"Thank you so very much." Akari bows. "I don't know how to say thank you enough for this gift."

"You have already thanked me enough by loving it. It pleases me to know that you will have the sister to Emi's painting. It's important to me that my girls and their dogs live in good homes."

Back upstairs, Masumi introduces us to a tall woman with her hair done up in a knot with a few tendrils loose around her face.

"Do you know who I am?" she asks.

"You're the wedding planner," I say. I am absolutely certain that this elegant person is the same woman to whom Emi wrote the letter. "I went to the shop. One of the women there remembered you." The woman smiles as though this is not a surprise to her. "May I ask if it was good advice? What Emi wrote to you?" I ask.

"To leave my job? Oh, yes. I became a tour guide for Japanese people who wanted to travel abroad. Then I started my own company with much smaller groups, and we run English classes so people can learn a bit of English first and have a more authentic experience of wherever we're visiting. No tonkatsu for two entire weeks." She laughs.

"So, you saw the world?" says Akari.

"Quite literally. And it's such an amazing world. I hope you'll both see it too."

An older man approaches with two glasses of champagne. "I've been instructed to bring these to you," he says. The man is tanned and lean. As I take the glass from him, I begin to laugh. I look at Akari and wait for the flicker of recognition. Finally, she gets it.

"You are the bartender," Akari says. "The bartender who was really a surfer."

"Yes." He passes her a glass.

"You and Emi are still friends?" I say.

Emi hears her name and joins us, slipping her arm around the surfer.

"More than friends." Emi and the bartender laugh. I hand my glass to Akari and applaud.

"In the journal, you wrote that it was not possible," Akari says.

"I wore her down with love," says the surfer.

"That's a great line," I say.

"It is, isn't it, Skye?" says Emi, looking fondly at her partner. "I may have to borrow that one. Now let's have a toast." She raises her glass.

"To what are we toasting, my dear?" asks the surfer.

"To stories."

# ACKNOWLEDGMENTS

So many people have encouraged and supported me. This book belongs to all of you.

*Thank you to the folks who helped me become a writer:*

My maternal grandmother Marjorie McBride and my mother Edith McDiarmid who introduced me to stories.

The writers of my childhood: Lucy Maud Montgomery, Louisa May Alcott, Johanna Spyri, Frances Hodgson Burnett, Madeleine L'Engle and Louise Fitzhugh.

My high school and university literature teachers who taught me theme and metaphor repeatedly until I got it. Special thanks to Dr. Rosemary Hooey, my teacher in my final year of high school.

The members of my first writing group: Dr. Rena Upitis, Callie Markotich and Lynda Wilde.

Writing teachers Sarah Selecky and Caroline Donahue who helped me understand a story from the inside out.

*Thank you to the humans who helped me write this book:*

Much of this book grew out of the thousands of conversations I've had with Japanese teenagers over a decade of living and working as a high school counsellor at international schools in Japan. It was both my job, and an honour, to witness their lives, and I'm grateful to all the students who trusted me with the stories of their friendships, families, cultures, academics, and their possible and impossible loves. Without their truths, Akari would not have a voice of her own.

My gratitude to Japanese sensitivity readers Sakurako Naka and Raveena Bhattacharjee who helped me spot and correct several errors and inaccuracies in the book. Any errors that remain are mine alone.

I'd like to thank my writing teacher and friend Rachael Herron and her amazing community of writers who have been some of this book's most enthusiastic cheerleaders.

Jun Sekiya was its first gentle reader when I was very nervous about receiving feedback.

My team of book-making miracle workers: Catriona Turner, Copy Editor. Annette Tomlinson, Proofreader. Caitlin B. Alexander, Book Cover Illustrator. Ed Giordano, Book Whisperer.

*Thank you to those who support my work and who love me:*

My guests on the *Ease Lessons* Podcast, the kind humans who support me on Patreon, my coaching clients and the amazing folks who take my courses. Working with you enriches my life.

Barb, Christine, Sarah, Genevieve, Kathy, Michelle, Ashley, Katy, Ann, Jaya, Cary, Adam, and Irina. I'm so grateful for your friendship.

My sister Megan Sunstrum who has always believed in me.

My partner Damien Pitter who makes all things possible through his unflappable commitment to me, my stories and to our shared life.

# ABOUT THE AUTHOR

Monna McDiarmid is a writer, international school counselor and life coach. She and her partner live in a tiny apartment in Yokohama, Japan and an old, wooden house in Nova Scotia, Canada.

Sign up for her newsletter at monnamcdiarmid.com, for updates about new novels, events, and courses.